"I'm not the kind of bodyguard who likes to remain undercover,"

Nikki said.

"Maybe you would. If you were undercover with someone you liked," Scott responded.

"Bodyguards and their subjects cannot get involved with each other," she whispered. "It's a cardinal rule."

"Yes, but we've grown beyond that, haven't we?" He searched her face for her answer.

Nikki lifted her face to his. "God help me, we have."

Dear Reader,

We're back with another fabulous month's worth of books, starting with the second of our Intimate Moments Extra titles. *Night of the Jaguar* by Merline Lovelace is the first of a new miniseries, Code Name: Danger. It's also a fabulously sexy, romantic and suspenseful tale of two people who never should have met but are clearly made for each other. And keep your eyes on two of the secondary characters, Maggie and Adam, because you're going to be seeing a lot more of them as this series continues.

Award-winner Justine Davis presents one of her irresistible tormented-but-oh-so-sexy heroes in *Out of the Dark*, another of her page-turning titles. And two miniseries continue: Kathleen Creighton's Into the Heartland, with *One Good Man*, and Beverly Bird's Wounded Warriors, with *A Man Without a Haven*. Welcome bestseller Linda Randall Wisdom back to Silhouette with her Intimate Moments debut, *No More Secrets*. And try out new-to-contemporaries author Elane Osborn, who offers *Shelter in His Arms*.

As promised, it's a great month—don't miss a single book.

Enjoy!

Leslie Wainger
Senior Editor and Editorial Coordinator

Please address questions and book requests to:
Silhouette Reader Service
U.S.: 3010 Walden Ave., P.O. Box 1325, Buffalo, NY 14269
Canadian: P.O. Box 609, Fort Erie, Ont. L2A 5X3

NO MORE SECRETS

LINDA RANDALL WISDOM

INTIMATE™MOMENTS®

Published by Silhouette Books

America's Publisher of Contemporary Romance

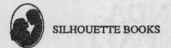

SILHOUETTE BOOKS

ISBN 0-373-07640-1

NO MORE SECRETS

This edition published by arrangement with Harlequin Enterprises B.V.

® and TM are trademarks of Harlequin Enterprises B.V., used under
license. Trademarks indicated with ® are registered in the United States
Patent and Trademark Office, the Canadian Trade Marks Office and in
other countries.

Printed in U.S.A.

LINDA RANDALL WISDOM

first sold to Silhouette Books on her wedding anniversary in 1979 and hasn't stopped since! She loves looking for the unusual when she comes up with an idea and only hopes her readers enjoy reading her stories as much as she enjoys writing them.

A native Californian, she is married and has two dogs, five parrots and a tortoise, so life is never boring—or quiet—in the Wisdom household. When she isn't writing, she enjoys going to the movies, reading, making jewelry and fabric painting.

To Leslie.
After all these years, they can't keep us down, can they?

Prologue

"How could it happen, Harvey? How did she get the poison?"

"Things just happen, Nik. You know it and I know it. She was guilty and obviously couldn't handle the idea of spending the rest of her life in a federal prison. She took the coward's way out." The man speaking tossed a file folder on his desk.

The file cabinet was typical government issue, even for the head of security—gray metal, with the requisite locked drawers. His fancy walnut desk and equally fancy office with the original paintings and Persian carpet weren't for public view. Right now he was in his public persona as they discussed the recent treason case that had covered the front pages of every newspaper across the globe for the past few months.

Nikki Price, the woman standing before him, was dressed in naval blues, with her hair trimmed just above the nape and no makeup highlighting her delicate cheekbones and uptilted, honey-brown eyes. She stood ramrod straight as she listened to the director of security explain the most recent development in the Renee Carter trial, a trial that wouldn't take place. The woman had committed suicide before a jury got the chance to find her guilty.

Nikki had been offered a chair, but considering that her superior officer was standing, she wasn't about to take a seat. When she had been called into his office, she hadn't expected to see the head of Naval Intelligence there, nor had she expected to learn there would be no follow-up on Renee Carter's death. As far as anyone in the intelligence community was concerned, the case was closed. The guilty party had been discovered, arrested and duly executed by her own hand, which according to him had saved the taxpayers a great deal of money. No emotion was written on Nikki's face as she heard the news. After all, she was an officer in the navy. A member of the intelligence community who had been commended for her undercover work ferreting out the security leak in the Washington, D.C., scientific community.

Shock waves had rippled through the tight clique when it came out that Renee Carter, wife of renowned scientist Scott Carter, was the leak. While the social-climbing woman hadn't been liked by most, no one had had any idea that she would be cruel enough to betray her husband and her country by handing over his research notes. He'd been working with a unique weapon, and to have that knowledge fall into enemy hands...

It was Nikki who'd begun to wonder if Renee might not be guilty, even though the evidence against the woman was overwhelming. Nikki herself had been the one to present that evidence to her superiors, and she'd been present when Renee was arrested, but even so she'd begun to feel that there had to be more to the story. What if Renee wasn't as guilty as the evidence indicated she was? Mrs. Carter was a trifle vain and selfish, but Nikki wouldn't have thought her stupid enough to hide incriminating papers where they could be so easily found. Wouldn't she have taken more care?

Maybe that was why this case bothered her so much. It had all been too easy, and Nikki couldn't remember the last time evidence had fallen into place so easily.

She shook her head. "Something's wrong here, Harvey. You know it, and so do I. Why can't I take the time to do a little digging and find out?"

"Nothing is wrong, Lieutenant Price. The woman was guilty."

Nikki turned to face the other man. Handsome in a grim-faced way, resplendent in his crisp uniform, he was the picture of correct military bearing.

"Her death left a child without a mother," she stated. "We shouldn't close the case before we know for sure she was guilty."

"It's already closed, Lieutenant. There are too many cases pending for us to worry about one that's been wrapped up so neatly." The officer checked his watch. "Now, I believe you have a meeting at two o'clock with Captain Gibson. He will be giving you your pick of assignments. He's very pleased with the way you handled this one, but I'm sure he'll be telling you that himself."

She thought of the folded sheet of paper tucked in her briefcase. She hadn't known of Renee Carter's death when she'd made her decision. Hearing about it had only strengthened her resolve. "All Captain Gibson will be doing is accepting my resignation."

Harvey was the first to react to her abrupt announcement. "Don't make any rash decisions, Nikki."

The other man shook his head. "Obviously you're allowing your emotions to speak instead of acting like the naval officer you're supposed to be. I would have thought Annapolis had pounded such behavior out of you."

Nikki refused to rise to the bait. "This is probably one of the most logical decisions I've made in a long time. I listened to Renee tell me she didn't know what was in those papers, and that she hadn't stolen them. The entire time she was in jail she was never worried about herself but about her daughter and what these accusations would do to her. Renee may have been selfish and thoughtless, but she did care about Heather. Does that sound like a traitor to you? There's something missing here. Because the evidence so conveniently pointed to her, we were willing to arrest her— it looked so cut and dried. That's what bothers me. It's too cut and dried. A case like this shouldn't be wrapped up this easily. If you cared to think about it, you'd see I'm right.''

The other man wasn't impressed. "She didn't care what the scandal would do to her husband, did she? Don't be a fool, Lieutenant. Put this aside and go on with your life. You have an excellent chance to advance after your work on this. Take advantage of it. Don't blow your career when you're finally on the way up.''

Nikki didn't bother answering. She picked up her briefcase and walked to the door, then looked over her shoulder at Harvey, who'd been her mentor during her budding military career. Then she turned to the other officer, who stared at her with contempt openly written in his gaze.

"I should have known you couldn't take it when things got rough. You just don't have it in you," he said.

A faint smile curved her unpainted mouth. She ignored Harvey's pleas to not do anything rash as she faced her superior.

"You know what? I think I'll take that as a compliment. Don't worry about my clouding your career. I won't even bother to send you a card next Father's Day, because I have a feeling you've just disowned your only daughter.''

She didn't look back as she walked out of the office.

Chapter 1

She watched the man cross the room, a mixture of pleasure and trepidation filling her mind. After all this time, what could he want? He wouldn't have tracked her down without a good reason.

"For once my horoscope was right. It said I'd be seeing a specter from my past, and here you are."

Harvey Larsen smiled. "I didn't think you believed in astrology."

"I do a lot of things I didn't use to do." Nikki Price reached down inside a bright purple gym bag and pulled out a blue print sweatshirt that matched her leotard and echoed the blue of her Lycra bike shorts. She drew the shirt on over her head, letting the folds drape around her slender hips. She cast a sharp eye over his impeccably tailored, dark gray suit, snowy white shirt and muted tie. "Don't you know that vacations mean you can leave your suits at home? But then, I can't remember you ever taking a vacation."

Harvey had to give her credit. She wasn't about to show him, by voice or manner, that she was surprised or unsettled by his unannounced arrival. But then, knowing Nikki as well as he did, he knew few things could unsettle her, and he doubted that five years would have changed her all that much.

He took a few seconds to study her. She was thinner than he remembered; probably because of the self-defense classes she taught. But there were other, more obvious changes. The hair she used to wear short was now longer, and worn in a style that released the curl, and there were hints of coppery light in the coffee-brown hue. He would even hazard a guess that there was mascara darkening her lashes and a hint of colored gloss on her lips. He wondered if the years away from military restrictions and her father's even harsher restrictions hadn't allowed the butterfly to finally begin to emerge. She might have been five years older, but she looked years younger.

"Like you, I've been doing things I hadn't considered before. Still, I had no idea it was considered a crime to come down to see my goddaughter." He held out his arms.

Nikki shook her head as she cast an amused glance at his immaculate attire. She knew the Louisiana weather was the same as always—hot and muggy—yet Harvey's white shirt didn't show a wrinkle, while she was less than fresh after teaching her advanced step-aerobics class. "I don't think you want me too close until I've taken my shower."

His arms dropped back to his sides. "Fine, you go take your shower, then we can go out for dinner. Your boss said this was your last class for the day."

Nikki didn't answer as she pulled off the bandanna knotted around her forehead to keep her shoulder-length hair out of her face while she taught. She shook her head, allowing the damp curls to settle around her cheeks. So Harvey had checked out her schedule ahead of time. That wasn't too surprising. He always liked to know what to expect when he approached someone.

"How could I refuse to consider such a charming invitation? But before I go anywhere with you, I'd like to know how you found me."

"Considering you hadn't bothered to let me know where you've been these past years, it wasn't all that easy. You covered your tracks well. Even accessing records didn't give me any answers. You went and got a new social security number, didn't you? You made sure you wouldn't be easy to find."

She smiled and inclined her head in response to his compliment.

"My break came when you ended up as front-page news down here when you caught a rapist. I heard he broke your nose. One of the detectives on the case figured you were more than your run-of-the-mill self-defense instructor and ran a check on you. The request was routed to my office. I talked to the man, received a description, realized he was talking about you and immediately assured him that you weren't a dangerous criminal on the run but an ex-naval officer who didn't like to talk about her specialized training."

Nikki's laughter held little humor. "Amazing. You risk life and limb to help the cops catch a major sleaze, and their macho egos get all bent out of shape because you accomplished what they couldn't. It must have been Pickett you heard from."

His nod was answer enough.

"He had a habit of calling me 'little lady' and figuratively patting me on the head. Still, it must have taken him a while to run the check. That story is old news around here."

"Old, but not forgotten. I read the police reports. If it hadn't been for you, that man might still be out there. You just went out one evening and brought him down."

She looked up, eyes blazing, and her voice throbbed with anger as she remembered the fear that had haunted the women as they left the club in the evenings. The fear that they might be the next victim of a malicious soul who hated women so much he viciously hurt them. If it hadn't been for the male instructors escorting clients to their cars, they would probably have had to close in the evenings.

"Damn straight I brought that bastard down. Women were afraid to be out at night because of him. At first I thought teaching them self-defense would give them some confidence, but it wasn't enough. He still had to be caught. I told the police they were putting out decoys who looked like decoys instead of prospective victims. They didn't believe me, so I went out with the right attitude and brought him down. Simple as that."

Harvey chuckled. "I gather he's since regretted choosing you for his victim of the evening."

She looked entirely pleased with herself. "He lost two teeth, ended up with a broken jaw and nose, and let's just say it was a long time before he even thought of looking at a woman. While the police weren't entirely happy about a civilian—and a female—catching him, the women at the club were ecstatic that another woman had the power to subdue her attacker. They realized that learning self-defense would do some good, and my classes almost tripled in attendance."

Harvey glanced at his watch. "Dinnertime's coming, darlin'."

Nikki shook her head, bemused by what she'd heard. "I haven't said I'd go yet. So thanks to a suspicious cop, you decided to come down and see me."

"I started looking for you when I didn't hear from you after six months. I wanted to give you time to come to terms with what happened. I didn't realize you'd be so stubborn about it. You made finding you harder by using your great-grandmother's maiden name," he admitted. "You look good, Nik. Real good."

Nikki shrugged. She knew Harvey hadn't traveled all the way to Baton Rouge just to exchange pleasantries, but she would wait and let him make the first move.

"Five days a week of teaching aerobics and self-defense classes tends to keep you fit."

He looked around, uneasy at the number of people giving him curious glances. "Little do they know just how accomplished a self-defense instructor they have."

Nikki was amused by Harvey's discomfort. "They probably think you want to sign up."

He turned back to her. "Dinner tonight?"

She studied the intense light in his gaze. "Why?"

"Because I haven't seen you in five years and I'd like to catch up. Find out how you're doing."

"Why?"

He drew a deep breath. "Nikki, I'm not your father. Don't treat me the way you treat him."

He was right, and she knew it. She shouldn't treat him this way, but too many memories intruded.

"Where are you staying?" She nodded when she heard the name of the hotel. "They have an excellent dining room. I'll meet you in the bar at seven."

Harvey held back his sigh of relief. For a moment he'd been positive she was going to refuse him altogether. He couldn't afford that; time was too important right now. He picked up her hand, squeezed it and walked away.

"Just as long as you're paying," she called after him.

Nikki remained in the room, watching Harvey push open the heavy glass doors and exit. She wondered what he wanted. She only hoped she would be strong enough to refuse him.

A heavy southern drawl intruded on her thoughts. "Darlin', you can do much better than someone like that. Besides, a man who dresses that borin' has got to work for the government! They have no fashion sense whatsoever!"

She looked up at Marcia Collins, the club owner, a woman who'd proven to be a good friend to Nikki even when the younger woman had flat out told her that all she wanted was a job and nothing more. Now Nikki appreciated Marcia's persistence in bringing her back to life.

"He's a family friend."

Marcia nodded at her explanation, but didn't entirely believe it. She hadn't missed the carefully banked anger lighting Nikki's eyes, turning them a deep golden color with only a hint of brown in the iris. She had always wondered about Nikki's background. While she was certainly qualified to teach aerobics, Marcia sensed that Nikki's qualifications went far beyond that.

"You have a nice time tonight."

Nikki hoisted her bag over her shoulder. "Maybe."

Nikki arrived at the hotel bar promptly at seven. Harvey's eyes lit up with pleasure when she walked toward his table, and he noticed that she ignored the numerous other male eyes watching her progress across the dimly lit room. Dressed in black silk trousers with a cummerbund waistband and a bronze silk blouse, she looked quite lovely.

Harvey watched her approach and realized she wasn't the woman he remembered from five years ago. It appeared Nikki had made a few changes along the way, and not just in her hairstyle. He liked what he saw.

"You're a pretty picture to this tired old man's eyes." He quickly stood up and grasped her hand in a warm grip before releasing it so he could hold her chair out for her. As she seated herself, he inhaled the warm floral scent coming from her skin. Another change. She'd never worn perfume before.

"Flattery will get you exactly nothing." She looked up as a waitress stopped at their table. "Scotch, no ice."

Harvey shook his head at the waitress's inquiry and informed her that he was fine. "Still trying to show how tough you are?"

"Some habits are hard to break."

Harvey sipped his drink. "Tell me about your work. Do you enjoy it?"

She laced her fingers together and placed them on the table. "Why don't we just cut to the chase? You've always said that small talk is necessary only at diplomatic functions. Let's make it easy on ourselves. You tell me why you're here, and I'll give you my answer—which will be a very sound no. Then we can have a nice dinner, catch up on old times and you can go back to D.C. knowing you've done your job, even if it wasn't successful." She presented the waitress with a warm, grateful smile as her drink was placed in front of her, then turned back to Harvey, the smile now wiped from her lips.

Harvey had to smile in turn. That was the Nikki he remembered.

"Three weeks ago, Dr. Scott Carter's car was blown up. The charge timer was set to go off after he was in the vehicle. That morning he happened to be running late. Otherwise, he would have been blown up with the car. A week later, someone broke into his house while he was attending a think tank where he works. His housekeeper managed to hit the panic button on the alarm, but was badly beaten for her efforts. His daughter was frightened into a near-catatonic trance."

"Poor Heather." The words slipped through her lips before she could call them back. But it didn't stop her from recalling a tiny elf of a girl with light blond hair, sapphire blue eyes and a ready grin no one could resist. When Nikki had worked in the house, she had tried so hard to keep Heather at arm's length, but the little girl had been so friendly and eager that it was almost impossible. If she regretted anything, it was that the girl had gotten emotionally hurt in the process. "Is she all right now?"

Harvey nodded, pleased he'd found a weak spot. "She's seeing a therapist to talk out her fears, and Dr. Carter has been working at home since the housekeeper resigned her position."

Nikki raised her drink to her lips. She savored the liquor sliding down her throat in a cool stream, only to explode in a ball of heat in her stomach. The sudden languor in her limbs told her that she should have eaten lunch today.

"I don't blame her for leaving. Being beaten isn't usually a part of the job description." She took a second sip. If it hadn't been for the slight dulling of her senses, she might have realized what her godfather was up to.

"We want you to come back and work for Dr. Carter again. Since you had worked there before, no one in the neighborhood would think twice of you returning. The cover story would be your hearing about the incident and wanting to come back to help out."

Only Nikki's tight grasp on her glass kept it from falling on the carpet. "I don't think that would be a good idea."

"You can do it, Nik. You did it before with great ease."

The heat blooming in her stomach suddenly turned into a ball of ice. Nikki hadn't told anyone about the dreams that still haunted her nights. She had lost count of the number of times she had woken up in a sweat and lain awake almost until dawn because she was afraid sleep would only bring the nightmares back. Nightmares about Renee Carter and her husband.

When she had worked undercover in the Carter home, she'd come to realize that Scott Carter was a thoughtful employer. Now that memory was overlaid with the memory of his open disgust when he'd learned that she was the one behind Renee's arrest.

She recalled her mixed feelings about Scott's reaction. She had always held a great respect for the man and if there had been other emotions blooming, she hadn't bothered to explore them since he was definitely off-limits. Now, though, he wasn't married. For a moment, she wondered if that wasn't why she had finally agreed to return. More for Scott than for Heather.

"Will it be easy to sleep at night knowing you've destroyed a family, Lieutenant?" It was the last thing she remembered him saying.

Little did he know.

She shrugged off the old memory. "You can't tell me that Captain Price would want me in this. I'd be his *last* choice, and I'm sure he'll tell you he can come up with someone much more qualified."

"The captain is now an admiral, and this isn't under the navy's jurisdiction, but mine." He quickly amended that last statement. "I pulled a few strings and made it mine."

"So he made admiral. He's reached the goal he was striving for all his life." She stared down at her drink. "But then, he always gets what he wants, doesn't he?"

Harvey glanced at her half-filled glass. "Shall we continue this during dinner?"

"It won't do any good to continue it. You'll still get the same answer."

He stood up. "Maybe a good steak will change your mind."

"Don't be so sure of yourself."

Harvey was clever enough to discuss anything but the mission as they were seated in the dining room, where Nikki ordered a seafood platter and he had his usual steak.

He was clever enough to wait until they were served and had begun eating, first catching up on old news before he returned to their original topic. "I need you for this, Nikki. You have the training to keep them both safe. You have to realize how important it is for you to come back."

Nikki didn't have to think twice. "Find someone else, Harvey." She looked down at her plate, glad they had resumed their argument near the end of the meal. At least she wouldn't have to walk out before she'd eaten. She pushed back her chair and stood up. "It was wonderful to see you. Perhaps next time you'll stop by because you want to *see* me instead of because you want something *from* me."

He looked up. His expression was weary, as if he wasn't able to continue the discussion. "Nikki, I'm not feeding you a story when I say I need you for this." His admission was quietly given and she instinctively knew it was from the heart. He wasn't one to plead.

She blamed herself for the telling pause that came next, because it gave him time to use his trump card.

"Think of Heather. She's already lost her mother. What will happen to her if she loses her father, too? Or worse, what if she's the one who ends up a victim?"

How could she sleep if she later learned Heather had lost her life because of improper security? Nikki didn't consider herself Superwoman, but she was an expert in security matters. She wasn't sure who she hated most—Harvey for doing this or herself for thinking of giving in.

"Give me a week to tie things up here," she finally replied in a low voice as she bent down to pick up her purse. "And tell my father not to worry that I'll contact him, because I won't." As she straightened, she looked at Harvey with a gaze that chilled him to the bone. She would have been furious if he'd told her just how much she resembled her father at that moment. "And, Harvey, don't ever try emotional blackmail on me again."

With that she walked out of the dining room, once again the subject of interest to several male diners.

Harvey almost collapsed in his chair with relief. "Try it again? I'm probably lucky I survived this time."

"I don't want you to go."

Scott Carter could hold his own with world-famous scientists. He could discuss scientific and mathematical problems with the same ease with which his housekeeper sorted out a recipe. Correction, *ex*-housekeeper. He had met with the president and the leaders of several foreign nations without breaking into a sweat. So why couldn't he handle one nine-year-old girl?

He combed his fingers through his hair. He was positive the longish strands were standing on end. They did that a lot lately. Every time he tried to reason with Heather he found himself feeling as if his hands were tied. Until now, he'd had no idea that his darling, sweet-natured daughter was as stubborn as a mule.

His deep blue eyes narrowed in exasperation as he studied the small face scrunched up in a pout. He wasn't sure how he'd accomplished it, but he could swear one of her pink-ribboned braids was longer than the other. He took a deep breath as he formulated his next argument.

"Heather, I told you, I have a very important meeting to go to this morning. I can't afford to be late."

"I can go with you. I'll take my books and sit in your office while you have your meeting."

He swallowed a sigh. "Honey, you can't go with me. That's why I asked Mrs. Donelli if she could come by and look after you until I get home."

Heather wrinkled her nose at the mention of the woman who worked as the neighbors' housekeeper. Her employers traveled frequently, and she enjoyed Heather's company. "Mrs. Donelli smells funny."

"She doesn't—" He bit off the rest of his argument. How could he say that, when the sweet, elderly lady did smell strongly of mothballs and lavender sachet? "Heather, that isn't a nice thing to say, and I don't ever want you to say that to Mrs. Donelli."

She crossed her arms in front of her narrow chest and looked at him as if he'd said the most ridiculous thing. "Daddy, I don't say rude things to anyone. I'm only telling you what I think."

Scott viewed the suddenly ringing telephone as a blessing. He snatched up the receiver.

"What?" he almost shouted.

"Your troubles are over, my boy," Harvey said jovially. "I know you've had trouble finding a housekeeper, so I'm sure you'll be happy to know I've found one for you."

Scott bit off a curse. Harvey had been pushing him to increase security around the house, including having armed guards on the property, but so far he had been able to placate the man with increased police surveillance and using a driver when he went to the institute. He wouldn't put it past Harvey to find him a housekeeper who could handle a semiautomatic as easily as she could handle a frying pan.

"Don't tell me. You've gone into handling domestics, too. Thanks but no thanks, Harvey. I'll find one on my own."

"Have you had any luck finding someone who can handle one strong-willed little girl and who won't go into hysterics when a gun is thrust into her face?"

Scott shuddered at the memory of what he'd once come home to. "I'm hoping that won't happen again."

"Hope won't keep your daughter safe, and you know it. But I guarantee that we can push the odds in your favor if you'll just listen to me," Harvey assured him. "The lady I've hired will be at your house any moment now. I wouldn't worry about Heather's reaction to her. I'm sure she'll adore her."

"Harvey, I don't want any.... Harvey?" He uttered a soft curse at the silence from the other end. The older man had already hung up. Scott thought of the seminar he wouldn't be able to attend because he wasn't about to trust a stranger, even one recommended by Harvey. "Terrific. Probably another one of his musclebound agents who told him she can boil water," he muttered.

Since Scott's car had been blown up and Heather almost kidnapped, Harvey had made sure the Carter household was under constant surveillance. Scott hated it with a passion. On an almost daily basis, he wondered why he had taken up a career that involved the government.

"We're getting a new housekeeper," he started to explain to Heather, only to be interrupted by the melodic tones of the door chimes.

"Who?" Heather's eyes turned wide. "Will I like her?"

"I have no idea." He headed for the front door and pulled it open. As he did, he wondered if he should tell Heather the woman probably knew more about semiautomatic weapons than little girls' games.

Whatever else he might have thought was instantly lost as he gazed at the woman standing on the doorstep. Fury mingled with shock as he gazed into eyes the rich shade of dark honey with floating specks of brown and green. He knew this woman could give his daughter the love and attention she craved, but she was the last person he wanted there. His hands flexed at his sides as if they wanted to be around her neck, squeezing slowly.

"I just want you to know I haven't changed my mind about certain things," Nikki calmly announced as she brushed past him and stepped into the entryway. "I still won't do windows."

Chapter 2

"Nikki!" Heather practically leapt into the woman's arms. "Are you here to take care of me?"

Nikki pretended to stagger from the girl's charge. Her mouth curved in a broad smile at her exuberance. "No, this can't be Heather! You're too tall to be that munchkin I used to run after. Look how much you've grown."

Scott clenched his hands into fists to keep them from tearing his daughter from Nikki's arms. "Heather, go to your room."

"But Nikki just got here," she argued before turning back to her. "Are you gonna stay with us?"

Nikki looked over Heather's head. Her eyes fairly danced with mockery as she answered the little girl's question. "Yes, I am. Is that all right with you?"

"Yes!" Nikki shouted with glee.

Rage filled Scott's being. Normally a quiet, self-contained man, he'd never thought of himself as someone with a temper. Not until five years ago, when he'd discovered that

Nikki Price was behind Renee's arrest and was therefore the person he blamed for Renee's death.

"Heather, go to your room. *Now.*"

Once she saw the cold light in her father's eyes, Heather knew better than to argue and quickly scuttled out of the room. Before she passed out of sight, she paused long enough to look over her shoulder at Nikki. "I missed you."

Her soft confession tore at Nikki's heart.

"I missed you, too, munchkin."

Scott waited until he heard Heather's steps at the top of the stairs and her bedroom door close.

"What the hell are you doing here?"

Nikki ran her fingertips across the top of the antique table that stood near the door. She studied the dust darkening her skin and shook her head.

"It isn't that easy to find good help nowadays, is it?"

Comprehension dawned with blinding reality. "You're the one Harvey called about."

Nikki didn't answer. She walked past the living room, heading straight for the kitchen.

"How about some coffee, Scott? I know I could use some. I've been on the road for hours and feel the need for some caffeine to give my system a kick start. I didn't stop once on the drive up."

Mumbling curses under his breath about stubborn women, he had no choice but to follow her. As he stepped into the kitchen, he experienced a startling déjà vu. How many mornings had he walked in here and found Nikki at the stove fixing breakfast and listening to Heather's chatter? Except this time the picture was very different. It took a few moments for him to figure out just what the difference was.

What he first noticed was the change in her hairstyle. She had allowed it to grow over the years. It now had a slight curl to it and was pulled up into a bouncy ponytail. She was much thinner than she used to be and her tailored shorts and vest were more colorful than the dark pants and white shirts she used to wear. She had once explained to him that they were her uniform. Although he had told her she was free to wear her personal clothing, she had insisted a uniform would be more professional.

But there were more subtle changes. He noticed her fingers, long and supple in their movements as she measured out coffee grounds. He remembered she had always kept the nails short and unpolished. Now they were glossy, coral ovals, the same color that brightened her mouth. And what about that slight bump on her nose? That was new, too. He wondered how she had broken it.

Was a man behind these incredible changes in her? Not that it should matter to him. He steeled himself against that type of thinking. He had to remember what kind of woman she was.

"I want you out of here now," he said between clenched teeth.

Nikki switched on the coffeemaker, then turned to lean against the counter.

"I see you've decided against the all-white decor." She nodded toward the bright blue-and-green-print curtains moving with the morning breeze. "I like what you've done."

His eyes blazed with fury. "The hell with the kitchen! I want you gone."

She went on as if he hadn't spoken. "I wouldn't have been here until tomorrow, but I understand you have an important meeting this morning, so I left a day early." She frowned as she looked down at her watch. "In fact, you don't have time for coffee right now, do you? Not if you want to get to your meeting. Don't worry, I can get my things squared away without any trouble. I remember where everything is."

Scott felt ready to explode. "I don't care if you can walk through the house blindfolded and not bump into one damned piece of furniture. Everything has already been arranged, so we don't need you. Heather will be staying at a neighbor's while I'm gone, and you will be leaving. Now."

"No can do, Scott. I'm here to stay whether you like it or not." Her humor was replaced by a cool gaze meant to intimidate. "Maybe you don't care if you get blown away, but there's another member of this household to consider. Right now, you should think about Heather's safety." She continued, blatantly ignoring the cloud of anger darkening his features. "Tell me something, Dr. Carter. Who would you prefer to have protecting your daughter—someone who wouldn't hesitate to pull the trigger or someone who would run at the first sound of gunfire and be too frightened to think about a defenseless little girl left behind to fend for herself?"

A muscle in his cheek twitched at her direct hit.

"I suppose you still have that room next to Heather's set up as a guest room?" she went on, as if this was nothing more than a normal, everyday chat. "I'll stay in there instead of the maid's room down here off the kitchen. It will be better if I'm closer to her." She turned to open a cabinet door and pull out a mug, then cocked her head at the sound of a measured knock at the door. "I assume that's your driver?" She moved forward. "I better start doing my job and make sure."

Scott held up his hand for her to stop. He was going to take charge of the situation, one way or another!

"You don't have to. That's his knock to let me know it's him." Indecision warred with his common sense. Heather did need someone with her, but the last person he wanted on the job was Nikki. He wished he could stick around and battle this out, but he couldn't miss this meeting. "We will talk when I get back." It was his terse way of giving in. For the moment.

At least, that was how Nikki saw it.

"Don't worry about a thing," she cheerfully answered. "If you have someone call to let me know when you're leaving, I can have something ready for dinner. I hate to ruin your expectations, but the past five years haven't improved my culinary skills all that much. I can promise not to poison you, which I'm sure is a comfort."

Scott stared at the ceiling and muttered several words under his breath. Nikki hid her smile from him. She knew he wouldn't have spoken that way if Heather had been present. She watched him stalk out of the room, pulling on the knot of his tie as if he was strangling someone. Nikki had no difficulty in identifying his victim.

"Have a nice afternoon," she called after him. "Oh—is there anything special you'd like for dinner?"

A slammed door was his reply.

Nikki reached out with one hand and grabbed hold of a nearby chair, dropping onto it before her legs gave out. As she sat there, cradling the mug of hot liquid between palms that felt ice cold, she could feel the sweat trickling down her back. Delayed reaction was setting in with a vengeance.

Not by a flicker of an eyelash had she allowed Scott to know how she'd truly felt during their conversation. She'd been prepared to find hate and disgust in his gaze. It was only natural, since he blamed her for Renee's death.

What she hadn't expected was to discover that the somewhat staid, button-down scientist had changed over the past five years, just as she had since her resignation from the military. And it seemed both of them had changed for the better.

Nikki stood in the kitchen and asked herself why she was there. She had begun a new life in Louisiana—had even dated a little, thanks to Marcia's less-than-subtle pushing. But so far, Nikki hadn't met a man she could see herself spending the next fifty years with. So why did looking at Scott give her such a strange feeling? A feeling of coming home?

"You were a fool to come back, Nikki, my girl," she muttered to herself, lifting her cup to her lips.

"Nikki?"

She looked up to find Heather standing uncertainly in the kitchen doorway. Nikki's heart melted the moment she saw her. She dredged up a smile and held out her arms. The little girl immediately ran over and climbed onto her lap, although Nikki privately hazarded a guess that Heather usually insisted she was much too old to sit on a person's lap these days.

"You are going to stay, aren't you? First Mommy went away, then you did, and I missed you so much. Didn't you love me anymore? Daddy was really mad at everybody then. When I asked him when you were coming back, he said you weren't." Her questions flew fast and furiously. "Daddy said I'd forget you when I got bigger, but I knew I wouldn't. And I didn't," she proudly added.

Damn him! Nikki swallowed the emotion filling her throat as she looked at the open adoration lighting up Heather's face. She couldn't remember the last time someone had displayed warm affection so easily. She had never seen it in her family; she'd grown up watching her friends' parents hug them and love them while she received only more rules to live by.

"I had to go because my own mommy was sick, munchkin." She hated lying to her, but she felt this was one time a lie was necessary. "She needed me to take care of her because I was all she had, and I knew you had your dad."

Heather's rosebud mouth rounded in a silent O. "Is she all better now? You can stay, can't you? You won't have to go away again?"

Nikki hugged her tightly. "Yes, I can stay until you get so tired of me, you'll beg me to leave."

The corners of her lips turned downward. "I'll never want you to leave. Daddy said Mommy won't ever be back, so you have to stay. I love you, Nikki."

Nikki remained quiet. For the moment, she was content to rock the girl back and forth in her arms as she rolled ideas over in her mind.

She knew she would have a fight on her hands when Scott returned. Harvey had warned her it wouldn't be easy, but she would have known that anyway. After all, the last time she'd faced Scott, he'd wished her in hell. It was apparent his feelings toward her hadn't changed. She couldn't blame him. She'd simply have to overrule him.

As she realized what conclusion she'd reached, she felt like laughing. For someone who hadn't wanted to come here in the first place, she was making a lot of plans to entrench herself in the household.

"Why don't you help me unpack?" she suggested, jiggling the girl. "I bet if you do a real good job, you might even find something in my bags that has your name on it."

Heather was off her lap in a flash and running for the door.

"Wait up!" Nikki ran after her. She held onto Heather's hand as she squatted down to the little girl's level. She willed Heather to look into her eyes as she made her point. "You have to promise me that you'll never go outside unless either your dad or I are with you."

She nodded.

Nikki forced herself to sound stern. "I'm very serious about this, Heather. It's important you do what I say. I don't want you going out by yourself."

"You're telling me this because that bad man came in here and hurt Mrs. Grainger and tried to hurt me," she said in a small whisper. "I don't want him to get me, Nikki."

"No one is going to get you. I'll make very sure of that." Nikki took a deep breath and smiled to lighten the mood. "Now let's bring my bags inside and get them unpacked."

Scott silently cursed Nikki during the drive to his meeting. He hadn't expected her reappearance in his life and right now was not a good time. During the meeting, he was constantly distracted as he tried to figure out what he was going to do about her. He was rudely pulled back to the present as he realized the debate going on had to do with him.

"I don't see what the problem is," he said in a clipped voice, directing his ire toward the closest target. "It's not as if the institute has been directly threatened."

"We all realize the past few weeks have been difficult for you, Dr. Carter, and you may not see things the way we do. It's just that we're not comfortable with the notoriety you've received from these threats on your person. The bombing of your car was horrifying, and that someone would break into your house and assault your housekeeper shows how serious this issue is," David Westin, one of the other department heads and unofficial team leader, intoned, looking at Scott over the top of his reading glasses. "We believe in keeping a low profile here. And it just isn't happening." Dressed in a muted-plaid, wool sport coat, cream-colored shirt and rep tie, he looked like the mathematics professor he had been for seventeen years before joining the institute.

"I can understand your concern. You must be relieved that the newspapers only stated I was working with a private institute and didn't bother naming it."

Scott's sarcasm didn't go unnoticed.

"That's not the point and you know it."

"Then what is the point, David?" Fed up with the direction of their talk, Scott shook his head. To think he hadn't wanted to miss this meeting! Little had he known he would be the main topic. "You were only too happy to have me join you when I left my post with the navy. You said you didn't even mind the fact that my wife had been branded a traitor, since I was shown to be squeaky clean. And even more important, I was willing to finish my work under the institute's banner." He spit out each word, with chilling results. "Or have you forgotten our first meeting, when you pontificated on how wonderful it would be to have a scientist with my background here?"

David's pursed lips indicated just how unhappy he was with Scott's derisive assessment. "I can tell you aren't seeing it the way we are. No matter what you believe, we are only thinking of you. With everything that's happened and the pressure you've been under, we thought you might prefer to work from your home."

Scott straightened up. "I'm curious, David. What changed your mind?"

"From the beginning you've known what a small and select group we are, Dr. Carter," one of the other men ventured to say in a halting voice. He stared at his notes, as if he was reading from a speech. "The rest of us are involved in experiments that don't command the public attention yours has." He held up his hands in a gesture of resignation. "We aren't used to being under so much public scrutiny. It makes us uncomfortable. Reporters standing by the doors, lurking in the parking lot. It's very... unnerving."

Scott swallowed the retort crawling up his throat. "Perhaps you're right—I'd hate to think I'd bring the institute any unwanted publicity. I can see only one way to handle this that will make everyone happy. You'll have my resignation on your desk within the hour." He reached down for his briefcase.

David sat up straight. "Dr. Carter, we weren't—"

Scott shot him a look that sliced to the bone. "Yes, you were."

"You, of course, will leave your records here," one of the other men said.

Scott's reply wasn't something the other men heard on a daily basis.

The scientist didn't flinch. "The contract you signed states that any research executed here belongs to the institute, Dr. Carter."

"It also states that any findings I come up with belong to me and only me."

"I think we can reach some sort of compromise here," David offered hastily. "After all, Dr. Carter's name did give the institute the opportunity to receive several very large grants last year. I'm sure we can find a reasonable solution."

Scott remained standing. "I'm nothing if not reasonable." He also knew a nice portion of the institute's funding would leave with him.

In the end, it was decided they would not object to Scott's use of the institute's laboratories on a part-time basis until the source of his trouble could be identified. His assistants would split their time between the lab and Scott's home.

Scott looked from one man to another. He wondered if one of them could be behind all his trouble. He respected all the men, even David Westin, with his stiff-necked ideas. He hated to think he had nowhere to call safe.

"Is that acceptable?" David asked.

"All I care about is getting on with my research," Scott replied. "As long as you allow that, everything is acceptable."

As Scott headed for his office, he thought of the confrontation he would be facing next. For the last two hours, he had tried to put it to the back of his mind so he could concentrate on the meeting. Now that it was over, he couldn't avoid his problem any longer. As he thought about it, he realized the lab's solution might work out even better than he had hoped, since it would allow him to adjust his hours to Heather's.

"It seems the esteemed Lieutenant Nikki Price won't be needed after all," he muttered, already relishing the idea of sending the lady on her way.

Scott headed downstairs with the intention of checking in his lab. He inserted his electronic key card in the slot by the door and waited until the light turned green before twisting the knob. The laboratory was filled with several computers, printers and various electronic equipment hooked up to the computers. One young woman sat at a monitor typing, only half listening as a man mumbled and cursed while he fiddled inside the computer terminal next to hers.

"Kay, there is nothing wrong here," he grumbled, settling his baseball cap on his head backward.

"Then why won't it boot up?" she argued.

"Hell if I know."

"Maybe if you'd treat it gently it would," Scott intoned. Both looked up, offering their boss broad smiles.

"About time you got down here," the young man groused, turning back to his work. "Aphrodite crashed."

Scott grimaced. "Dammit, Cully, why didn't you call me?"

"You were already on your way when it happened." He straightened up and dropped into a nearby chair, long legs sprawled in front of him. In his early twenties, Cully O'Brien was a rising star in computer technology, having graduated from a top university with a variety of advanced degrees by the time he was twenty-one. So engrossed in his work he often forgot to eat, he looked almost frail in his tattered jeans and T-shirt. He took off his glasses and rubbed his eyes.

"Hey, Kay, how come the boss gets to go home while we stay here and slave away?" He flashed Scott a grin.

"Because he knows we're stupid enough to get the little stuff done." She didn't pause in her data inputting. Dressed as casually as Cully in jeans and a T-shirt, Kay Garvey looked more like a teenager than a young woman of twenty-five.

Scott gazed at the two people he had handpicked for his team. It wasn't difficult to find good assistants who could put up with him. It *was* difficult to find people he could feel comfortable with; Cully, with his irreverence for the world, and Kay, who shared the same lighthearted manner, were a perfect complement for Scott's more-serious side.

He walked over to the computer Cully had been cursing. "Let's get this fixed. Then I want you two out of here. From now on, we'll be alternating our work between here and my home lab."

"Cool." Cully reached for several tools. "I'd like this place a hell of a lot better if it had a pool."

"As if you'd ever use it," Kay gibed.

As Scott went to work on the downed computer, thoughts of what would be waiting for him at home left his mind.

The first thing Scott heard when he walked into the house was the sound of Heather's laughter. He couldn't remember the last time he'd heard his daughter laugh so freely. He wasn't happy to acknowledge who was behind that laughter. He followed the sound to the backyard, where he found Heather sitting cross-legged in the grass with Nikki facing her. Dolls and an elaborate tea set were placed between them.

He stood in the doorway for several moments, watching the domestic scene unfolding before him. He didn't like what he saw; Heather was already growing close to Nikki, and he didn't want that. The little girl had had enough pain in her life. What would happen to her when Nikki left again?

He noticed that Heather's hair had been rebrushed and rebraided. Her bright pink-and-white-striped T-shirt and pink shorts were rumpled from her play. But it was the sight of her cheeks flushed with happiness and the sound of musical laughter that struck him in the heart. Had Nikki, in the course of a couple hours, been able to accomplish what others, especially himself, hadn't managed in months?

Jealousy billowed upward for a moment, but he quickly tamped it down.

As he watched them, he noted again the many changes in Nikki. That last time he had seen her she had worn her dress blues, looking every inch a naval officer.

The rust-colored, pleated shorts and rust-and-turquoise-striped vest she wore today left her throat and arms exposed. As she stretched out her bare legs in front of her, he noticed they were the same sun-kissed color as her arms. He couldn't remember ever seeing her hair styled in anything as youthful as the ponytail she sported now, nor did he remember the burnished copper lights shining in her hair. And if he wasn't wrong, he'd swear she was wearing makeup. He felt as if a fist had planted itself in the pit of his stomach as he stared at Nikki, who seemed to be taking the doll party as seriously as Heather was. Why would he allow himself to feel these threads of attraction for a woman who had caused so much turmoil for his family?

"Daddy!" Heather's squeal of delight brought him back to the present. He pasted a smile on his face and held out his arms as she ran toward him.

"What are you up to?" he asked, forcing himself to act as if nothing was wrong.

"Nikki and I are playing Barbie." As she gestured behind her, she leaned back dangerously, but she had no fear her father would accidentally drop her. "I told her sometimes I think I'm too old for dolls, but she said you're never too old for Barbie. She brought me a playhouse for my dolls," she confided. "She promised to help me put it together in my room."

Scott's facial muscles tightened at the allusion to Nikki's staying.

"I have good news for you, honey. I won't be working at the institute every day." He purposely made it sound like the beginning of a grand party. "I'll be doing a lot of my research here at home, so you'll have me all to yourself."

"How generous of them." Nikki arched an eyebrow as she approached them at a languid pace. "I didn't think they'd allow someone so important to work away from their all-seeing eye. From what I've read about the Sanborn Institute, they like to keep pretty close tabs on their people. Why, I bet you even have to sign out to go to the bathroom."

He stared at her over his daughter's head. "We worked things out." He turned back to Heather. "Sweetie, why don't you go inside and change your clothes? We'll treat ourselves to dinner out. Anything you want."

"Pizza!" she shouted as she jumped from his arms and ran inside.

It wasn't until then that Scott realized being alone with Nikki, even for a few moments, was a mistake. A hint of perfume floated in his direction, and his senses abruptly teased him into visualizing a background more seductive than his grassy backyard. He was sure Nikki couldn't be enticing him deliberately and had to blame his celibate lifestyle for allowing him to fantasize about the first woman who'd stomped into his life.

"After your previous success in my household, I'm surprised the navy would give you the time off to play housekeeper again. Or do they think Heather is taking up where her mother left off and is now selling military secrets to her classmates?" Only a darkening in the depth of Nikki's eyes told him he'd hit his mark. "After all, she's in school now. Who knows what tidbits she's passing on to the other kids?"

"Just as the navy no longer has jurisdiction over you, they no longer have any over me. I'm here at Harvey's request."

"If you think that will make your presence here any more tolerable, you're very wrong." He leaned over her, grateful that while she was tall, he was taller. He figured she was a good four inches shorter than his six foot three and he intended to make that difference known.

He soon learned it wouldn't work. Because of the family she grew up in, physical intimidation seemed to have no effect on Nikki. She stared back at him without an ounce of fear.

She shrugged as if it wasn't all that important. "It just means that I gave up uniforms in favor of a more-casual wardrobe. I discovered that clothes shopping could be a lot of fun." She looked completely relaxed under his growing fury. "I'm surprised the old fogies at the institute didn't force you to resign. I understand Sanborn hates anything that smacks of unwanted publicity and will do anything to avoid it. They must hate you a lot right now."

Even though he wanted to remain angry with her, Scott had to smile at her description of his colleagues.

"I'm not sure all of them would fall into the 'old fogey' category, but I'd say it covers most of them." He pretended to think about it. "David Westin with his closeminded ideas probably comes closest to that description. But, no, resignation wasn't mentioned," he lied. "They were willing to compromise as long as I was."

"I thought all scientists have to have an open mind, so they can look beyond what's in front of their crossed little eyes. Otherwise, they wouldn't be able to come up with all those new, handy-dandy little gadgets for the public."

Scott shook his head. "You can't have too open a mind when you're worried about investors." His chest rose and fell with the deep breath he took. "Look, I know Harvey had some devious plan in sending you out here, because he's been bound and determined to turn this place into an armed camp. But that doesn't mean I have to like it or go along with it."

"Maybe not, but he's only thinking of your welfare," she said quietly. She smiled at his look of surprise. "I may not have the off-the-scale IQ you have, but I can tell when I'm unwanted. Especially when someone is as blatant about it as you are. Be honest, Scott. You don't want me here because I bring back bad memories. When you see me, you remember what happened to Renee and you blame me for it."

Scott's features darkened at her less-than-subtle reminder. How could he have forgotten how blunt she was? "I suggest you leave before I strangle you." He turned away.

"No!" Nikki grabbed his arm and jerked him back around. "We need to have this out!"

Scott was so stunned he couldn't respond for a moment. As he looked into her eyes, blazing with fury, and saw her haughty expression, a sudden thought flashed through his mind: how would she react if he pulled her into his arms and kissed her until no air was left in their lungs? As that thought blossomed in his mind, a darker thought took its place—a memory. A memory of that day when two federal officers had come to the door, informing him that they were under orders to take Renee Carter into custody. The charge—treason.

"Believe me, Lieutenant, you don't want to have it out," Scott said through gritted teeth. "Because you won't like what I'll have to say." He turned to face her fully and grabbed hold of her arms in a punishing grip. "Damn you for even bringing it up."

He had to give her credit. She still didn't back down from his fury. She stood there unflinching as she took his verbal abuse.

He kept hold of her hand and dragged her through the kitchen and down a stairway leading to a windowless room that she knew housed his lab. He released her as suddenly as he'd grabbed her and walked over to a drafting table set up next to two technologically advanced computers.

"Heather," she cautioned, giving a token protest, although she knew it wouldn't do any good.

"I can hear her from here and she knows how to use the intercom," he said in a clipped voice. At the drafting table he turned around, bracing himself against its edge. "You came into my house more than five years ago, allowing us to think you were an experienced housekeeper. I guess I should have known better when you really couldn't cook worth a damn. I never had so much indigestion in my life. I thought I was going to have to live on antacids and even told Renee we should let you go. But Renee insisted on keeping you because you were so good with Heather."

"No one bothered to check out my culinary credentials before giving me the assignment," Nikki interjected. "I was told to come in, observe all of you and report back my observations."

His eyes turned a steely blue. "Assignment. That's all we were to you, weren't we? A damn assignment. You came into this house, became a part of the family until Heather idolized you. Then you upset everything by falsely accusing Renee of treason."

Her gaze blandly met his. "Considering the evidence found, we had no choice but to take Renee in for questioning. It was an open-and-shut case. We only wished we could have gotten the name of her contact."

His opinion of her idea of "questioning" was decidedly profane.

As if he couldn't stand looking at her, Scott spun around. His back was straight and he braced his hands on his hips as he tipped back his head and stared upward. But he could find no answers on the ceiling, only stark white insulation tiles.

"I admit Renee was vain at times and she was selfish. Not to mention she resented my work like hell," he said finally, still looking up at the ceiling. "But she would never have taken my notes and sold them. She never went into the lab or broke into my files. I don't see how anyone could think she would, since she'd never bothered learning how to use a computer, much less my own."

Nikki stood there staring at his broad expanse of back covered in soft green cotton. A part of her noticed the way his dark hair curled over his collar. She couldn't remember his ever wearing his hair in anything other than a short, almost-military cut. Now it looked soft and silky. She wondered if it would feel that way if she sifted her fingers through the strands. Would his back muscles flex under her fingertips if she dared touch him? As she realized the direction her thoughts were taking her, she reined them in immediately.

She thought of telling him she'd resigned because she'd felt as if Renee's death might have been her fault. Except she couldn't find the right words . . . if such words even existed.

"Why don't we just agree that we'll disagree on this and go on from there," she suggested.

He turned back around. "What do you mean, go on from there?"

"That even if you're going to work here on a part-time basis, you'll still need me here. Heather isn't in school twenty-four hours a day. She needs to have someone close by. You might even want to think about sending her away until the perpetrator is caught.''

''No!'' He suddenly shook his head in rapid movement, signifying a silent apology for his abruptness. When he spoke, his voice was so quiet she almost couldn't hear him. ''When our last housekeeper was assaulted, I said something about sending Heather to her grandparents and she promptly went into hysterics. She didn't want to be away from me. It's only been in the past week that she hasn't thrown a tantrum when I've had to go to the institute. She needs to know I'll never be far from her.'' His eyes pierced her with laser brightness. ''The therapist she's been seeing says she's afraid I'll go away and not come back, the way her mother did. I intend to show her that won't happen. If she's at her grandparents, she'll constantly worry about me.''

The remark shouldn't have hurt. After all, Nikki knew Scott wanted her gone and would do anything to force her out.

''With me here, you won't have to worry about that.''

''The way I was told not to worry when Renee was arrested? The way I was told it was nothing more than standard procedure and everything would be all right once it was cleared up? I want you gone.''

It was on the tip of her tongue to tell him she had her own suspicions about the evidence that had mounted up so quickly against Renee.

But what good would it do for her to tell him that the more she thought about it, the more she felt his dead wife was innocent? That she had even begun to wonder if Renee's death was really a suicide? If she voiced her thoughts, she'd feel even more compelled to find out if she was right, and the danger Scott was in would increase tenfold.

No, she'd keep quiet for the time being, until she could do a little discreet investigating. But if he intended to wound her, she would not only show him she wasn't hurt, she'd fight back.

"I came back here because I felt Heather needed some-one on her side. Someone willing to go that extra mile to protect her. You'll never have to worry about her safety as long as I'm here. I'll go you one better than that," she of-fered. "I'll guarantee you'll come out of this alive."

Chapter 3

The room was dark except for a lamp shining a tiny pool of light onto the desk surface. The lack of clutter on the polished cherrywood top had nothing to do with the owner's habits, but with the need for ensuring that no incriminating papers were left out where they could be found.

The man sitting at the desk had been staring at the photo in his hand for several moments. He didn't look up when the alarm on his watch beeped several times. He picked up the telephone and punched out a series of numbers. He waited, listening to the series of clicks and tones that indicated the call was making its way through several exchanges until it reached its destination without any worry of detection.

"Yes?"

"She's installed in the house." No names were given. There was no need, when the two men were partners in many ways.

"Why was she brought back?"

"It was decided the little girl should have someone she knows and trusts around. That way, Carter's guard will be lowered, since he won't be worrying about his daughter."

The man chuckled. "After what happened before, I can't imagine Dr. Carter would want Price in his home."

"The way I heard it, the powers that be wanted her there whether he wanted her or not."

"Do you honestly think she's going to let us walk in and obtain Carter's final pages?"

"No. I've heard she's very good at what she does, but I've done some research on her and she seems to have a few blind spots. By working on those, we'll have the papers before anyone realizes what's happened. We won't have to worry about leaving any tracks thanks to the computer age. Evidence will suddenly appear showing that Nikki Price framed Renee Carter five years ago. She'll be filled with remorse for what she's done and will kill herself over it. Naturally, her father will have to resign from the navy because of the scandal, and her brothers' careers will also suffer from the fallout. She'll be dead, her father will live out his days in disgrace and we will be very wealthy gentlemen. Anything wrong with that?"

"Not a thing."

Chapter 4

It didn't take Scott long to realize sleep would not be part of his agenda that night. What made him think he could sleep when all his senses were centered on the woman residing in the guest bedroom two doors down the hallway?

The liquid red numerals on his clock mocked him as they advanced every sixty seconds, ticking off the minutes and hours as he lay on sheets that seemed to suffocate him.

"Damn her," he muttered, rolling over and punching his pillow for what was probably the twentieth time that night. He was convinced by morning it would be flat as a pancake. "Why couldn't she have stayed wherever she came from? Why did she have to reappear and stir things up just when I felt as if my life had returned to normal?"

He froze as he heard a barely audible sound coming from the hallway. Just as quickly, he relaxed. He didn't need to look out to know it was Nikki doing her job. He strained his ears but couldn't hear anything more. She was good. Very good.

He had to wonder what she had been doing the past five years. Where she had gone? And what had brought about the changes in her? He decided if he wasn't going to be allowed to sleep, he might as well do something useful—such as try to figure out Nikki Price.

The woman who had insinuated herself into his household five years ago had been unobtrusive and so quiet he'd once joked to Renee that he wondered if she wasn't some sort of android—he'd be anxious to meet her creator! It wasn't until later that he came to understand why she acted so aloof. She was a member of Naval Intelligence and had a job to do. And since she was also the daughter of a naval officer who, rumor had it, probably had more power and contacts than most members of the Pentagon and government agencies rolled up into one, she did her job very well.

Scott had dealt with Adam Price in the past and wasn't shy in voicing his opinion of the man. He figured only someone without a soul could rise as high and as swiftly as Price had. And Nikki was obviously just like her father.

No, he corrected himself. The woman he'd seen today was nothing like her father, nor like the Nikki he remembered.

Unwillingly, a question rose in Scott's head as he mulled over his unwanted houseguest. What had it been like for Nikki, growing up in an all-male household? Her brothers were all in the military and rising with the same single-minded purpose her father had displayed. There was no question they were career officers. And Nikki had shown that same purpose. So why had she resigned from the navy when she had just made the arrest that would seal her career? It would have insured her pick of assignments—she'd become the darling of the navy because she'd discovered a traitor. Instead, she'd tendered her resignation and abruptly disappeared.

He suddenly swore under his breath. What was he doing? The last thing he wanted to do was think about her. Then the memory of her perfume burst inside his mind. The exotic fragrance held a hint of vanilla and cinnamon. Why had he ever thought those two scents were common? He thought of deserted islands in the Pacific when he stood close to her. He thought of cool sheets on a hot night. He only wished he didn't feel something so elemental and arousing when around her.

He breathed a huge sigh. And this was only the first day! Scott dreaded the days to come; he knew she would insinuate herself into his family again no matter how badly he wanted her gone. Another fear took place. She had brought sorrow to them before. What kind of heartache would she leave behind this time?

He stiffened as he once more sensed movement in the hallway, then heard the faint click of a door closing.

"Damn her," he muttered, closing his eyes and firmly willing himself to sleep.

"Mrs. Grainger used to make really good muffins for breakfast." Heather climbed up on the stool at the breakfast bar so she could watch Nikki cook breakfast.

"She did?" Nikki pulled a carton of eggs and a package of bacon out of the refrigerator. "What kind did she make?"

"All kinds. Sometimes they were lemon or orange or they had blueberries in them, and once she made strawberry muffins." The little girl's voice was filled with awe.

Nikki checked her smile. "Obviously Mrs. Grainger was a much more accomplished cook than I am. I'm afraid if you have muffins they'll either come from a mix or a bakery. More likely the bakery."

"That's okay. I bet you can make other good stuff."

"Obviously, you don't remember Ms. Price's cooking." Scott walked into the kitchen and headed straight for the coffeemaker. He waved Nikki away when she moved to pour him a cup and took care of it himself.

He curved an arm around Heather's shoulder and dropped a kiss on her brow as he passed by her. That was one thing Nikki had noticed from the very beginning—Scott had never been afraid to show his love and affection for his wife and daughter. He was free with hugs, kisses; he'd even pick Heather up and spin her around in a circle—anything to show them he cared. Nikki couldn't remember the last time her own father had touched her, shown any affection—if indeed, he ever had. Seeing Scott display warmth toward Heather brought a strange feeling to the pit of her stomach.

Scott used his foot to snag the stool next to his daughter and sat down.

As Nikki cracked eggs into a bowl and beat them into a frothy mixture, she was keenly aware of Scott's gaze focused on her. She didn't bother to ask him how he'd slept. She couldn't imagine anyone missing his bloodshot eyes or the way he gulped his coffee. She hid her smile as she noticed him wincing when the hot liquid touched his lips.

"Is there any reason you make it strong enough to float the entire navy?" he muttered, grimacing as the caffeine exploded in his veins.

Nikki smiled. "It's better than a wake-up call."

"I think I'd prefer the call." He took careful sips of his coffee after that, staring into the dark brown depths as if they held all the answers to his problems. "So what's your agenda, Lieutenant?"

"After breakfast, I'll take Heather to school, then come back here." She carefully laid strips of bacon on the hot griddle. "I'll make enough appearances outside so your neighbors will know you have a housekeeper again. I understand the Sandersons are in Barbados right now." She didn't bother to wait for his reply. "Julia Willis is still their housekeeper, and Wilma Andrews still works for the Matthewes, although they have a new nanny, Christine Abbott. She's been checked out and shows a clean background, although not squeaky clean. She was considered a troublemaker in the fourth grade because she refused to be a wicked witch in the school play. She insisted the witch couldn't be all bad."

That was one thing Scott hated: how easily Nikki—and other people in power—could obtain the most personal and obscure information on people. "What else do you know about her? Did she kick her mother too many times while still in the womb?"

Nikki slid a glance toward Heather, who seemed oblivious to the conversation. "Nothing you'd be interested in," she answered, preferring to ignore his sarcasm.

"Maybe I would be."

"I don't think so." As far as she was concerned, the subject was now closed.

Nikki served breakfast with the crisp efficiency Scott had come to expect and cleaned up while Heather returned to her room to retrieve her book bag.

"When do you eat?" he asked. He hadn't missed her brief sideways glance. It was obvious she expected him to leave. He wasn't about to make it that easy for her.

"I already have."

His gaze swept over the bright coral tank top that ended just below her trim hips and the coral-and-black-print Lycra shorts that hugged her lower body. Her hair was again pulled up in a curly ponytail, caught in a matching coral hair twist. As his gaze wandered over her, he noticed she was also barefoot. When she bent over to place plates in the dishwasher, her tank top gaped open and he caught a hint of her cleavage. He hastily gulped his coffee and almost swore as the still-too-hot liquid burned his mouth.

"I don't think anyone in the neighborhood is going to recognize the new you."

Nikki's laughter caught him off balance.

"What did I say that was so funny?" he asked in an irritated tone.

"Calling this a neighborhood." She swept her hand outward. "Tell me, do you really *know* any of your neighbors? None of the houses in this immediate area are under five thousand square feet. They all sit on five-acre lots, with swimming pools. Many have horses and or tennis courts."

She closed the dishwasher door. "All the children attend private school because they're expected to. After all, we're talking about the privileged progeny of highly placed government officials, leaders in industry, old-money families. They wouldn't know what a real life is." She speared him with eyes that glowed a rich honey brown.

"And you would?" he challenged, stung by her description. He'd worked damn hard to afford this house, and listening to her disparage it didn't improve his mood any.

"Damn straight." She turned and stared at him. "Would you like to know what a real neighborhood is?"

"Sure, tell me." Caught up by her intensity, he had no choice but to rise to her bait.

Nikki took a deep breath. "A neighborhood is more than just houses on a street. It's what's inside those houses that count. A mom and dad and kids. Bicycles and other toys littering the front yards and dads working on their cars in the driveway. Dogs sleeping on front porches or eyeing the neighbors' cats. Kids playing in the park at the end of the block. Having the neighbors over for barbecues on Saturday nights or Sunday afternoons. Wondering how you're going to pay for the kids' college tuition or if you're really going to let your daughter wear that low-cut dress to the prom. And can your son honestly handle that job he's taken after school because he wants to buy a car? In a real neighborhood, you have friends, not just people you nod to every morning when you go outside to get the morning paper." Her body fairly quivered with indignation. "That's what a neighborhood is."

Scott was stunned by Nikki's words. "I didn't think a military brat would know about these things."

All life in her eyes died as his words sunk in. When she straightened, he saw a trace of the cool, assured woman he remembered.

"It is true that base housing doesn't exactly qualify as a neighborhood, Dr. Carter. Now, if you'll excuse me, I need to take your daughter to school." She walked out of the kitchen, leaving behind a heavy, tension-filled atmosphere Scott doubted would dissipate anytime soon.

He stared at the doorway she had just disappeared through.

"So the lady has a bit of a temper," he mused, lifting his cup to his lips. This time, the coffee could have been pure acid and he wouldn't have noticed.

Nikki operated on automatic pilot, barely listening to Heather's chatter as she drove to the private school Heather attended. But it didn't stop her from continually checking the rearview mirror to ensure they weren't being followed.

She soon pulled up in front of the sprawling, two-story stone building, with the ivy-covered sign announcing that Butler Academy had been forming young minds since 1872.

"Are you going to pick me up after classes?" the girl asked as she gathered up her book bag.

"I'll be here."

Heather nodded. She hesitated before climbing out of Nikki's four-wheel-drive vehicle.

"I'm really glad you're back." Her elfin face suddenly lit up with a smile before she jumped to the sidewalk and ran off with a quick wave over her shoulder. Nikki remained at the curb, watching Heather join a small group of girls, then walk into the building.

She'd barely left the vicinity of the school when her car phone beeped. She waited a few seconds before picking it up. She didn't need to hear the caller's voice to know his identity.

"Perfect timing, Harvey. I just dropped Heather off at school."

"I've always had excellent timing. How are things going?"

She laughed briefly. "I didn't expect to be welcomed with open arms, so I wasn't surprised when I wasn't. He hates my part in Renee's arrest and naturally blames me for her death. Heather's excited I'm here, but Dr. Carter wants me gone— now."

"You know we need you there, Nikki."

She grimaced as a small sports car cut in front of her, forcing her to slow down. She mouthed a pithy curse at the driver as she adjusted the receiver in her palm. "I didn't say I was leaving. No matter what obstacles he puts in my path, I intend to stay, Harvey. And if anything else happens, I intend to see Heather out of there and in a safe place."

"I'm here if you need me."

Nikki smiled. "Good, because if Dr. Carter gets any nastier, I'm going to demand a hefty raise."

"It will be yours. One day, when things are quiet, I want us to meet for lunch."

She had to laugh at that. "Harvey, life for you is never quiet."

"All right, we'll just plan to have lunch no matter what. I'll see you soon."

Nikki replaced the phone in the cradle and quickly downshifted, changing lanes and sliding around the small sports car with the ease of a New York taxi driver. She laughed when the driver made an obscene gesture as she raced off. That little show of defiance on Nikki's part cheered her like nothing else could have as she drove back to the house.

She parked her truck in the three-car garage and got out. She walked around the roomy interior, looking into dark corners, behind boxes stacked against the wall. She noted the gardening tools placed neatly in one corner and a bright blue bicycle, obviously Heather's, resting against a wall alongside two larger mountain bikes. A pair of child-size Rollerblades was nearby. She ran her fingertips along the side of Scott's dark-colored sedan parked next to her truck as she headed toward the tarp-covered mound at the rear of the garage. She picked up a corner and peered underneath.

"My, my, look what we have here," she murmured, pulling the tarp up farther to reveal a black-and-chrome motorcycle. "How many sides does he have?"

"Snooping?"

Unperturbed at being caught, Nikki took her time to straighten and turn around. She draped the tarp back over the seat so she could better admire the smooth leather.

"This is one heavy-duty machine," she commented. "Do you have the leathers and tattoos to go with it?"

"Not the tattoos." He reached past her and flicked the tarp over the motorcycle again. "Everything is kept in its place here. Windows are clean and it's well lit. You won't find any easy hiding places in here."

"I like to see that for myself."

"Naturally."

Nikki took a moment to compose herself. She couldn't remember anyone ever irritating her the way Scott was just now. She reminded herself that the man standing before her wasn't the Scott Carter she remembered. This one was even more devastating, because he exuded a presence that was almost a raw masculinity. She wondered where that idea had come from; she couldn't remember the last time she'd thought of a man in that sense, and Scott Carter would have been the last man she'd expect to think of in that way. For Nikki, a woman who never feared anything or anyone, the idea was more than a little unnerving.

"Don't you have work to do?" She purposely made her tone crisp.

Scott's mouth curved in a faint smile. "Trying to run me off, Lieutenant?"

Damn him, he was trying to unnerve her again. Her gaze was cold enough to turn him into a block of ice.

"As you well know, Doctor, I'm no longer in the navy, so the title is not necessary."

"I think I prefer it over calling you Miss Price. Or would you prefer Ms.?" He crossed his arms in front of him and cocked his head to one side, watching her. She sensed he was gauging her reaction, as if he was deliberately goading her.

"I prefer Nikki to all of the above." She turned away. "Will you be keeping set hours in your laboratory or work-

ing only when the muse hits you? I'd like to have an idea
when you'll be in there and when you won't."

Scott straightened. It wasn't any fun playing a game no
one cared to play along with. "I will work here two to three
days a week, and the rest of the time at the institute. My assistants will be coming in to work with me. Don't worry,
they've all been checked out and passed with flying colors.
I can't give you a set schedule because it depends on how
well the work is going."

He started walking out of the garage and added over his
shoulder, "When I'm in my lab, you can reach me on the
house intercom by punching 07. Don't worry if I don't answer right away. I was once told I tend to forget the outside
world when I'm working. And don't worry about keeping
up appearances by fixing me lunch. Although I admit, having a housekeeper who looks like you feeding me would be
an interesting idea."

Nikki braced her hip against the motorcycle and watched
him head for the back door. She knew he would reach his
laboratory in the cellar from there. Since he didn't work
with chemicals, volatile or otherwise, at home, having the
lab inside the house wasn't considered dangerous. But that
wasn't what snagged her attention. What she noticed now
was the way his faded jeans hugged a very firm rear end,
how his light blue polo shirt molded to a very nice upper
body and how his tanned features were undeniably good-
looking. She couldn't stop staring, even though the threat
of his turning to catch her loomed bright.

"What happened to the geek?" she murmured thought-
fully.

Nikki spent a quiet morning straightening the house. Although Heather had made an attempt at neatness, her idea
of making her bed was pulling the covers up to her pillow.
Nikki picked up the damp towels from Heather's bathroom, then went on to make her own bed. She stopped in

front of the master bedroom. There was no mistaking that Scott had closed the door as an unwritten Keep Out sign.

"Silly man," she told herself, clasping the cold metal knob and turning it. She knew he wouldn't go so far as to lock it, and the door easily swung open at her touch. "As if that had ever stopped me before."

The moment she stepped inside the room, she felt the difference. She froze in the doorway, assimilating the many changes.

Gone was the white-washed bedroom set. Renee's dresser, littered with jewelry, perfume bottles and ornate jars filled with body creams, had been replaced with a dark wood armoire that opened up to reveal a television set and stereo system. The scrolled-wood headboard was also gone, with a brass one standing in its place. Even the air was different. The floral scent Renee had preferred was gone, and all Nikki could smell was a lingering hint of lime. The bed, covered with a quilt brightly designed in shades of cobalt blue, emerald and fuchsia, was neatly made, with even the pillow shams in place.

She peeked inside the bathroom and found the towels folded neatly on the racks, the mirror wiped clean, even though there was still a hint of humidity in the room left from Scott's shower. The floral wallpaper she remembered had been painted over in a soft cream color.

As Nikki looked around the room, a strange feeling came over her. For a moment she almost felt as if she was suffocating. Had Scott tried to wipe Renee out of his life by replacing furniture and repainting rooms? She knew the couple's marriage hadn't been perfect, but she hadn't thought it had been that bad, either. Feeling as if she had stumbled into something she shouldn't have, she quickly left the room. It wasn't until she stood out in the hallway that she started to breathe normally again.

Nikki stopped in her bedroom long enough to unlock her suitcase and pull out a large manila envelope she had rolled up and stashed in a side pocket. Carrying it in one hand, she headed for the family room, stopping off in the kitchen first for a second cup of coffee. She dropped the envelope on the coffee table, set her cup down on a coaster and settled on the floor beside the low table, curling her legs under her.

Nikki spilled the envelope's contents out in front of her and sorted through the papers and photographs. She barely glanced at the latter, preferring to concentrate on the typewritten papers first. Especially the papers detailing one Dr. Scott Reynolds Carter, age thirty-seven. Born in Bethesda, Maryland, to Robert Alan Carter and Marilyn Carter. Tested as a genius at the age of seven, advanced to third grade at that time and skipped grades several times after that. Graduated with honors from MIT at the ripe old age of seventeen and returned to school to add another degree and row of letters to his name. His expertise was in the field of computers and laser weaponry development.

"Odd combination," she murmured, using a fingernail to hold her place as she picked up her cup of coffee. She grimaced at the cooling liquid, but that didn't stop her from drinking it; she had drunk much worse than cold coffee in the past. She continued reading the basic report about Scott's work with a manufacturer under government contract, then his move to Tellis Industries, where he began research on an advanced laser weapon. That was where his troubles had started. He had insisted on having complete control over his projects and refused to release any of his findings until he was ready to. Neither the company nor the government appreciated his policy, but they had no choice but to comply—when he was well ahead of anyone else in the field.

Nikki sifted through the reports to find the one detailing his marriage to Renee Anne Winthrop twelve years ago. As Renee was the treasured only daughter of former ambassador to Brazil Randolph Winthrop and socialite Lucille Alberton Winthrop, her wedding had been the social event of the season. Accompanying newspaper clippings proved it. As Nikki read them, she remembered going through the same reports five years ago just before she'd entered the Carter household as housekeeper.

Discarding those, she dug for the report describing the recent attacks on Scott and his household. As before, reading the crisply written report of Heather's being terrorized by the masked man brought a tightness to the pit of her stomach and anger roiling deep inside like a virulent acid. Realizing she was losing her perspective, she put the report to one side. She couldn't afford to get emotional.

"That bastard will not get away again," she fiercely vowed, moving on to another report.

She lingered over the candid photographs taken of Scott standing in front of the institute or playing with Heather. The more Nikki read, the more her brow furrowed in confusion as a brief thought kept flitting through her mind. Then it hit her.

As well constructed and up-to-date as the reports were, she'd found none detailing Renee's arrest and subsequent death. Even more surprising was that there was no mention of Scott's motorcycle. She wondered how he'd kept its existence a secret and had to admire him for doing so.

Nikki unfolded her body and stretched across the table to snag the cordless phone. She quickly punched out the number that would connect her to Harvey's private line.

"Yes."

"There's something missing here, Harvey," she said, without bothering to identify herself.

"Such as?"

"Such as the reports on Renee Carter's arrest." She chose not to mention the motorcycle. It could hardly pertain to the case, and she instinctively realized—and respected—Scott's desire to keep at least part of his private life... private.

"Those aren't necessary at this time."

She swallowed her sigh. "To you, maybe, but I'd like to read them. I might find something that connects to what's going on now."

"There wasn't any reason for you to read them then and there isn't now."

She was rapidly losing her patience. "Dammit, Harvey, I want the reports!"

"They're not part of my department, Nikki," he argued.

She drummed her fingers against the tabletop in frustration. "Harvey, you have access to paperwork even the president of the United States can't touch. All you'd have to do is make one call and you'd have them. Why are you keeping me from those reports?"

There was momentary silence on the other end. "You went through a rough time back then. I wanted to spare you that."

"Harvey, if I'm to do my job here, I want to have everything at my fingertips." She decided to try charm this time around. "You can help me with that."

"All right, you'll have the reports within the hour. But you keep them away from Carter," he warned.

She breathed a sigh of relief. "No problem there. He hates to spend more than five minutes with me as it is. Thanks."

"You owe me more than lunch for this."

Nikki laughed. "And you shall have it."

Harvey's voice suddenly turned serious. "Your father wants to see you."

Her fingers tightened on the receiver. "Why? To remind me what a mistake I made in resigning?"

"I don't think that's it at all. You need to talk to him, Nikki."

"He didn't want to talk to me when I left five years ago. I have nothing to talk to him about now. Thank you for the reports, Harvey." She hung up before he could argue with her any further. When it came to the subject of her father, she had nothing more to say.

Nikki pushed all the papers back into the envelope. She carried it to her bedroom and put it in its hiding place again, making sure all was secure before she left the room.

As promised, within the hour a packet bearing a confidential seal was delivered to Nikki by special courier. She put it in her hiding place next to the other envelope, deciding she'd read it later.

She glanced at the clock and realized it was way past the lunch hour.

"No matter what the good doctor says, I guess I should feed him," she murmured, walking toward the kitchen. "Harvey would say I'm not doing my job if I let him starve."

Harvey had just received the signed receipt for the papers sent to Nikki when his visitor was announced.

The erect figure was dressed in navy blues, his admiral stars gleaming. Adam Price entered the office with the dignity befitting his rank.

"Adam, what a surprise." Harvey stood up and offered his hand. "To what do I owe this visit?"

Adam Price hadn't gotten where he was by beating around the bush. He wasn't about to start now.

"I understand Nicole is back in Carter's house," he began without preamble. "Why her and not someone from Naval Intelligence?"

Harvey chuckled. "I wondered when you'd hear the news. Tracking her down took a bit longer than I had expected, but I finally succeeded."

Adam didn't see any humor in his statement. "Why did you do that when there are agents more qualified for that kind of work and who have the proper clearance?"

"Because she has the right skills and is familiar with working undercover. Her reinstated clearance was no problem."

"Replace her."

Harvey's smile disappeared. "You forget something, Adam—in this area, I'm in charge, not you. Nikki stays."

"If she had done her job properly five years ago she would have learned the identity of Renee Carter's contact and we wouldn't have this hellish mess now,'' Adam said crisply, standing up. "All right, Harvey. As you reminded me, you're in charge of this case. I only hope you're prepared for the fallout when Nicole screws up again.'' His eyes, the same golden brown as Nikki's but with none of the warmth, speared the other man. "If they get to Carter, you have only yourself to blame.''

Harvey refused to back down. "I can live with it.''

Adam mumbled a brief curse and walked out.

"Nice to see you again, Adam,'' Harvey called after him. "Let's have lunch sometime when you're in the mood.''

He didn't expect an answer and didn't receive one.

"Dr. Carter, lunchtime!'' Nikki called out in her cheeriest voice. She waited at the closed door but heard nothing. "Dr. Carter?''

The door was opened to a recitation of curses.

"Very good,'' she said, complimenting him. "I never thought of that one. Do you think it's anatomically possible? You're the scientist. You should know that kind of thing.''

His glare rivaled one of his lasers in its intensity. "What the hell do you want?''

"I made lunch.''

Scott pulled off his glasses and rubbed his eyes. "I told you not to bother me when I'm working.''

"I made extra and didn't want it to go to waste.'' She tried to look over his shoulder, but he effectively blocked her. "Don't worry, I have a very high security clearance,'' she added.

"Good for you, but it still isn't high enough to get you in here.'' Scott glanced at the tray she held in her hands.

She noticed the direction of his gaze. "If you're through chewing my ear, I'll leave your lunch with you.'' She pushed the tray at his chest none too gently, secretly pleased when a whoosh of air escaped his lungs. With a mock bow, she walked away.

"Honey, if I was going to chew your ear, it wouldn't be in anger."

Nikki felt a faint wave of heat pass through her body at his comment.

It was only a draft of warm air, she decided as she climbed the stairs a bit more quickly than usual. There was no way she would believe Scott was deliberately goading her.

Chapter 5

Scott regretted his decision to split his work between the institute and home. Since his home computer was linked into the computers in his lab, there was no problem with that. But at the institute he didn't have to think about his bodyguard walking overhead, or showing up with a roast beef sandwich and sassy comments on the side.

He thought of calling Harvey and begging him to send Nikki away, promising anything in return. But he already knew it wouldn't do any good. Harvey was determined to keep him under surveillance and Scott realized that most of the behemoths Harvey had working for him would be worse to have around. Could there even be a part of him that wanted Nikki to stay?

He stared at the computer monitor, but couldn't have told anyone what it said.

"No wonder they call it a cursor," he muttered, using two fingers to tap several keys in rapid succession. He studied the diagram taking place on the screen, swore under his breath and began again. He hadn't told anyone of his past failure with the design. They all thought his work was further along than it really was. He had even kept his fears from Kay and Cully, which was the way Scott preferred it. Even though his crew was topnotch he sometimes caught himself wondering if they were as honest as they appeared to be.

"And here I thought only the CIA was paranoid," he muttered, tapping the Enter key and watching graphics unfurl on the monitor.

In the past, he had been hounded by government representatives demanding timetables, instant results, access to products before they were ready. If they thought he wasn't far enough along, they demanded to know why. He usually told them he was on the homestretch, so they would leave him alone and would be able to finish faster. Scott refused to take the time to figure out how their minds worked. He only wished he could be left entirely alone until he was ready to unveil each creation.

As he picked up the second half of his sandwich, he briefly imagined he could still smell Nikki's perfume. Acting purely on whim, he reached for his phone and tapped the speakerphone button. Within moments, he heard Harvey's private line ringing.

"Larsen."

"Scott Carter here." He squinted at the computer monitor as he talked and made a minor correction. "I need an answer."

Harvey chuckled. "Make it an easy question and I'll do my best."

"Why did Nikki Price leave the navy?"

"Did you ask her?"

"Anytime I bring it up, she basically tells me to go to hell and what I can do when I get there."

The older man's chuckle echoed in the room. "That's my Nikki." He grew serious. "That's up to her to tell you. I can't do that."

"You can do whatever you want, and in the past, you've done exactly that. She's living in my house, Harvey, protecting me and my daughter. I have the right to know."

"You have the right to know you have one of the best people available protecting you."

"One of the best who's been away from Naval Intelligence for five years, and, for all I know, is out of practice," he corrected. "Or has she been out in Hollywood protecting the rich and infamous since then?"

"Scott, I would not send in anyone I didn't feel was qualified to handle the job. That's all you need to know. How is your work going?"

"Fine," he lied without a qualm.

"Good, good! Now if you'll excuse me, I have a meeting at the White House within the hour and I need to gather my papers. I'll speak to you soon."

Scott hung up, feeling more frustrated than before.

"What next?"

When raised voices sounded overhead, Scott's first reaction was panic. Without bothering to shut down his computer, he leapt from his chair and practically raced up the stairs.

"I don't see why I can't!" Heather shouted, stomping into the kitchen and throwing her book bag on the floor.

Nikki followed her at a more leisurely pace. "You can't because I said so. Now, are you going to pick up that bag or are you going to leave it there until you need it again in the morning?"

Scott froze in the doorway. Instead of finding an intruder battling with Nikki as he'd feared, he found himself smack in the middle of an argument. Heather's anger was nothing new to him. She'd had tantrums off and on since Renee's death. The psychologist had explained it was her way of dealing with the facts behind her mother's death and, more recently, the attempts on her father's life.

"What the hell is going on here?"

His roar effectively checked anything further Heather might have said. She spun around, presenting him with the militant expression he had seen a few too many times in the recent past. And had hoped he wouldn't have to see again.

"Nikki told me I couldn't get the mail. I told her I always get it." She pressed her fists on nonexistent hips. "Tell her I can get the mail." Her voice rose with her indignation.

Nikki dropped a small stack of envelopes on the counter and placed her purse next to it. "I can see she'll have a brilliant future as a dramatic actress."

Scott sent her a telling glance before turning his attention back to his daughter. "I'm sure Nikki has an excellent reason for saying you can't."

Heather wasn't about to be appeased. "She told me she doesn't have to give me one."

Scott closed his eyes for a moment. The headache that had threatened to burst inside his skull was now doing its job with a vengeance.

"Heather, pick up your book bag and carry it to your room."

Her pursed lips tightened. "Aren't you going to tell Nikki I can get the mail?"

"Go. Now." The last word sent the girl scurrying; she had apparently realized she had pushed her father about as far as he was willing to go. She threw a mutinous glance at Nikki on her way out.

"We saw no problem in her retrieving the mail, since there's a man parked at the end of the block who's keeping watch on the house. Because she's under constant surveillance out there, I figured it's okay to let her do it," he said quietly. "It makes her feel more grown up."

Nikki went through the envelopes one by one, balanced each on her fingertips and studied the flap, then turned it over to examine the front.

"Wasn't it somewhere in Georgia where a judge was killed by a letter bomb? Or was it a bomb planted in the mailbox?

I always get the two mixed up.'' She spoke as casually as if she was discussing the weather. "I'm surprised Harvey didn't think of that problem. Obviously, his people out here aren't very alert. It's amazing how many oddities go through the mail. You really should have everything delivered to a private box."

The shock of her words almost drove Scott to his knees. He groped for a chair and sat down then gazed at her eyes, dark and serious against her pale features. Even then he felt as if he wanted to strangle her.

"That was a hell of a thing to say!"

Nikki didn't look the least bit apologetic. "Get real, Doc. The other attempts were their idea of playing with you. But there will come a time when playtime will be over. If they truly want to bring you down, they'll choose Heather for their victim. If it's only scare tactics, they'll still use her to get to you, because they know she's your soft spot. They'll naturally attack where you're most vulnerable."

He braced his elbows on the table and buried his face in his hands. "We figured there was nothing wrong in Heather getting the mail." His words were slightly muffled. "Harvey did say something about being careful regarding delivery-men and mailmen, but our mailman has had this route for more than fifteen years and Harvey had him checked out. We had no reason to suspect him."

"He can't be aware of the contents of every piece of mail he carries. And, just to play devil's advocate, I'd like to point out that large amounts of money have changed some very honest people," she said, setting two envelopes to one side. "I still feel Heather should be sent away someplace where she'll be safe. I also want to explain to her exactly why I don't feel she should pick up the mail for the time being."

Scott grimaced. "Does she have to know?"

"Scott, she's almost ten years old. She lost her mother at a young age, and she was terrorized at a time when she shouldn't have to worry about anything more serious than a boy sticking a frog in her face. She needs to know exactly what's going on."

He felt control of his life slipping out of his fingers. "Then why the hell didn't you tell her when she first asked you?"

"Because of the way she asked. She has to learn to accept my rules without question. Just as you need to." She deliberately kept her face expressionless. "I also want her to learn some self-defense moves."

"For God's sake, she's only nine!"

"Even nine-year-olds can learn to do some damage."

Scott's eyes were dull blue stones as he tried to assimilate the probability of even more changes in his life. He wondered what would spiral out of control next.

"Your life was put in my hands. I won't allow anything to threaten my control."

A tiny voice deep inside prompted Scott to ask, "You've never lost control?"

She looked at him squarely. "Never."

He eyed her, his mouth was lifted in an appealing curve.

"Never, huh? That's good to know." He stood up and carefully slid the chair against the table. "It's fine with me if you want to talk to Heather. I'll be honest—I don't want to send her away, and will do so only as a last resort. She's my breath of sanity in this world. But if you feel it's necessary, I'll make the arrangements for her."

"I didn't want to take this assignment to begin with," Nikki said unwillingly, sensing his pain.

"At least you didn't have to worry about Harvey asking you to rejoin the navy." He paused for a moment, then added, "Although you never did say why you resigned."

"Go to hell." There was no heat in her comment.

"Maybe I should ask your father. I'm sure he knows." He knew he'd made a mistake the moment he uttered the words.

Nikki's movements were slow and deliberate as she picked up her purse. Scott wondered if he should get ready to duck.

"If you have any brain matter that's not designated to design some hotshot, supersonic weapon to kill off more people, I suggest you use it to reconsider your statement. Because if you want to live, the admiral's name is to never come up in conversation, casual or otherwise." She matter of factly slung the bag over her shoulder and walked out of the kitchen.

It took Scott a few minutes before he could find the bottle of aspirin in one of the cabinets.

"Triple strength would have been much better," he muttered, popping two into his mouth and swallowing them dry. He felt that, for the moment, the disgusting taste in his mouth was the best punishment he could give himself.

Nikki dropped her purse off in her bedroom before going on to Heather's room. She paused in front of the closed door, hearing the girl slamming drawers and muttering angrily. Respecting her privacy, she rapped her knuckles against the wood panel instead of walking in without an invitation.

"Heather, may I come in?"

Silence reigned on the other side before the door slowly opened. Heather had already changed out of her school uniform into a pair of lavender tights and a long blue-and-lavender-print T-shirt. One of her braids had come loose and now hung in wavy tangles over her shoulder. But it was the expression on her face that tore a tiny hole in Nikki's heart. She could have sworn she had once faced her own father with that same militant expression. Each time she had dared do something he wouldn't approve of, she'd faced him as if she were one of his officers, although the results were usually a great deal worse. She deliberately closed her mind to that recollection.

"I guess if I say no, you'll come in anyway." Heather crossed the room and plopped herself on the bed. Her lower lip stuck out even more.

"No, I wouldn't. This is your room and I wouldn't think of coming in without your consent, unless it was an emergency."

As she stepped into the room, Nikki looked around. More changes. Heather's room was the perfect hideaway for a young girl, complete with a white, French-provincial canopy bed draped in pink-and-white lace. The wallpaper was a mural of a flower-strewn field and birds and butterflies flying against the blue sky. Snowy white clouds were painted on the ceiling. Nikki looked around at the shelves filled with dolls and stuffed animals that were obviously loved and played with, not just there for show. A little-girl-size table and chairs sat in one corner. It was the room Nikki would have killed for as a child. A room she never had.

But what drew her attention most was the elaborate Victorian dollhouse set on its own table near the window. She walked over and sank down on her heels, fingering a lace curtain hanging in the dining room. "I wanted a dollhouse like this when I was your age," she murmured.

Heather dropped onto her bed and sat up with her legs crossed Indian style. With Nikki's back to her, the girl couldn't see her expression, filled with longing mingled with regret.

"Daddy gave it to me for my birthday. Did you get yours for your birthday?"

Nikki shook her head as she slowly rose to her feet. "Because my dad was in the navy, we moved around a lot. My dad said I didn't need anything that would only get broken during one of the moves and he didn't feel it was appropriate for a navy brat." By the time she turned to face Heather, there was no hint of her thoughts written on her face.

Heather's brow furrowed in thought. "But if you packed it really good, it might not have gotten broken, and if it had, couldn't your daddy fix it?"

Nikki smiled as she sat on the bed beside her. "He wasn't around a lot, either. But that was a long time ago." She quickly changed the subject. "Let's deal with the present, shall we? Such as the mail. You already know someone wants to hurt your dad, and they even tried to hurt you."

Heather's head bobbed up and down. Sensing the serious intent of the conversation, she prudently remained quiet.

Nikki took a deep breath. "Sometimes they try to hurt a person in other ways than just coming into a house and physically attacking him. They can put bombs in a letter or a box and mail it to the person they want to hurt. Or they can even rig the mailbox itself. That's why I'm here—to protect you and your dad."

Heather looked puzzled. "But you're a housekeeper."

Nikki shook her head. "No, sweetheart, I was in the navy for a while and I learned special skills that enable me to protect people."

Heather's narrow shoulders rose and fell as she sighed. "I wish you could have used them when my mom was in trouble."

Nikki knew there was no way she could tell Heather exactly why she had been in the house back then. That was one truth the girl didn't need to know.

"That's why as long as I'm here, I'll pick up the mail."

Heather's shimmering blue eyes echoed her distress. "But if they could hurt us, they could hurt you, too."

"I'll be very careful. Besides, it's my job. All right?"

Heather thought about it, then nodded. "I hope they get the bad person real soon so I can get the mail again."

Nikki laughed. "I hope they do, too."

"I'm sorry I yelled at you," the girl said. "Daddy says it doesn't do any good to yell, but sometimes I get scared and I don't know what to do."

"Then yelling is the perfect thing to do to help you feel better," Nikki told her. "In fact, I'm going to arrange something for you where yelling is what you're supposed to do."

Heather's eyes widened. "Really? You mean I'd be able to yell all I want and I wouldn't get in trouble?"

"Really." Nikki released the young girl's other braid and combed the hair over her shoulder with her fingers. "Why don't you clean up in here, then you can come out and help me with dinner."

Heather jumped up and down on the bed. "All right! Mrs. Grainger never let me cook."

Nikki wasn't sure if having a nine-year-old help her cook was a good idea, but while she could, she wanted to give the girl a few positive memories of this time in her life.

But this shared time with Heather might not be quite so beneficial to Nikki. She was quickly discovering that spending time here was bringing back memories from her childhood she had no desire to explore.

One thing Scott enjoyed doing each night was tucking Heather into bed and reading her a story. Even though Heather occasionally protested that she was too old for the routine, she then relented, saying she knew it made her dear old dad feel better. Since the attack, Heather had refused to sleep in a dark room; after making sure her night-light was working properly, he dropped a kiss on her forehead and left her to sleep.

Needing to unwind, he stopped in the kitchen and poured himself a glass of wine. Movement in the backyard caught his eye and he looked out to see Nikki sitting on the pool coping, dangling her feet in the water. Occasionally, she lifted a leg, watching the water sprinkle down from her calf. Without stopping to think, he reached for the bottle and poured a second glass, then slipped off his sneakers and walked outside.

"How about something to cap off the day?" He held a glass in front of her face.

She looked up, clearly surprised to see him, and accepted the glass. "Thanks." She sipped the liquid, pleased to find it cool and tart on her tongue. "This is very good." She noticed he was still standing beside her. "Pull up a chair and sit a spell."

Scott chuckled as he dropped to the ground beside her. "Why don't you just go in for a swim? It's more than warm enough tonight."

She shook her head. "No, this is fine for me." She took another sip. "I'd forgotten how pretty spring is back here."

He decided that asking a semipersonal question might not hurt. "Where have you been living?"

Obviously, the wine was already starting to mellow her a little. "Baton Rouge."

"I was in New Orleans a few years ago for a scientific seminar and visited Baton Rouge. Nice area." He wisely left it at that. He thought if he could ask a question every so often he might get enough answers.

He glanced at the ponytail bouncing between her shoulder blades and wondered if her hair would feel as silky as it looked. Before his fingers could give in to what his mind was asking, he sternly reminded himself that she wasn't a woman he'd invited over for the evening. She was his bodyguard. A woman he had once blamed for Renee's death, until he'd come to realize that it wasn't Nikki's fault Renee had killed herself. Obviously Renee hadn't been strong enough to fight the scandal and come back to her child. He'd never expected her to come back to him. He'd lost her long before then.

He looked into his glass and wondered if the wine wasn't making him maudlin. Or was it the sight of a bare-legged Nikki?

Did she look this good before? he asked himself, sending a few sideways glances at shapely, golden-tanned legs that moved slowly back and forth in the water. *Or have I been without a woman so long anyone would look good?*

"Does the peace offering mean you're not going to throw me out?"

"It means that after suffering through my tantrum and Heather's today, you deserve a little pick-me-up."

"If you thought I deserved a little pick-me-up, I wish you had brought something a bit stronger. Like a double whiskey."

Scott smiled. "That bad, huh?"

"That bad," she agreed. "Children throwing tantrums are fine. Adults throwing tantrums deserve broken bones in return."

"What saved me?"

"I knew I couldn't break a finger or an arm, and I had the hardest time trying to decide whether to break your right leg or your left." Her brow furrowed in a frown. "Is your car manual? If you don't have to worry about a clutch, it would be easier to figure out which leg to go for."

Scott continued sipping his wine. "You've developed a sense of humor over the years."

"Don't act so surprised. I've always had it. It just works a little slower around some people." Nikki lifted her feet out of the water and sat cross-legged on the concrete. She rolled her wineglass between her palms as if the motion was calming. She lifted her head. In the faint evening light, her face was a mere shadow. "Perhaps we should get a few things out of the way now. Five years ago, I was doing my job, nothing more. I didn't come here on a witch hunt. Renee was the last person we would have suspected of any wrongdoing." She dampened her lips with her tongue as she paused. "In fact, the person at the top of our suspect list was Jeffrey Gardner."

Scott straightened at the mention of a man he'd known since school and worked closely with for a while. He wondered how many other friends they had investigated. "Jeff? You honestly thought he wanted my files?"

"There were suspicious deposits in his bank account on a fairly regular basis, and he had a few friends who didn't exactly have a clean background," she replied. "A further check was done, and the deposits were proven legitimate. As for those friends, it only showed he had bad taste." She set

her glass to one side on the ground. "I was sent here because they wanted someone working undercover in the
household to see who might be showing too much interest
in your work. It was a little difficult, since you didn't em-
ploy a large household staff." Her lips twisted in a wry
smile. "I was one of the unlucky few who had a working
knowledge of what a kitchen looked like. They didn't realize that meant I only knew how to work the microwave."

"But that wasn't why you were chosen, was it?" He went
for the wild guess that he figured wasn't so wild, after all.
"Your father wanted you here because he saw the possibil-
ity of a case being blown wide open and a promotion for you
coming out of it. Or were you the one after the promotion?
After all, that kind of arrest must have turned you into the
darling of Naval Intelligence. Too bad you resigned. You
might have ended up with a tropical-beach assignment
somewhere."

Scott understood the phrase "faster than the speed of
light" in scientific terms. He just hadn't seen it applied to a
person until he realized Nikki was now on her feet and the
contents of her wineglass were dripping off his face. He
couldn't even remember seeing it happen. He wiped his wet
face with his hand.

"Don't tell me I hit a nerve, Ms. Price?" he asked with a
sardonic twist of the lips. "The way you act, I didn't think
you had any."

"Be careful, Doctor." Her level tone was more chilling
than blatant anger would have been. "You're treading on
very dangerous territory. Why don't we just concentrate on
keeping you protected? When the job is over, I'll be gone
and you can have your life back."

Scott didn't have a chance to say a word as Nikki stalked
off. He winced when the back door slammed hard enough
to make the windows quiver. As she passed through the
kitchen, the open windows allowed him to hear her mut-

tered curses on his ancestors, grooming habits and general personality.

He picked up his glass in a mocking salute before draining the last of his wine. "I'll tell you this, old boy. You have to admire a woman who can rain that number of creative curses on a man without once repeating herself."

"That son of a..." Nikki walked through the house, not bothering to turn on a light; her night vision was excellent. Even though she was furious with Scott and wanted to throttle him, her sense of responsibility sent her gaze out the windows facing the front. The yard was large, extending down to the two-lane, paved road, which she couldn't see very well thanks to the row of shrubs separating it from the wide expanse of lawn. She knew a car was parked unobtrusively up the road, with a man posted to keep watch. But how could she be sure the car's occupant was on their side?

"Friend or foe?" The words left her mouth before she realized their meaning. Just who could she trust besides Harvey and, God help her, her father? The manila envelope containing reports about Renee Carter might be locked away, but that didn't stop its siren call.

For five years Nikki had refused to think about that period. But now that she was back in Virginia, back where it all began, she couldn't help wondering if there was a reason behind her deliberate memory loss. Did her refusal have a hidden meaning?

She walked back to the kitchen and stood far enough from the window that she couldn't be seen as she looked outside. Scott had placed his wineglass on the glass-topped table near the pool and was pulling his shirt over his head. He unfastened his shorts and allowed them to drop to the ground, revealing only a pair of briefs that hugged a tight, muscular rear end. His lean torso could make a woman's mouth water, Nikki mused, as he walked to the pool's edge and dove in with barely a splash.

It wasn't until he began swimming laps, stretching his arms out in front of him in even strokes, that Nikki realized she had been holding her breath as she watched him.

While Scott spent the next hour in the pool, working off his pent-up energy, Nikki went into her bathroom and took a cold shower.

Chapter 6

Nikki deliberately waited a week before she made her first public appearance in the neighborhood. Her destination was the small shopping center a short distance from the house, where a good many members of the neighborhood's domestic staff did the shopping.

She first stopped at Scott's lab and informed him she would be out picking up a few things; she warned him not to leave the house.

"Considering the way my morning is going, I won't be leaving this room for the next ten years," he practically bellowed at her. "Cully and Kay are coming by in about an hour to go over data. I'm sure they'll be adequate baby-sitters until you return."

"I shouldn't even be leaving, but I need to keep my cover as your housekeeper intact. In case we're under observation, I want to keep things looking as normal as possible."

Scott raked his fingers through his hair. The equation he needed was just out of his reach and stubbornly refused to come any closer. He'd been up most of the night working on it and hadn't made any progress.

"Go."

"Anything special you'd like?"

You, in a sheer red nightgown, came unbidden to his mind. He bent over the computer keyboard before he was tempted to say it out loud. Luckily, he thought of a safer alternative.

"Can you fix spaghetti?"

She thought for a moment. "Boil water, throw the stuff in it, stir a few times. Make sure it isn't too soggy and pour sauce over it. No problem."

"Then pick up some pasta. It's one of Heather's and my favorites for dinner," he muttered, forcing himself to stare at the screen instead of back at Nikki. When she had barged in, dressed in a bright blue skirt that didn't even come close to her knees and a blue-and-yellow-print, short-sleeved top, she'd looked like a breath of spring.

Scott began to wish Nikki would return to the dark pants and white blouses. When she'd worn the sexless outfits, she hadn't inspired these late-night fantasies. Fantasies he still couldn't understand. Where had his rage toward her gone? For a man who lived on logic, he was feeling some very illogical emotions.

"I thought this would be a good day to go out, since Julia and Wilma shop on Thursdays. I'm sure by now they've heard I'm back. And they'll be certain to pass on any news, since word travels fast through the domestics' grapevine. I may even pick up some hot gossip if I run into them."

Scott turned his head when he heard her explanation. "Oh great, you're going to gossip with the neighbors' help. That will be real interesting. Tell me something. How do you plan to explain the new you?" He nodded toward her outfit.

Instead of the bouncy ponytail she usually wore, she had pulled her hair back in a French braid with a blue ribbon interwoven through it. Heather had been so entranced with the hairdo that morning, she had asked Nikki to fix her hair the same way. She had left for school with her hair pulled back in an intricate braid tied with a black hair twist.

"You look about as much like a housekeeper as I look like a monkey," he muttered.

"Don't worry, I get the hint, Cheetah. I'll add peanuts to my list." She patted him on the cheek and walked out.

"Ha, ha, very funny," Scott called after her. When he returned to his work, he had a smile on his face and felt just a little bit lighter. While he groused about having her in the house, he had to admit he was already getting used to hearing her tuneless whistles as she fussed about the place, though several times he had been tempted to tell her she couldn't carry a tune if her life depended on it. Even more important, he did appreciate having someone here who could protect Heather.

Except having Nikki here also brought up a lot of memories he'd successfully buried. And posed a lot of questions. He couldn't miss the fleeting expression of what he could only call regret that would cross her face when she'd stand at the kitchen window and watch him in the backyard with Heather as they took their late-afternoon swim. Although she was repeatedly asked to join them, she would always put them off with an excuse. Scott was caught between curiosity about seeing Nikki in a bathing suit and gratitude for her leaving him and his daughter alone.

Since he had dealt with Admiral Price in the past and gotten to know the man better than he would have liked to, he couldn't help but wonder what kind of childhood Nikki had had with the cold, unfeeling man as a father. Or had he shrugged off that militaristic persona when he was home among his family? Scott couldn't imagine him doing that.

He told himself there was no reason to wonder about her. He shouldn't be interested in her as a woman. She was here to do a job. That was all.

Then he'd watch her working in the kitchen, patiently enduring Heather's idea of assistance, or he'd catch her

unawares during the day and wonder what she would do if
he sneaked up and kissed her. He had a suspicion it could
merit him a few broken bones, but it might be worth it.

Nikki planned it carefully and had it timed to the minute. She parked her truck in a far corner of the parking lot
and watched the main entrance until she saw Wilma and
Julia arrive in their respective cars and park not far from the
grocery store. She surmised their routine wouldn't have
changed over the years, and she was glad to see she wasn't
wrong. She knew from past experience they would first meet
in the coffee shop two doors down from the grocery, have
lunch and then do their food shopping. She deliberately
waited about ten minutes before exiting the truck and
heading for the plaza.

Nikki stepped inside the coffee shop with the air of
someone there to have a bite to eat and not intending to meet
anyone. Out of the corner of her eye, she could see Wilma,
a plump brunette, widen her eyes in surprise, nudge her
friend and gesture toward her. Nikki made sure not to look
in their direction as she searched the counter for an empty
stool.

"Nikki?" Wilma touched her shoulder. The woman's
pale blue eyes were still wide with astonishment. "It *is* you.
I can't believe it!"

"Wilma!" She affected pleasure in her tone. "How are
you?"

"Nikki, darlin', come on over here." Julia's husky
Southern drawl rang out over the lunch chatter.

"Julia!" Nikki smiled at the other woman as she and
Wilma walked back to the booth. She slid in next to Julia.
"What a surprise to see you here."

Julia's dark eyes swept over Nikki with a thoroughness
that secretly amused the younger woman. Nikki had always felt Julia would have a talent for intelligence work.

"Honey, you look good." Julia's down-home Georgia
drawl poured over her like warm honey. "Where've you

been all this time? And what brought you back here? Not to mention, what have you done to yourself? Sweetheart, you look gorgeous.''

"I was working in Louisiana." She believed in keeping to the truth as much as possible. That way it was much easier to keep track of what lies had been told to whom. "And I came back because Dr. Carter tracked me down and asked if I'd work for him again." She heaved a deep sigh. "Poor little Heather! I can't believe the things that have gone on in my absence."

"You missed a lot of excitement," Wilma chimed in. "I suppose you heard about Mrs. Carter."

Nikki nodded. "I saw it in the papers. It was so hard to believe. The woman was always a wonderful employer." She turned back to Julia. "As for me, I worked for a publicist who believed in image more than a clean house. The first thing she did was insist on a complete makeover."

"She did a good job." Julia fingered Nikki's sleeve. "But then, if I was a good eighty pounds lighter, I'd dress that way too instead of like this." She looked down at her pale pink uniform. "'Course, the Sandersons never did have much imagination in how their household help should dress."

"Did Dr. Carter tell you his house was broken into?" Wilma asked. She lowered her voice. "Normally, we don't gossip, especially about Dr. Carter, since he's a wonderful man. But you've been out of town all this time, so you might not know everything that's gone on."

"He mentioned the break-in and that his other house-keeper had been terrorized," Nikki said carefully.

"Terrorized?" Wilma shook her head. "I talked to Luanna Grainger the day after it happened. The poor woman was a basket case. She said there were two men there and they were horrible, disgusting creatures who said terrible things to her." She shuddered, although there was an avid gleam in her eye.

Nikki didn't think the woman was as horrified as she pretended to be. Of course, in that neighborhood, excitement was someone's dog setting off a perimeter alarm.

Wilma leaned forward and confided, "She was afraid they would molest her."

"No man in his right mind would have wanted to tangle with that woman," Julia argued, rolling her eyes. "She might have been good at her work, but there was always something about her that didn't ring right with me."

That one sentence pricked Nikki's curiosity. "Really? Why?"

The housekeeper nodded. "She was too curious about everyone else. Wilma refuses to call what we do gossiping, but I'm not afraid to use the word. At the same time, we don't say anything that would hurt anyone. Personally, I think she was hoping to latch onto a better job. She wanted to care for a bigger and better house and she figured Dr. Carter was a good stepping stone."

"Nothing like wanting to advance yourself," Nikki murmured. She paused as a harried-looking waitress stopped by to take their orders. She ordered the same as the other two ladies—a club sandwich and ice tea. "So, tell me, what other boring stories can you tell me about Morning Glory Court?"

Julia's laughter rang out. "Where would you like us to start? With Mrs. Phillips, caught playing around in the hot tub with the pool man? Or how about when the maid accidentally walked in on Mr. Abbott and found him wearing his wife's underwear? Then there was Mrs. Williams, whose gardener did a hell of a lot more than weed her flower garden!" She erupted in hearty laughter.

Nikki's eyes widened as she visualized the stern-visaged man who had been president of a large financial institution for years until his retirement. "Mr. Abbott in his wife's underwear? He always came across as so stodgy. That must have been a sight."

Julia's chuckle rumbled through her body. "He wasn't so stodgy when Paula caught him wearing his wife's good French lace undies."

The three women stopped their talk and looked up, smiling, as the waitress deposited their orders.

When Nikki bit into her sandwich, a movement that didn't seem right caught her eye. Pretending to reach over for the salt shaker, she shot a covert glance out the window. Now she knew why her senses had gone on alert. She noticed a heavy-duty pickup truck parked next to her four-wheel-drive vehicle. While that might not have looked suspicious to most people, it did to Nikki. She had deliberately parked in an area of the lot that was almost empty of cars, and there were no stores close enough to warrant anyone else parking there. The beat-up condition of the truck told her the owner wasn't parking there to protect his precious vehicle. She also noticed that the driver hadn't gotten out of the truck and was sitting behind the wheel with a cellular telephone in one hand.

Are we calling a girlfriend or are we calling someone about me? The prickles of unease crawling up her spine suggested the latter. Her fingers itched to pull her own cellular phone out of her bag and call Scott to make sure everything was all right. But another sense, hidden deep down, told her she would sense if anything was wrong with him. Instead, she forced herself to concentrate on the conversation flowing around her and eat her lunch as if nothing unusual was going on.

"So you're here to do some grocery shopping?" Wilma asked as the three women walked outside.

Nikki nodded. "I noticed the cupboards were getting a little bare."

As she entered the grocery store, she noticed the truck was still parked beside hers and the driver was still seated behind the wheel. From here, she could see he wore mirrored sunglasses that shimmered as the afternoon sun bounced off the lenses. And he was most definitely watching her. She didn't think he realized she was likewise watching him, but she knew better than to assume anything. She carried a scar curved along her left side because she didn't think a sweet-faced seaman would carry a knife along with his cocaine stash. If her sixth sense hadn't kicked in, she would have been gutted by the deadly blade handled by a man crazed by drugs. She kept her gaze directed away from her unknown admirer as she selected a shopping cart and entered the store with the two women.

"Keep Thursdays as your main shopping day," Julia advised, as they later parted company. Wilma had already hurried to her car, explaining that she still had to pick up dry cleaning and prescriptions. "We can always use another voice as we figure out who's doing what to whom in the neighborhood."

"Thanks, I will."

"Nikki?"

She turned to Julia.

The older woman peered at her with a discerning gaze. "It's surprisin' you showin' up just when all this trouble is happenin'. And here you left right when the other blew up."

"I always miss all the fun," Nikki said lightly.

Julia merely smiled. "Maybe." She started toward the station wagon she drove. She stopped and turned around. "Did I ever tell you I once worked for a director of one of those government secret agencies?"

"No." She feigned interest. "You must have some fascinating stories about your boss. Were there secret passwords and phones you weren't supposed to answer?"

"One thing I learned was that his people always had a certain look about them, as if they heard every word you said but their minds were miles off as they checked out what was going on around them." Julia paused. "The same kind of look you have." She unlocked the rear door and pushed it upward. "You take care of yourself, darlin'. I don't think that house is all too safe at times."

Nikki knew when to continue a masquerade and play dumb and when to just drop it. This was definitely a drop-it time.

"Don't worry, I can yell with the best of them." She waved and walked toward her vehicle. She noticed the pickup truck was gone, but she wasn't worried. She had tucked the license-plate number into her memory. As she drove out of the parking lot, she called Harvey and requested he run a check on the license number.

"You're not getting paranoid, are you?" Harvey demanded, after taking down the information.

"Only when ugly trucks park next to my beautiful chariot." She kept one eye moving between the rearview and side-view mirrors. She wouldn't be surprised to find the truck lurking in the background somewhere.

"How's Carter's research coming?"

"He sits at that computer of his, drawing things and muttering a lot to himself. He doesn't say too much about it to me."

Nikki glanced in her rearview mirror again and wondered about the dark sedan traveling a few car lengths behind her. She wasn't able to see the license plate. Testing him, she slowed down and pulled into a gas station.

"Get him to talk about it."

"Considering he's tolerating me better than he had in the beginning, I don't think I care to push my luck. Goodbye, Harvey." She was pleased to have the last word as she ended the call.

Nikki pretended to ignore passing traffic, especially the dark sedan, as she handled the gas pump and inserted the nozzle in the tank. While ostensibly watching the gallons click off, she noted the sedan slow down a half block away and pull over to the curb.

"So the trucker has a friend," she murmured, leaning against the rear fender and crossing her legs at the ankle. "I feel so popular having all these men following me. What a shame they're so shy they can't just come up to me and ask for a date."

After Nikki paid for the gas, she pulled back into traffic and allowed the sedan to easily join the other cars on the road. Even then, the car remained far enough back that she couldn't see the license plate. As she drove along, she wondered how many stops she could make and frustrate the other driver at the same time. And she wondered how many more were out there.

"Better one I don't know than one I don't see."

The unsettled feeling plagued Nikki all the way back to the house. As she drove past the tiny side road where one of Harvey's operatives' was parked, she nodded slightly and drove on.

"Do you need any help?" Scott sauntered outside after she pulled into the garage and hopped out of her truck. She opened the rear hatch and pulled out shopping bags.

"Thanks." She promptly handed him three.

He quickly adjusted his bundles. "Obviously you believe in equal opportunity."

"I had no choice, considering the way I was raised." She gathered up the last bags and closed the hatch. "Where are your gremlins?"

"I locked them downstairs where they belong. I had to take a call from Heather's grandparents." His lips twisted in a wry smile. He walked toward the kitchen door. "They've been bombarding me with calls since the incident with Mrs. Grainger. They're convinced Heather will be killed if she stays with me and seem to enjoy driving that point home."

"Sounds as if you had an enjoyable couple of hours." She dropped her bags on the counter and began emptying them. "So, are they the same lighthearted couple they've always been?"

"Worse, since..." He bit his lower lip.

Since Renee's death. She could have finished for him, but chose not to say it out loud. Which reminded her she still had to look through that file she'd had Harvey send over.

They both froze when the doorbell chimed.

"I really should have an electric gate installed at the end of the driveway," Scott muttered, starting to move toward the door.

She grabbed hold of his arm. "No, Dr. Carter, that's my job."

The moment Nikki looked through the spy hole, she wished she had let Scott answer it. After taking a deep breath to still the slow-boiling fury deep inside, she pulled the door open. And immediately wished she could slam it shut.

"Admiral." She faced the man who had helped in conceiving her; she could never use the word *father* when referring to him. She realized five years wasn't long enough to help her resolve the feelings she had toward him.

Adam Price inclined his head. Formal in his uniform, he looked as intimidating as ever. "Nicole." He waited for an invitation to enter.

"Please, come in," she said mockingly, standing back. "I'll tell Dr. Carter you're here. He's in the kitchen."

"I'm not here to see Carter. I'm here to see you." He headed unerringly for the living room without bothering to see if she was following him.

Nikki mouthed a curse and tagged along behind.

Adam seated himself on a stiff-backed chair, his hat settled on his knee. His gaze, as it wandered over her casual dress and equally casual hair, was disapproving.

"Shouldn't you be wearing something a bit more... appropriate?"

She stood by the fireplace, forcing herself not to cross her arms in front of her for self-protection or do anything else that would show her father how unsettled she felt in seeing him without any warning. She noted that he looked thinner and that there was a heavier concentration of gray scattered along his temples and forehead. The lines radiating from his eyes and mouth indicated life had not been kind to him the past couple of years. "That was in another life. Don't you believe in announcing your visits in advance?"

"I knew if I called first you wouldn't be here."

She inclined her head in silent agreement. "I do have a cover to keep up in this community. A navy admiral coming to see a mere housekeeper wouldn't look right."

Adam's features, so like his daughter's, tightened. Except his held a cold anger directed at her.

"You are a fool to come back into this house after what happened."

She mentally shrugged off his insult. "Who better than me? I have the training, I know the house, the routine, and I'm a fairly familiar face in the area. I don't see it making me a fool."

"Carter has very important research to finish and I can't imagine his peace of mind could be intact with you here. After all, you were the cause of his wife's death," he pressed. "Some wonder if you might have even had something to do with it."

Nikki silently congratulated herself on not visibly reacting to his accusation. She refused to give him any more ammunition, because Adam Price had always believed in going for the jugular when warranted.

"Since I didn't see Mrs. Carter after her arrest, there was no way I could have had anything to do with her death, and you know it. As for Dr. Carter, if he doesn't mind my being here, there's no reason you should."

"You were gone for five years. You didn't send any word to your brothers. I, of course, didn't expect any after your little tantrum in Larsen's office."

"They would have cared as little as you did," she cut in. "The last time I saw Matt he told me I was a fool for resigning, and all Brad was concerned about was making sure anything I did didn't affect his own career. Once he realized he'd be fine, he forgave my so-called stupidity. Now, why don't you tell me exactly why you're here? I have things to do."

Adam met her gaze head on. "I can have your commission reinstated. You might have to settle for some scut assignments to show you're serious, but it's only fair."

Nikki spoke slowly and distinctly. She didn't want Adam to say he didn't understand. "I have no desire to return to the navy."

"What will you do?"

"Right now, I'm not sure. Maybe work for Harvey on a full-time basis after this. Maybe I'll work for someone else or go back to school, but no matter what I do, it won't have anything to do with the navy." Her voice grew hoarse with the emotion she was trying so hard to suppress. Her nails dug into her palms as she held her arms stiffly at her sides. "You never gave a damn about me while I was growing up. All you cared about was that I could hold my own with Matt and Brad. All you cared about was that I didn't embarrass you. So, to please you, I excelled in everything I could. I even applied to the Academy and endured hell because I had two strikes against me—I was female and I had you for a father. The instructors went out of their way to make sure no one could accuse them of giving me special treatment."

Sparks of fury flashed in her eyes. "But I showed the navy I was worthy of being your daughter by graduating with honors. I went into intelligence to prove to you I was as good as you, although you wouldn't have admitted it if your life depended on it. I put away a drug dealer and I even helped find a murderer down in Pensacola. All my prisoners stayed alive! They didn't kill themselves!" Lost in her anger, she didn't notice the set expression on his face.

"She killed herself because she couldn't face her guilt over what she'd done. She was afraid to stand trial."

Nikki shook her head. "That's too pat an answer and you know it."

Adam slowly rose to his feet. "Obviously, you aren't going to listen to reason." He looked her over from head to toe, clearly still displeased with her appearance. "Do you have any idea what your job here could entail?"

She knew exactly what he meant and she bristled at his implied insult.

"Don't worry, Admiral. If the time comes, I'll step out in front and take that bullet." She pronounced each word through gritted teeth.

Nikki didn't offer to show him to the door, but she did follow him. She wanted to make sure he was gone.

Before Adam walked out, he looked back. "If you're so sure she wasn't guilty, what are you going to do about it?"

She didn't have to think about an answer. It had been lingering in the back of her mind for some time. "I'll do what I can to find out who was."

His lips tightened. "After this length of time, it won't be easy."

Nikki faced him; she needed to, to hold on to her self-respect. "After this length of time, the guilty party will have relaxed, convinced he or she is in the clear and has nothing to worry about."

"You're still a fool, Nicole. I'd hoped you would have learned to temper your judgment by now. I guess I was wrong." These were his parting words, each intended to wound, even if his victim refused to allow them to.

She watched him walk down to the sedan, where his driver was waiting for him. He climbed into the back seat without bothering to look at her. It wasn't until the car had left her line of sight that she realized it was a dark sedan.

Chapter 7

"**A**nyone can see that you and your father are a wonderful example of a close, loving relationship. He wasn't exactly father-of-the-year material during your formative years, was he?"

Nikki muttered a curse. She should have known Scott wasn't above a little eavesdropping if he thought he could get some questions answered.

"Oh, yeah, we're straight out of a TV sitcom," she said heavily, pushing the door closed. She wanted nothing more than to lean against it and shut her eyes. She wanted the pain and remorse to wash over her, wanted to indulge in a bout of self-pity. But there was no way she'd show any sign of weakness in front of Scott. Her glare sliced right through him. "Don't you have work to do?"

Scott leaned against the door jamb, his arms crossed in front of him as he studied her with those deep sapphire eyes that seemed as penetrating as the lasers he worked with.

Was it her imagination, or was she looking at thick, dark eyelashes any woman would kill for? And where had that dimple come from? She couldn't believe he'd had it the last time she'd seen him smile. What was going on here? What about her did he find so funny? She felt the tension coil inside her like a rattlesnake ready to strike.

"What?"

He quirked a brow at her peevish tone. "What, what?"

Nikki pushed herself away from the door to stalk down the hallway, but suddenly found herself facing his chest. She couldn't believe she hadn't seen him move sideways to block her way.

"Don't let your father get to you, Nikki. I have an idea that's what he's hoping he'll do."

She could have handled anything but his gentleness. She looked anywhere but at him.

"I told you before. My father's and my relationship is none of your business. Stay out of it."

"It is my business if you let him affect you so much you can't do your job properly. In case you've forgotten, my life is at stake here and I need you in top emotional shape." He was deliberately goading her. He preferred facing her temper than to see her indulging in self-pity.

Nikki's head whipped upward. Her deep gold eyes glowed like an angry cat's as she visually bored holes into him.

"One thing you'll never have to worry about, Dr. Carter, is my ability to protect you." Her words may have dripped ice, but Scott appeared impervious to the drop in surrounding temperature. "I know what my job is, and if push comes to shove, I will be the one doing the shoving."

"Contrary to what you think, I've never worried about your ability to protect me, Nikki." His gentleness hadn't disappeared despite her anger. "My worry was more about you." As he spoke, he stroked the back of his fingers across her cheek. "You have very nice skin," he murmured. "Like silk."

Nikki reared back as if stung. "Don't." The word was forced from deep within her soul. She refused to admit his touch affected her.

"Why not? You have skin made to be touched."

She blindly stared at his mouth, noting the way it opened and stretched with the words he spoke, but she didn't hear any of them. She was too lost in the streak of sensation that ran along her cheek. She had trouble finding her breath.

"Obviously, you've forgotten why I'm here," she said.

His somber gaze was replaced by his smile. "I haven't forgotten anything, Nikki, but I've been doing a lot of thinking about us. And I've come to the conclusion that I let my anger and bitterness blind me. I shouldn't have blamed you for doing your job. You were trained to do as you were ordered, without questioning those orders. I shouldn't blame you for something that was beyond your control."

Only Nikki's training kept her from telling Scott she had obtained Renee's file and planned to study it further. She told herself she was remaining quiet because there was no reason to say anything to him when she didn't know what she would find.

She brushed past him and continued down the hall. When she reached the end, she turned around.

"You mentioned my refusing to wear anything close to a uniform. When I resigned from the navy, I vowed to never wear a piece of clothing that looked even close to a uniform," she said quietly, but with great feeling. "I don't even wear the same colors. For now, if what I wear makes me stand out a little, that's all right. Anyone interested in the doings of this house won't see me as a threat." She turned to leave.

"Oh, you're a threat all right, Nicole Price," he murmured. "I'm not sure if it's more to the enemy or to me."

Nikki felt raw, almost exposed. Two confrontations within the space of an hour was two too many in her estimation. The first thing she did was head for her bedroom and put in a call to Harvey.

"You tell the admiral to stay away from me," she said the moment she heard that the phone on the other end had been picked up.

Harvey's long-suffering sigh could be heard over the line. "No matter what, Nikki, he is your father and he was worried about you. Besides, have you ever known him to listen to me?"

"He gave up the right to fatherhood years ago. As for his worrying, he was only worrying about my screwing up here and people connecting me with him," she stated baldly.

Harvey chose not to say anything. The truth was too apparent in his silence.

"Did you find out anything about that pickup truck I called you about?"

"The usual. It was reported stolen the night before."

She muttered a curse. "Anything else?"

"One of our operatives learned that a small faction wants the weapon for themselves. They figure if they have all the paperwork in hand and Scott's dead, no one will be able to come up with anything close for years."

She was stunned. "That's how far ahead of everyone else he is?"

"That and more. The man exceeded the supergenius level years ago. That's why everyone bows to his whims. We didn't argue with his resigning from the institute and we didn't suggest he take his research to a laboratory of our choosing or demand he move into a safe house for a while. He refuses to work that way. He's a loner where his work is concerned. So, while we don't like the way he orders us around, we feel we have no choice. But if things get too hot, all of you will be yanked out of there whether you like it or not."

Nikki caught a glimpse of herself in the mirror and grimaced as she spied the tension lines now radiating from her mouth. She thought she had resolved her feelings for her father long ago. Today proved she hadn't.

"I won't let you down, Harvey."

"I know you won't, Nikki. I have faith in you to do exactly what I need for this assignment."

"Excuse me?"

Nikki looked up and found a woman in her twenties standing in the doorway. Dressed in denim cutoffs and a red T-shirt that barely covered her flat midriff, the young woman made Nikki feel very old.

"Hi, I'm Kay," she said breezily. "Dr. Carter said you'd be able to fix a snack for us."

Nikki dredged up a smile. "I think I can do that for you." She walked into the kitchen, wondering what she could fix in a hurry.

"You know, what I can't understand is why you and the doc would cook up such a hokey story," Kay commented, keeping close on Nikki's heels.

Nikki arched an eyebrow. She had a pretty good idea what was coming, but she wanted Kay to put her foot in her mouth very securely. "Story?"

The younger woman nodded. "It's the nineties—who cares what you do nowadays? Or is it because of the kid?"

Nikki turned around and leaned back against the counter. "Instead of dancing around the subject, why don't you just spell it out, Kay?"

"True, we are adults here." The younger woman dropped onto one of the kitchen stools. "I mean, it's obvious you and the doc are having an affair, but for some reason you're keeping it under wraps. Now, whether it's because of his daughter or because you used to work for him when his wife was alive and something might have been going on then—"

"Kay, if I were you, I would never mention such a thing to Dr. Carter." Nikki's chilling voice brought her upright. "But then, perhaps you don't plan to work for him much longer."

The graduate student's eyes sparked in displeasure. "Everyone thinks you two are an item."

"I don't think *everyone* thinks that," Nikki countered. "I can't believe you would listen to gossip about your superior. Even implying Dr. Carter was unfaithful to his wife years ago would be disparaging a wonderful man, and you should be ashamed of yourself for thinking such a thing."

She held back her amusement as she saw the dull red creeping up Kay's cheeks. She wasn't surprised when anger replaced the embarrassment and Scott's assistant hopped off the stool.

"It may surprise you to learn that I'm well over twenty-one and Dr. Carter has noticed more than my mind. And when he finishes this project, I'll be climbing up that success ladder right alongside him. And you won't even know what's going on. You can bring down the snacks when you're finished. We'll all want dinner later." She stalked out of the kitchen.

"Obviously we don't appreciate having our young age and lack of tact pointed out to us," Nikki murmured, pulling a box of cheese-flavored crackers out of a cabinet.

As she poured the crackers into a bowl, she replayed the conversation in her mind. What kept coming back to her was the expression in Kay's eyes. It was clear she wasn't quite what she claimed to be.

"Surprises happening all the time," Nikki murmured, glancing at the clock, relieved to see it was time to pick up Heather. She carried the tray downstairs and knocked on the door. "I'm going to get Heather now, Dr. Carter," she said in her best housekeeper voice. She could hear muttered voices in the background. "We have a few errands to run, so we'll be a little later than usual." She smiled as she thought about what kind of errands she and Heather would be running. Since Kay and Cully had passed Harvey's background checks, she knew Scott would be safe with them.

"That's fine." Judging from his absent tone, he was lost in his work and probably hadn't heard half of what she'd said.

"I think I'll fix broccoli for dinner," she murmured, running back upstairs. "With cheese sauce." She knew Scott hated broccoli, even with cheese sauce, but it didn't matter to her.

Nikki quickly changed into Lycra shorts and a T-shirt and went into Heather's room to get her a change of clothing before going outside. She decided it was time to keep her promise.

"Where are we going?" Heather asked once she realized they weren't heading straight home.

"To a place where you're going to yell and learn how to protect yourself," Nikki told her, pulling into a small parking lot.

Heather looked around the area, noticing that the buildings were old and somewhat shabby. "Are we safe here?" She tucked her hand in Nikki's.

"Very safe." Nikki tugged at her hand and helped her jump out of the vehicle.

The sign on the door said Dragon's Lair. Inside was controlled confusion. A woven-mat-covered floor was filled with boys and girls wearing white *gis* as they shouted, practiced hand movements and kicked outward.

"You can change in there." Nikki handed Heather the small bag and pointed toward the dressing room.

"It is about time you came to see your master. You are a very rude girl."

Nikki broke into a broad smile. She bowed to the elderly Asian man who faced her with a frown on his lips and a smile in his dark eyes. Dressed in simple black cotton pants and a white cotton shirt, he looked about as threatening as a butterfly.

"If I am rude, my lord, it is because you trained me that way. Master Chang, this is Heather Carter."

Heather hesitantly bowed the way Nikki had.

Chang beamed. "Such a polite young one. Not like another girl I know."

"Thank you for allowing me to use one of your private rooms to teach Heather some basic self-defense moves."

"You will have a mediocre teacher," Chang told the girl, "but she will do the best she can."

"He's joking," Nikki murmured to Heather, whose head whipped from one to the other. "Go change." She waited until Heather disappeared into the dressing room. "I want her to have a chance if anyone ever tries to hurt her."

"I heard of your troubles. She may need to know as much as you can teach her."

Nikki had to smile. Chang had never been involved with any government agency other than to offer advanced training to special operatives, but that hadn't stopped him from finding out classified information on his own. His training methods were world reknowned and his classes always filled to capacity. Many people had been surprised when he had insisted on teaching women, children and teenagers self-defense instead of working exclusively with men who trained to step up each rung of the martial-arts ladder as he had for so many years.

For Nikki, he had been the father figure she'd never felt she had at home. When her father had been transferred to Washington, D.C., all those years ago and learned of Chang's skills, he had enrolled Nikki and his sons. The two boys had dropped out, but Nikki had refused to give up. At first it had been to show her father she could do something her brothers couldn't. Chang had taken her under his wing, had listened to her fears and her anger toward her father and had showed her how to direct those emotions in a more positive way.

"You made me suffer a lot of years."

He smiled. "You were a rude child. You deserved to suffer." He turned as Heather came out wearing a leotard and looking a bit uncertain. "If the little butterfly does not mind this old man watching, I will make sure this arrogant girl teaches you properly."

Heather immediately relaxed under his gentle teasing. "Only if you don't laugh. When Nikki said she was going to take me to a place where I could yell, I didn't expect it to be here."

He looked her over from head to toe. "You will do well. Come." He led them to the rear of the building and a small room at the end of the hall. He carefully closed the door behind them.

Nikki showed Heather how to stretch first, explaining the importance of warming up her muscles.

"There are several places where a man can be hurt," she then told the girl.

Heather blushed. "I know of one."

Nikki nodded. "But that's not your best bet. Aim for the knee. He won't expect it. Or, if you're able, try for the throat or eyes." On Heather's body she touched each area she mentioned.

"But why the yelling?"

"It makes you sound scarier," Nikki whispered, laughing softly.

For the next two hours, Nikki ruthlessly drilled Heather in technique for yelling out the word *no,* kicking or using the side of her palm against an assailant's knee or throat and running immediately after that. The entire time, Chang squatted on his haunches against the wall in a position most would find extremely uncomfortable, although he looked as if he was reclining in an easy chair. He didn't speak until toward the end of the second hour, when he straightened and walked to the door with a smooth, gliding step that made it appear he was floating.

"Now she must go up against someone other than herself to see if she remembers your lessons." He opened the door and called out a name.

Heather looked nervous as a burly man entered the room. He wore a chest protector and knee pads. "I can't do anything to him," she protested.

Nikki understood what Chang was attempting and approved of his method. "Yes, you can. Just remember what I showed you. With the right kind of balance, you can even throw him."

"You will take this little girl," Chang commanded.

Heather drew a deep breath when the man advanced on her.

"Come on, honey," he coaxed, gesturing with a come hither wave of the hand.

"No!" she said forcefully.

"Come on, little girl, don't make me get tough." He walked even closer. "I don't want to hurt you."

"No! Back off!" Her voice rang out. Whirling like a tiny dervish, Heather kicked him in the knee twice before she quickly backed off herself.

"She's learning," the man groaned, looking up at Chang from the floor, where he'd fallen.

Nikki couldn't have looked prouder if Heather had been her own daughter.

"You are learning very fast." She hugged her. "And now I want you to do it again."

"Easy for you to say," the man joked, slowly getting to his feet.

"John works as our target here," Chang explained.

This time, the Asian man made suggestions and showed Heather more fine-tuned techniques. Nikki stood back, pleased to see the girl taking his comments seriously.

"You will be back," Chang predicted as Nikki waited for Heather to change her clothing. "She has found a way to feel safe, and she will want to return to learn more. She is very much like you."

"No, she doesn't have a home life she wants to escape from." Nikki looked at Chang more closely and noticed the heavier lines in his weathered face, although he still stood straight and tall. She couldn't help asking, "Have you heard anything?"

Chang seemed to look inward. "Who do you trust?"

"Myself. You."

He nodded slowly. "Trust no one. I feel there is a thread no one will see until it is too late."

A chill skittered up her spine. "If you hear anything..."

"I will contact you. But I suggest you come here three times a week. The butterfly will need to practice and you should practice also." He eyed her with his all-seeing gaze. "You were very clumsy in there when you worked with her, although you remembered what needed to be done. The grace I worked so hard to instill in you is gone. I fear you will need to struggle very long and hard to bring it back."

Nikki bowed. She didn't take his comments to heart. Chang believed that to build one up, you must tear him down first.

"I will do as you say."

"This was fun!" Heather bounced out. "Are we coming back?"

Chang bowed to her. "You will return the day after tomorrow. Practice what you have learned today and you will learn more the next time."

Not as intimidated by Chang by now, she swallowed her giggle and bowed back.

"What is known to me will be known to you," he murmured to Nikki as they took their leave.

"He's like someone out of those karate movies," Heather said on the way home. "Can we really practice tomorrow?"

Nikki nodded. "We'll practice some, although I think you'll find your muscles are a little sore after today."

"I feel fine!"

"You won't by later tonight," she predicted. "When we get home, I want you to take a hot shower and then help me with dinner. Your father's assistants are staying."

"What are we having?"

"Spaghetti."

"Oh, good! You can't burn spaghetti!"

"What a comforting thought."

*   *   *

Time seemed to pass slowly as Nikki struggled to keep from lowering her guard. She knew the moment things were most quiet was when they could rapidly fire up. But not even Chang had heard anything, as he told her on the days she and Heather visited the *dojo*.

One Saturday Nikki stood at the kitchen sink, rinsing vegetables in preparation for making a salad for lunch. As a squeal of laughter rang out, she quickly looked up, her heart in her throat. But none of her fears were taking shape. There was no masked gunman chasing Heather, only her father swimming after her as she tried to evade him, and Heather splashing him in return. Looking at them, no one would guess that their lives were in danger or that anything bad had ever happened to them. When Scott picked up Heather and threw her into the water, the little girl howled with laughter and begged for more.

Had her own father ever played with her that way? Nikki couldn't remember any scenes like this in her lifetime. All she remembered were scathing words if her room wasn't cleaned up to Adam's specifications. If the sheets weren't tucked in so tightly a quarter could bounce off them, she was grounded for a week. She couldn't remember him ever hugging her or offering words of comfort as she'd suffered and stumbled through the emotional years of being a teenager. No wonder she'd grown up feeling like a misfit.

Mercifully, Scott hadn't asked her any more probing questions about her reasons for leaving the navy. But that hadn't stopped him from studying her with an intensity that unnerved her. While Nikki wasn't a virgin and had had her share of male admirers, she had kept them at arm's length. It was as if Scott refused to keep that distance and purposely invaded her space every chance he got. She didn't count him as an admirer, but there was something sizzling between them and she wasn't sure how to handle it. She felt like she was on an emotional roller coaster that seemed to accelerate more each day, and she wanted to hate him for making her feel so off balance.

Nikki paused when her eyesight began to dim. It was a moment before she realized tears were filling her eyes. She angrily blinked them away and began ripping lettuce leaves into smaller pieces.

"I should have stayed in Baton Rouge," she muttered, peeling carrots with a vengeance.

"Come swimming with us!" Heather called out.

Nikki managed a smile and a shake of the head. "Someone has to fix lunch."

"Oh, swimming's much more fun!" Heather climbed out of the pool, then ran toward the deep end, cannonballing into the water.

Scott roared with mock ferocity as he climbed out of the pool. "Cute, kid! Time to climb out and dry off," he told her. He waited until she was out of the pool, had a towel draped around her and was sitting on the grass before he walked into the house.

"You're dripping on the floor," Nikki told him. She kept her eyes firmly averted from his almost-bare body.

"I wouldn't worry. It's a warm day. It will dry." Unconcerned, he opened the refrigerator door and peered inside. "Since it's a nice day, why don't we eat outside? Do you want cola or ice tea?"

Nikki set the salad bowl to one side. "Ice tea. While you're in there, you may as well pull out the salad dressing. I'll get the rolls out of the oven."

Scott straightened up and turned to Nikki. "Why won't you swim with us?"

She turned to pick up a pot holder. "I just don't care to."

He reached over and took it out of her hand. "No, it's more than that. Why?"

"I don't want to, okay?" Her tone was more defensive than angry.

He held up his hands in surrender. "All right, I'll back off. For now."

Nikki hated to see her own hands trembling. "That's your problem. You constantly have to probe and dig as if you're fooling with a bad tooth. Why can't you just leave it alone?" She should have known he wouldn't listen to her plea. He stood so close to her she could detect the clean smell of chlorine on his skin.

"For the last five years I thought I hated you. I quickly learned that that isn't the case anymore." He tipped her chin upward. "You're full of prickles and you constantly back-pedal, but that only makes me want to find out what makes you tick. What makes you tick, Nicole Price?"

She tried to pull away, but his grip tightened. "Nothing all that interesting. Are you going to release me or will I have to hurt you?"

Tempted by the indignation lighting her eyes and flushing her cheeks, Scott lowered his head.

"Go ahead," he whispered, "hurt me."

Nikki's mistake was in opening her mouth to protest. Her next mistake was in not pushing Scott away when his mouth covered hers. It was already too late as she drowned in a multitude of sensations—the warmth of his skin against her T-shirt, the feel of droplets of water that fairly sizzled under her touch as she placed her hands on his shoulders. Encouraged by her response, he slipped his arms around her waist and pulled her closer against him. Her T-shirt absorbed the moisture from his skin as their bodies melded together.

Scott's tongue curled around Nikki's, probing in a way that sent tremors throughout her body.

"Come on, Nikki, relax," he whispered as his mouth paved a path along her jawline. He found her earlobe and nibbled on it. "Show me a little of that fire I see in your eyes."

Nikki moaned softly under his sensual onslaught as his teeth found a sensitive spot just behind her ear. She held on tightly for fear her knees would give out. A wave of heat washed over her body as she felt the contour of the counter against her back and the hard ridge of Scott's arousal against the juncture of her thighs. Wild thoughts raced through her mind—Scott pulling off her T-shirt, unfastening her shorts. Right now, the idea of making love on the kitchen floor didn't seem all that decadent to her.

"Nikki," Scott breathed, resting the flat of his hand against her abdomen.

"Dad! Nikki!"

A cold shower couldn't have been more effective. Nikki tried to pull away, but Scott was slower. His hand lingered against her midriff before dropping to his side. He took a quick glance out the kitchen window.

"She's still outside," he assured her.

Nikki quickly sidestepped and reached for the salad bowl. She dropped her hands just as quickly when she realized how badly they were trembling.

"Dad, are we gonna eat soon? I'm starvin'," Heather called.

"We'll be out in a minute," he yelled back. He glanced at Nikki and reached for her hand. He was stunned to find it cold to the touch. "Are you all right?"

She nodded jerkily. "You better go out before she comes in. I guess we should be grateful she didn't walk in on us. Talk about advanced education." Her laughter was forced.

Scott started for the door, then halted and looked over his shoulder. "This isn't finished, Nikki," he told her before he walked outside.

She wiped her hands down the sides of her shorts. "Yes, it is."

Chapter 8

Nothing was going right. Scott stared at the diagram on the computer monitor until the graphics swam in front of his eyes. He wondered how something that looked so right could be so wrong. He took off his glasses and rubbed his eyes. Then he slipped his glasses on and gazed at the monitor again. The design looked the same—all wrong. He was positive his professional life was in the toilet.

"Why can't we build the prototype from this?" Cully had demanded at the institute lab, where he and Scott and Kay had labored most of the night.

"Because something isn't right," Scott argued, still staring at the monitor and hoping the error would pop out at him and announce itself.

"But you don't know what's wrong! How do you know the prototype won't give you a chance to see exactly where the error is?"

He waved a hand dismissively. "Because it won't."

"We've gone over the calibrations four times, checked the power packs, the housing, you name it. Face it, it's ready to build and you just don't want to admit it," Kay chimed in.

"Dammit, I told you, it's not ready!" Scott's verbal explosion stunned his staff. He took several deep breaths to still his pounding pulse. He felt so tired, and frustrated that he had nothing to show for it. "It's not ready."

"The big guys expect to see something by the end of the month," Kay said softly.

Scott's expression could have been carved in stone. "They can wait."

"They won't and you know it. They're already mad because you're late in getting this together."

Cully winced at his co-worker's persistence. "Kay—"

She waved him off as she kept her attention on their boss. "This is big time, Scott. Not some penny-ante toy. We're talking lasers used as weapons. Weapons that can be carried the same as a hand gun."

He heaved a sigh. "You know, it was a hell of a lot more fun to break into NASA's computer than to come up with this. It would have been a lot easier if I'd gone into toy designing."

"I remember breaking into the university's computer and flunking all the idiots who called me a brain," Cully said reminiscently, leaning so far back in his chair he almost fell over. "One was the dean's son, who wasn't too smart to begin with."

"Cracking the phone company's computer and deleting all the long-distance charges from my bill," Scott added.

"Hey, I've got a better one. Erasing department-store charges."

Kay threw up her hands. "Oh, for heaven's sake! You're both impossible! All of that was juvenile stuff. We're talking adult now. Do you realize what we have here? We're on the stepping stone to success and you're both blowing it by sitting around and talking about the practical jokes you played in school. Guess what, guys, *you're not kids any-more!*"

"She was a lot more fun before she took that assertive-ness class," Cully griped. "It turned her into a regular witch."

Scott glanced at his watch and cursed. "I've got to get home."

"Afraid your *housekeeper* will get jealous you're with us instead of with her?"

He looked up at Kay, trying to decipher her coy remark. "Considering she's there to take care of the house and Heather, I'm sure she's happier when I'm not around to dirty up the place," he lied. With a guard seated just inside the laboratory door, Nikki's identity was kept safe.

"Yes, but can you trust her?" Kay pushed.

"Meaning?" His quiet tone should have been a warning for her.

"Well, what do you know about her? The way I hear it, she took off right after your wife killed herself. And then she showed up again right after all this trouble started." Kay fingered a stack of computer printouts. She looked up, her dark eyes speculative. "For all you know, she might have had something to do with it. Or maybe with what's hap-pened to you lately. I mean, you had all that trouble, then once she shows up, nothing happens. Doesn't that make you suspicious?"

Scott's jaw muscle flexed as he labored to keep his anger contained. He tried to tell himself that Kay was making these accusations only because she had no idea why Nikki was in his house. And things *had* been quiet lately, which made life even more worrisome for him.

"Kay, you are begging for a good swift kick in the pants," Cully muttered, returning to the safety of his computer. His fingers raced over the keys as he studied Scott's notes and reconfigured one of his earlier formulas. "And I'd be will-ing to help him give it to you."

Unfortunately, he only invited her wrath to rain on him.

"You are just as bad." She advanced on Cully with nostrils flared and eyes narrowed in anger. "Why can't you think of the significance of this project? Dr. Westin has! He knows how important it is! He's always asking me about it."

"He's what?" Scott interjected. "What has he said?"

Kay backed off only a fraction. "He said he can't get any straight answers from you, so he asked me."

"Westin doesn't have the brains of a slug," Cully declared.

For a moment, the young man wasn't sure whether he should duck. Kay stood over him, breathing hard, looking ready to kill. Luckily for him, she turned away.

"The next time Dr. Westin asks you anything about this project, you tell him to come to me. You *do not* say one word to him," Scott insisted. "Do you understand?"

Kay was too caught up in her own fury to act sensibly. "Don't worry, I won't say anything more to him. I don't know why I bother. Neither of you are taking this seriously." She picked up the backpack that doubled as her purse and stomped out of the laboratory.

"Think it's PMS?" Cully mused, wincing as the metal door banged shut.

"I wouldn't be brave enough to ask. She's mad enough at both of us to start throwing things." Scott tapped the Enter key, saved his notes to a disk and began the process of shutting down his system. "Let's just close up for the night and get back to this tomorrow."

Cully nodded and began his own shutdown process. "Why won't you go with the prototype? We're as ready with it as we'll ever be."

Scott inserted the disk in a special sleeve and put it in his briefcase. "Because if it's wrong, the prototype could severely injure, if not kill, the person trying it out."

"We could use robotics for the test."

He nodded. "I'll think about it. Who knows, maybe tomorrow will bring that magic thought that will put everything in place. Good night, Cully."

Cully watched as Scott and his guard left the laboratory. The moment they were gone, he returned to the computer and quickly typed in his password. Within moments, he was scrolling through the directory.

Scott had his driver drop him off by the front door late that afternoon. He hid his irritation when the man insisted on ringing the bell and when no one arrived, taking Scott's key from him and unlocking the door.

"This is necessary," he informed Scott as he entered the house first, gun in hand.

Scott felt a few nervous ticks as he realized the house was empty.

"Dr. Carter," the driver called from the kitchen. He walked out, smiling. "They're in the backyard. Have a nice evening." He closed the front door on his way out.

Scott rapidly headed for the kitchen window. What he saw and heard was unexpected. Rhythmic music that made a person think of dancing had the woman and girl doing just that.

"Left foot back," Nikki instructed, her hands holding Heather's as they swayed, their bare feet moving in time to the music.

The late-afternoon sun enveloped them, adding a golden brilliance to their clothing. Nikki's filmy skirt floated around her bare calves in colors of pink, blue, light green, lavender, peach and yellow, and her cream-colored tank top clung to her upper body in a loving caress. Heather, in bright pink shorts and a T-shirt-styled top, was equally colorful. She turned her head when she saw a movement in the kitchen window and her face lit up.

"Daddy!" She waved excitedly. "Nikki's teaching me Cajun dancing. This is so much fun! Come out!"

Scott couldn't stop staring when Nikki turned her head. The sun cast a glow across her narrow features. Even at this distance he saw the bright peach gloss on her lips and the touch of color on her eyelids. What was more important was the fleeting expression of joy on her face before she masked it behind a pleasant facade that said nothing at all. He wondered what it would take to get her to shake herself loose.

Intrigued, he walked outside.

"Cajun dancing, huh?" He caught Heather up in his arms and spun her around, while Nikki walked over to the cassette player and shut it off. The quiet was almost deafening.

Heather's head bobbed up and down. "Nikki learned it when she lived in Louisiana. And Cajuns have parties and dance a lot. Even the kids!"

"Sounds like fun." He looked at Nikki over his daughter's head. "Think she'll teach me?"

Heather slid out of his grasp. "If you ask her nice, I bet she will." She turned to Nikki. "Won't you?"

Nikki's gaze was focussed on Scott. "If he wants to learn."

He stared back at her, his expression as carefully masked as hers, but the heated look in his eyes told her his real feelings. "I want."

Nikki's eyes locked on Scott's as she walked toward him with easy grace. Her slender hips moved with the same sinuous movement a cat made stalking an unsuspecting mouse. The soft cotton of her tank top faithfully outlined her unfettered breasts, the neckline revealing the shadowed cleavage.

Scott's jaw flexed. The idea of his being a mouse was more fanciful than any thought he'd ever conjured up. After all, scientists weren't supposed to have whimsical thoughts. But looking at Nikki in her utterly feminine clothing had him thinking a lot about other, more-physical pursuits.

"I'm not exactly dressed for a dance." He gestured toward his jeans and white shirt with the sleeves rolled up to his elbows.

Nikki smiled. "You don't dress up at these kind of parties." She held out her arms in dance position. "Heather, would you please turn on the music again?"

The moment Scott took her in his own arms, he knew this was meant to be. Nikki stood in his embrace as if she was made for him. Barefoot as she was, she was tucked perfectly under his chin. He took a quick look downward and noticed her bare toes bore a bright pink nail polish. He wondered if he'd start dreaming about those colorful toes.

"Lead with your right foot," she murmured, swaying in that direction.

That was the first and last direction she gave him. The voices singing in the Cajun language of the Deep South sent them moving across the lawn as if they had danced together all their lives.

They didn't look down or take their eyes off each other as they whirled around the yard, their steps moving faster in time to the music. They didn't notice Heather sitting on the grass, watching them with a speculative eye for a while, then quietly slipping into the house.

When the song changed to a plaintive ballad, Scott drew Nikki closer and their movements slowed.

The heat generated by the dance had warmed Nikki's skin so that the erotic scent of her perfume seemed to flow around her body, blending with the crisper hint of lime on Scott. Not for a second had they looked away from each other. He didn't need to lead because he knew she would turn at the same moment he did. They could have been the only two people in the world.

"You've done this before." She was the first to break the charged silence between them.

"When I was in New Orleans I met a fellow computer specialist who had grown up in the bayou country. He showed me around." Not a hint of a smile softened his taut expression. "What about you?"

"One of my clients invited me to her family's parties. She felt I needed a more active social life. I spent a lot of time with them and they practically adopted me. Her grandmother felt I needed a good Cajun boy to make me happy."

"And what did *you* feel you needed to make you happy?"

He noticed she didn't answer right away and wondered if she was going to ignore his question the way she had so many others. He watched her tongue slide across her lower lip, leaving it shiny with moisture. He ached to follow that path.

"To be appreciated for who I am."

That telling remark said a lot.

"Nikki, you are appreciated." He slowed his steps until they merely swayed to the music.

"You don't know me." She tipped her head back and looked up with her deep golden eyes.

"I know you well enough."

He felt triumphant when she didn't stiffen or back off as she had before.

"You can't carry a tune worth a damn, although that doesn't stop you from singing in the shower. You don't mind spending time with Heather and you've taught her how to protect herself. You don't mind being the talk of the neighborhood with the new you." His gaze traveled over her bare arms. "And *I* don't mind looking at the new you, either."

Nikki shrugged. "I'm not the kind of bodyguard who likes to remain undercover."

"Maybe you would...if you were undercover with someone you liked." He trailed his fingers down her arms until they reached her wrists. With thumb and forefinger, he encircled each wrist, clasping lightly.

"Bodyguards and their subjects cannot get involved with each other," she whispered. "It's a cardinal rule."

"Yes, but we've grown beyond that, haven't we?" He searched her face for an answer.

She lifted her eyes. "God help me, we have."

That was all he needed. Scott lowered his head and nipped at her lower lip, tasting the sweetness that was her. Her hands still hung at her sides, his fingers circling her wrists.

He released her and slipped his arms around her waist so he could pull her closer to him. She flowed against him like a silken scarf as she stepped into his embrace. Her mouth softened against his inviting tongue.

For the moment, Nikki's only thought of protection was that involved in defending herself against Scott. It wasn't easy to do when the warmth of his body surrounded her and his mouth was doing incredible things to her, nipping her lower lip, the tender skin at the base of her throat.

"Beautiful," he muttered, pulling up her tank top slightly and finding skin even softer than the cotton covering her. Her breast fit his hand perfectly; her nipple became distended against his cupped palm. He wondered what color it was—a soft pink like the inside of a seashell or a deeper rose shade? He hungered to find out, but knew this wasn't the best place, even if he wanted her skin warmed by the sun. Instead, he soothed another hunger by returning to her mouth.

For once, Scott was in control. He had Nikki almost where he wanted her and intended to enjoy this magical moment for as long as he could.

"Scott." Her voice was breathless, and tremors coursed through her upper body as he cupped her breast, his thumb rubbing the sensitized nipple.

"Say it again," he said thickly, transferring his mouth to her earlobe. The tiny gold flower in her lobe invited his tongue to trace the delicate swirls, to swoop upward and outline the shell-like contour. "Say my name the way you'll say it in bed."

"*Scott.*" The word was a breathless whisper, but he heard it loud and clear in his senses. What it meant raced through his bloodstream, igniting nerve endings and arousing him to such a degree he wondered if he would ever get enough of her even if he had the chance to make love with her.

"I don't know when it began," he kept muttering over and over as he rained kisses on her face. He moved his hips against hers, feeling her softness cradle his arousal. "When I first wanted you so badly."

She closed her eyes, drowning in the sensations he was arousing in her. Then she opened them again. Sanity was rearing its ugly head and she was rapidly growing powerless against it. After all, they were in the backyard, where someone could arrive at any moment and see them. And Heather...

"Heather!" she gasped.

"She went into the house." He pulled her even tighter against him.

But the mood was now gone and they both knew it. Scott straightened and watched Nikki take a step back, a tiny step that kept her in his loose embrace.

"Thank you for the dancing lesson," he said formally.

"You're very welcome." She was equally formal. She took another step backward. "You'll have time for a swim to cool off before dinner."

His mouth curved upward in a crooked smile. "You could always join me in the pool."

Her answering smile warmed him more than the sun. "Yes, but then you wouldn't cool off, would you?"

"So how about we turn it to steam? We'll have a hell of a lot more fun."

With her skirt floating around her legs, she walked back to the house. Scott remained where he was, watching her every step of the way.

"Maybe a dip would help," he finally muttered.

The atmosphere between them was charged all evening. Nikki was grateful that Heather seemed oblivious to what was going on around her. Dinner was filled with long silences and heated looks from Scott. Nikki worked hard to keep things normal, encouraging Heather to talk about school and the end-of-the-year activities going on.

"I'll be able to go to the Smithsonian with my class next week, won't I?" she asked her father. She looked first at him, then at Nikki. "I'll stay with them the whole time. I promise. I won't even go to the bathroom."

"Those are pretty drastic measures." Scott turned to Nikki. "What do you think?"

Nikki knew she should say no. She should remind Heather that sometimes special treats had to be given up. Except there had been too many instances when that had happened to her.

"I think we can work something out."

"Yes!" Heather pumped her arm up and down in the air. She immediately straightened in her chair and adopted an angelic expression. "Thank you."

"Don't try that Miss Innocence act or we'll all think you're up to something," Scott teased, playfully pulling on a strand of her curly hair.

"No, I'm just showing you how grown up I'm getting." She picked up her plate and carried it to the sink. She returned to the table and picked up the rest of the plates. "I'll do the dishes. You two go outside and talk," she ordered.

"Maybe your father wants to go down to his lab and work," Nikki said.

Scott stood up and walked around the table, stopping near Nikki. "Maybe her father wants to go outside and talk. Let's make the little dictator happy."

As they walked outside, Nikki was glad she had changed from the skirt and tank top she'd worn for Heather's dancing lesson into denim shorts and a red T-shirt. She glanced toward the garage, with its motion-detector lights set up along the gutters.

"When did you buy the motorcycle?"

He was surprised by her abrupt question. "About two years ago. One day things were getting to me. Heather had been throwing a lot of tantrums and life just didn't seem to want to work out for me. I passed by this motorcycle shop and saw the bike in the window. It was love at first sight. Sometimes, at night, I'd just climb on and take off. It helped clear away the cobwebs." He pulled out a chair for her by the patio table and took the other one, swinging it around so he could rest his arms on the back. "How about a swim after Heather goes to bed?"

She shook her head.

"Afraid of going swimming with me?"

Nikki's eyes glinted with the same dangerous lights reflected in Scott's deep sapphire orbs. "I'm not afraid of anything."

"Then why don't you swim?"

"Because I don't like to swim." She said it in a way that told him she was serious.

"Really?"

"Really."

"I thought all navy brats were part fish."

"This navy brat would have flunked the swimming tests if it hadn't been for sheer determination."

Scott shook his head. "Obviously, you weren't with the right people."

"I enjoy remaining on solid ground."

"No wonder you went into intelligence work. You didn't have to worry about boarding a ship and floating out to sea."

"I went into intelligence work because the admiral said I wouldn't last," she countered, for the first time not appearing so tense when she talked about her father. "My first commanding officer was one of his old buddies, a real jerk who did his best to make my life miserable. I outlasted him and lucked out with my next commanding officer. He hated the admiral and did everything he could to help me advance. Unfortunately, the admiral must have figured things out and pulled some strings to get me transferred. But by then I was known for going in and getting the job done."

"Yes, I know."

Nikki reached across and covered his hand with hers. "I can't offer any hope, but I got hold of Renee's case file."

His head snapped up at her news. "And?"

"And I've glanced over it and plan to study it further, but I feel as if there's something missing."

His lips thinned. "Besides her so-called accomplice?"

"The accomplice no one ever heard about and who's not been seen since. And also how she was able to break into your files when she didn't know how to turn on a computer."

"Someone could have written out explicit instructions."

She shook her head. "No, there's something there. I just have to find it, and I'm afraid when I do, neither one of us will like what we see."

"You're thinking that person is still around?"

Nikki slowly nodded. "And knows what I am."

"Which is why nothing has happened since you appeared on the scene." He was guessing, but sensed it was the truth.

She nodded again.

"So your cover is no good?"

"It's only a hunch."

"But your sixth sense has never let you down, has it?"

She looked away. "It did once."

Scott took a deep breath. "No, I think you were so overwhelmed with the evidence that you felt you had no choice but to arrest her." He offered her a crooked smile.

"I didn't have the authority to arrest her. I left that to the feds, but now I feel I should have done a little more digging before I alerted them," she admitted.

Scott lowered his head to rest his chin on his folded hands as he stared at the house. He could see the light go on in Heather's bedroom window a minute after the kitchen light went out. "Renee was a lot of things, but she wasn't stupid," he mused. "If only she had given me a chance to prove she wasn't guilty."

It was the stillness of her body he noticed first. He glanced up. "You don't think she killed herself, either."

"Would Renee have honestly known how to obtain poison in a federal jail? She didn't have any visitors those last two days, so she couldn't have talked someone into smuggling it in for her," Nikki said candidly, aware her news might hurt him. "There are ways of getting anything you need if you know who to ask, but I doubt anyone with those connections ran in Renee's social circle."

She studied Scott, seeing the tension lines bracketing his mouth. "I'm sorry." She knew the words were inadequate, but they were all she had to offer him.

He held up his hand. "No." Violence vibrated in his voice. "I don't want to hear your apologies. I want something done about it." Even in the dark, his eyes glowed.

"I can talk to Harvey, have him run an investigation."

"No!" He took a deep breath. "I don't want you telling anyone your assumptions."

"Harvey is perfectly trustworthy," she argued.

"I don't care. I don't want you talking to him." At that moment, Scott looked far from the picture of a scientist. He looked like a warrior.

"I don't have the resources Harvey does."

"You're a smart lady. You'll handle it."

As they sat at the table, hands clasped, they had no idea a young girl was watching them from the window with a broad grin on her face.

The office was dimly lit as always, the occupant seated at a desk with the phone set squarely in the middle of the cleared surface.

"He's holding something back. He claims he isn't finished. For some reason he's refusing to let go."

"What can be done?" the voice on the other end of the phone line asked.

"With Price in there, he thinks he's well protected. I suggest we show him he isn't."

Chapter 9

"Can we go to the zoo today?" Heather pleaded, as she poked at the carrot shavings with her fork. "Please?"

Scott shook his head. "You were just at the Smithsonian last week!"

"That was school, not us." She bounced up and down on her chair. "So can we go, please?"

Scott glanced at Nikki. "Can you think of any reason why we can't?"

"I could probably state many reasons, but I'm sure you'd shoot each one down," she said quietly, catching Heather's hopeful expression. "Though are you sure she's been good enough this past week?"

"I practiced my throws, I did all my homework, which wasn't all that much anyway, and I even did dishes for two nights. Isn't that enough?" Heather wailed.

"Sounds like enough to me," Scott agreed.

He laid his fork down and studied Nikki. She had been quiet during the meal, which wasn't unusual, but this time seemed different. If he didn't know better, he'd swear she was trying to distance herself from them. Especially from him. He knew she had gone through Renee's files again. He'd asked to see them but she'd refused, saying it was better that he not read them. He'd tried arguing but had gotten nowhere. In the end, he'd decided she was right.

"I can't imagine anyone would try anything in a busy place like the zoo," he said finally. "If Miss Heather is willing to help with the dishes, I don't see why we all can't leave within the hour."

Nikki looked up. "I am not here to participate in family outings," she said softly, under the cover of Heather's excited squeals.

He held her gaze. "No, but you are here to protect us, so I guess you'll have to go where we go whether you want to or not. Not to mention you're the one who keeps talking about keeping up appearances. If we're under observation, they'll assume you're along for Heather's sake."

Unable to eat any more, Nikki picked up her plate and carried it to the sink.

"You can help Heather with the dishes. I have a few things to do first," she said before making her escape.

"Daddy, is Nikki mad about something?" she could hear Heather ask her father as she left the kitchen.

"No, honey, she's just got a lot on her mind. That's why I think your suggestion of the zoo will be a good idea. We've been cooped up here too long."

Nikki entered her bedroom and immediately headed for the closet. She pulled a small leather holster off a shelf and threaded it through her belt, allowing her gun to nestle snugly against the small of her back. For reinforcement, she added an ankle holster.

She changed into jeans and an aqua cotton T-shirt that billowed comfortably. As a last touch, she added a denim-billed cap and pulled her ponytail through the opening in the back. When she walked into the bathroom, she caught a glimpse of herself in the mirror.

"Just Mom, Dad and the kid on a day's outing." Brushing the thought from her mind, she picked up a coral lipstick. As she applied it to her lips, she could hear the doorbell chiming softly in the background.

"Special delivery for Dr. Carter." The words, called out in response to Scott's query, penetrated her concentration with the sureness of a heat-seeking missile and told her that something was very wrong. One thing Nikki had learned early on was to trust her instincts, because they never let her down. She didn't hesitate.

She wasn't even aware of dropping her lipstick and racing out of the room.

"Don't open anything!" she shouted, racing toward the family room. Voices rang loudly in her head.

"I bet it's my surprise from Grandma!" Heather was saying excitedly. "Is it, Daddy?"

"We'll have to see, kiddo."

"No!" As Nikki skidded to a stop inside the room, the scene before her froze in her mind like a surrealistic painting.

Heather was kneeling in front of Scott, who sat in an easy chair with a box nestled in his lap. Wrapping paper already flared out from the sides and Scott was just starting to lift one of the flaps. He looked up at the sound of Nikki's shout, took in the wildness in her eyes and grasped the situation within milliseconds. For a brief time he had forgotten his life wasn't all that normal, after all.

"Heather, get away!" He used his foot to push his daughter back just as the other box flap suddenly flew up. As it did, a whooshing sound echoed in the room and white powder flew into the air.

Scott intuitively covered his face with his hands, but that didn't stop his harsh curses as the powder burned a path along the back of his hands and arms.

"Heather, call 911!" Nikki ordered as she raced toward Scott. She didn't bother to see if the girl had followed her instructions, but grabbed hold of his wrists, careful not to touch the powdered surface. "Scott, take your hands away from your face. You mustn't touch your skin. Touching it will only make it worse."

He struggled in her grasp. "Damn, it burns like the devil!" he rasped, his face contorted.

"Just try to remain calm." She winced as she saw the angry raw patches of skin appearing under the dusting of powder. She had no idea what the caustic agent was, but she knew it was inflicting terrible pain.

She continued kneeling in front of him, holding on to his hands and talking softly. She didn't move from her spot even as she heard the strident sound of a siren echoing outside, until it stopped and someone pounded on the door.

"I have to let them in, Scott. Don't touch your face." She carefully removed her hands and ran for the door. She looked over the paramedics and ushered them in. She directed them to the family room and waited in the background as they took over.

"Any idea what this was?" one of the men asked, as he carefully applied wet packs to Scott's face.

Nikki shook her head. "The burning effect was almost immediate."

As Scott was loaded onto a gurney, Nikki noticed Heather standing off to the side. The stricken look on her face tore at her heart and she quickly hurried to the little girl.

"He'll be fine," she assured her, gathering her in her arms.

"I told him it was from Grandma," she sobbed. "She said she was sending me a surprise. I know you said we shouldn't open boxes without you, but I thought it was from her." She buried her face against Nikki's shoulder.

"I know, darling. Heather, you have to calm yourself. We need to go with your dad." She stopped long enough to grab her wallet and hurried out to her truck with the intention of following the ambulance.

During the harrowing drive, Nikki alternately comforted Heather and managed to call Harvey to apprise him of the situation.

"How is he?" Harvey demanded.

"Burned. We're not sure how badly." She winced as she ran a red light in order to keep up with the ambulance, then slowed down again. The last thing she needed now was an accident. "Can you send someone out for backup?"

"I'll have someone there within the hour. Let me know how he's doing."

Nikki hung up and managed a quick look at Heather. The girl still looked frightened but was calmer than she had been earlier.

Heather turned her head and stared at the lump visible between Nikki's back and the seat. "Do you have a gun there?" she whispered.

Nikki nodded. She refused to hide anything from the girl. "I have to wear it if we are going out somewhere. I need to protect you and your father."

"Is he going to die?" Her sapphire eyes, so much like her father's, were shadowed with fear.

"No, but he's going to hurt for a little while. Like when you get a bad sunburn," she explained, pulling to a stop in front of the hospital's emergency room, where she could see Scott being wheeled inside. She parked the truck and hurried after him, only to be told she and Heather would have to wait until the doctor finished his examination.

As Nikki waited, she thought of the many times she had been in a hospital in the past. How many times had she or one of her brothers been treated for various injuries and broken bones? She hadn't liked hospitals then and she liked them even less now. She settled Heather on one of the vinyl couches and coaxed her into closing her eyes in hopes that she would relax. Nikki did the opposite, pacing the room with the restless energy of a wildcat. As she paced, she wished she hadn't stopped smoking a year ago. At the moment, she felt only a cigarette would help curb the agitation running through her.

"Ms. Price?"

Nikki spun on her heel and faced the doctor. Dressed in rumpled surgical scrubs, the gray-haired man offered her a reassuring smile.

"Dr. Carter's eyes were spared," he told her, as he drew her to a corner of the room. "The powder did most of its damage on his arms and the back of his hands. I understand you kept him from touching his face. That quick thinking spared him even more pain and injury. We still aren't sure what kind of powder was used, so we don't know if there will be any scarring from the burns. Some areas are very raw."

Nikki rotated her shoulders to relieve some of the tension. "But he'll be all right?"

He nodded. "I wouldn't suggest he do any work for a few weeks, until the healing is completed, and we'll want to keep him here at least overnight. But I'd say the prognosis looks very good. He's a lucky man."

Nikki glanced over her shoulder at Heather, who lay stretched out on the couch. "I'll want to stay with Dr. Carter as soon as I make arrangements for his daughter."

He nodded. "I'll send a nurse out to tell you once he's settled in a room."

Nikki took out her wallet, looking for the small sheet of paper containing phone numbers as she searched for a pay phone.

"Scott, forgive me," she murmured, using her calling card to punch out a series of numbers. "But right now, I have no other options."

Scott felt as if his world had been wrapped in cotton wool. Sounds were muted, senses muffled, and he felt as if he was floating on air. The fuzzy part of his brain said not to worry. The more rational part warned him he'd have a hell of a lot to worry about once the pain medication wore off. He knew which part of his brain he wanted to listen to.

He tried to open his eyes and soon discovered they would open only a crack. When he tried again, waves of pain shot through his head. He groaned.

"Hey." A cool palm cupped his cheek. "Don't attempt anything too macho. Right now, you're wrapped up tighter than King Tut for a very good reason."

Without moving his head, he managed to glance down at his chest. Fear replaced the pain when he saw his arms wrapped in bulky bandages.

"My hands," he croaked, trying to lift them but failing miserably. "What happened to my hands?" All he had were fractured memories of his holding a box, Heather's excitement, then Nikki's panicked shout and something burning his skin.

"They're all right," she quickly assured him, gently pushing him back onto the pillows. "They were burned by the powder and have to be kept wrapped for a while. It's so you won't irritate the skin. It's very tender right now. The doctor said you were very lucky the powder didn't get on your face. Harvey's lab is analyzing it. They were able to scrape some off your arms."

Scott's stomach lurched at her matter-of-fact statement. While he didn't have a weak stomach, the events of the day and the idea of having his skin scraped was a bit much for him. Another fear suddenly arose.

"Is Heather all right?" he suddenly demanded, struggling to sit up. "I want to see her."

"Heather is fine and better be sound asleep, since it's almost two in the morning."

He dropped back onto the pillows. "If you're here, who's with her?"

Nikki paused. "I didn't have much of a choice. I didn't want to leave her with an agent, because she was frightened enough over what happened. She needed to be with people she knew and trusted."

Scott didn't wait for more of an explanation. "You called Renee's parents, didn't you?" The accusation was clear. "You called her damn parents." This time his groan wasn't from pain. "Do you realize what you've done? They've wanted to take her since this all began. Once they've got her locked behind those gates of theirs, they won't let her back out. They'll keep her a prisoner there and I'll never see her."

"Scott, calm down," she ordered, holding on to his shoulders. "If you don't settle down right away, the nurse will be in here like a flash and will give you a sedative." She waited until he stopped thrashing. "All right. Are you ready to listen to me now?" His sullen nod was enough. She lowered one of the bed rails and sat on the side of the mattress. "Heather needed something familiar. I didn't want her staying here at the hospital, since she couldn't come any farther than the waiting room. I also knew she wouldn't want to go back to the house with one of Harvey's agents."

She chose not to tell him of her meeting with Randolph and Lucille Winthrop. Their manner was as cold as the North Pole; accusations were left unspoken, but she read them loud and clear in Randolph's dark eyes. Nikki would have worried about Heather leaving with them if she hadn't seen the love they felt for their only granddaughter and known Heather would be safe with them.

"They'll have Heather call you first thing in the morning. I made sure to get their promise on that," she said.

He nodded.

"Poor kid. This is the last thing she needed after everything that's happened." He stared off into space. "We all would have been a lot better off if I had decided to design computer games instead of giving in to my fascination with war toys. The government would have left me alone and I could have had a normal life."

And I never would have met you. The bleak words bounced around in Nikki's brain.

Scott couldn't fight the weariness taking over, now that he had been reassured everyone was safe.

"That painkiller must be time released," he mumbled. "I think the second bombardment just kicked in." He closed his eyes, unable to fight the exhaustion that racked his body as heavily as the pain did. Within seconds, his breathing was even and deep.

With him sleeping soundly, Nikki felt brave enough to brush a strand of hair back from his forehead. His skin was warm and dry under her fingertips. His ordinarily tanned features were gray against the white cotton pillowcase and his lips were tight with the pain he must have felt even in his sleep. Even so, she couldn't remember ever seeing a more striking man, one who could turn her world upside down with just a smile.

As Nikki studied him, she felt another kind of fear surface—the fear that her emotions were taking over more than they should. It was dangerous for Scott. And dangerous for her.

She remained awake the rest of the night, watching Scott sleep and dream. Disjointed sentences left his lips as his dreams became real in his drugged mind. And she heard things she wished she hadn't.

She listened to Scott's fevered ramblings about the problems with his relationship as Renee had discovered being married to a world-famous scientist didn't mean excitement and parties. She listened to a sad story of love and lust that disintegrated over time. And she heard him talk about his anger and bitterness over Renee's defection and death.

Nikki slouched down in a chair that grew increasingly more uncomfortable with each passing hour. As she continued to watch Scott, she realized that her feelings toward him were growing too quickly for comfort. She thought of calling Harvey and demanding that she be taken off the assignment. She knew in this kind of work emotions had to be kept in cold storage. If they weren't, lives could be lost. But she knew she would do anything in her power to ensure Scott's safety. And her protective instincts hadn't kicked in simply because it was her job.

A corner of her mouth twisted in a wry smile.

"I guess the admiral was right after all. I need to learn to keep things in perspective."

"I don't give a damn what the doctor says. I want out of here now." If looks could kill, Nikki would have been struck dead by Scott's lethal gaze.

Unfazed by his anger, she calmly picked up the plastic pitcher and refilled his drinking cup.

"I don't want any more water."

She returned to the chair she had staked out as her own and settled down with a book in her lap. "Try and remember you are an adult. You have to stay an extra day because your temperature spiked last night, so you may as well behave yourself. There isn't anything you can do about it."

He merely glared in reply. "I want to see Heather."

Nikki didn't look up from her book. "You know very well hospital rules forbid her to come in."

He flopped back against his pillows. He knew he was acting like a spoiled child, but he didn't care. Right now, he'd give anything to upset that calm demeanor Nikki was displaying.

"Grandparent rules, you mean." He turned his head and frowned at Nikki, who looked as relaxed as if she was at the beach.

Anyone who didn't know her would think she was sitting there engrossed in her book, but he knew she didn't miss a thing. She had left his side only long enough to return to the house, shower, change and bring a set of clean clothes for him.

During the time she was gone, an agent had remained in the room with Scott, even when Harvey stopped by and kept him company. David Westin had also stopped by, and Kay and Cully had called to see how he was doing. Kay told him she and Cully would continue with the work and assured him with a teasing note in her voice that they wouldn't screw anything up until he returned.

Nikki's linen walking shorts and vest were the rose-pink color of ripe watermelons. She was the only bright spot in the sterile-looking room.

"You talked to Heather on the phone this morning," she reminded him.

"Sure, and she told me about the horse her grandfather 'just happened to find' and how her grandmother was taking her to a grown-up tea."

She calmly turned the page. "You're grumbling."

"You'd grumble too if you were a prisoner in this damn bed, where sadistic nurses poke and prod you and ask how you're doing when they should know." He changed his position and winced. "Not one of them knows how to give a shot without inflicting a great deal of pain."

Nikki tightened her lips to keep her smile from blossoming. She had heard that men made horrible patients. Scott was proving that story wasn't a myth.

"I brought more books with me. Try one. You might like it." She dug into her purse and pulled out several paperbacks, tossing them onto the bed near Scott's hand, the one that hadn't been burned as badly and was now unbandaged in hopes it would heal faster. The skin was an angry red and looked painful to the touch. Scott was careful as he picked each book up, studying the cover first, then reading the back blurb and opening to the teaser page.

"Horror, mystery, psychological thriller," he muttered, before finally selecting one. "You have a sick mind."

"Takes one to know one." This time when she dug in her purse, she pulled out a bag of candy-coated peanuts. She opened it and popped several into her mouth. "Sorry, you're not allowed them," she said without a trace of apology.

Scott put the book down. "I don't want to read."

She looked up under the cover of her lashes. "What do you want to do?"

"Why don't we talk instead?"

Nikki was instantly wary. "Talk about what?"

He shrugged. "Anything. Everything. I know what—I'll ask a question and you answer it honestly. Then you ask me one and I'll do the same."

"Such as?"

He thought for a moment. "What was the name of your second-grade teacher?"

"Mrs. Fitzsimmons. She believed group activities taught us more, so we were involved in I don't know how many projects." Her expression suddenly sobered. "Not long into the second semester, the admiral was transferred to another base to whip their intelligence section into shape. I went from her to an old crone who was waiting out her retirement." Nikki smiled as she realized it was her turn. "What position did you play in baseball when you were in school?"

"None. My parents didn't want me participating in sports. They were afraid I'd be critically injured." He suddenly grinned. "I made up for it by playing touch football in grad school. I was still in the gangly stage, but I could run like a bat out of hell. What about you? Did you play baseball?"

"I played shortstop. The admiral thought girls' softball was for sissies. I also played volleyball, touch football, field hockey and basketball. While other girls took ballet and tap dancing, I took martial arts and attended weapons classes three times a week." She thought for a moment. "If you could do anything over in your life, what would it be?"

He didn't hesitate. "I would have given Renee her divorce when she wanted it. Maybe then she wouldn't have died so needlessly." He wondered if this was the right moment to move in for the kill and decided it was as good a time as any. "Why did you resign from the navy?"

Nikki set her book to one side. "I think this little game of yours has gone on long enough. I'm going to stretch my legs."

Scott waited until she reached the door.

"You'll have to talk about it sometime, Nikki. It will do you good."

She looked over her shoulder. "Maybe I will, but not to-day."

She slapped the door with the flat of her hand and walked out. The door had barely swung shut before it opened again and Nikki walked back in.

Scott stared at her, noting the tightness around lips col-ored the same bright shade as her outfit. He was positive the color staining her cheeks didn't come from a compact.

"Why do you have to keep pushing?" She kept her voice low, her temper in check. But it was apparent she was walk-ing a fine line. "Okay, you're a scientist and you feel you have to know everything. Well, you don't have to know everything about *me.*"

"Maybe I want to."

She threw her hands up in disgust. "Why?"

"Because I find you a very lovely lady and I'd like to learn about the real you instead of that hard exterior you feel you have to portray to the world. You may like people to think you're tough, but you're not as tough as you want to be," he softly concluded. "You're hurting inside, Nikki. You'd be better off if you could let it all go."

Nikki stepped forward until she leaned over him, using her position to intimidate. "A degree in computer science and a high IQ do not give you the right to know every-thing."

Without a hint of warning, Scott caught Nikki off bal-ance, causing her to fall over him. She gasped and reached for the rail still raised on the other side of the bed, which proved to be a mistake since it caused her to stretch across his body even more. When his free arm curled around her waist, she had no way of regaining her balance.

"Let me up," she ordered.

A corner of his mouth twitched at her imperious tone.

"Say please."

The word she spat out had nothing to do with etiquette. Scott arched an eyebrow in surprise as Nikki's threats rained on his head.

"Are you sure that's anatomically possible?"

"*I'll* make it possible." Her expression promised dire consequences if he didn't obey her warning. "Scott, let me up."

He shook his head. "No way. I think I like you better this way. Besides, if one of the bad guys shows up, you've already thrown yourself into proper position to protect me."

Nikki tried to shift out of his grip and only succeeded in sliding further over him. She also discovered he was less than immune to her wiggling as she felt his arousal nudge her.

"Hey, do that again." His voice emerged husky and his eyes turned a deeper blue than usual. "I may be in a hospital, but I'm not so sick I can't get . . . interested."

"This isn't a good idea." Her husky voice matched his in intimate tones.

"Why not? You've got me where you want me. I can't go anywhere. A lot of women would love to have a man in this position."

Nikki's laughter burst unwillingly from her throat. "Don't do this, Scott. I'd rather remain angry at you."

He took a chance and lifted his hand to trace the outline of her lips. "I keep remembering the times I kissed you. And every time I do I get hard as a rock and want to kiss you again. But I'm greedy. I want more."

Her breath caught in her throat at his matter-of-fact statement.

"Don't . . ."

Scott's crooked grin turned Nikki's stomach into a roller coaster. "At least you didn't try to tear my head off when I told you."

"I saw no reason to injure you when we're within easy reach of medical assistance."

"Great." Scott lifted his head and pressed his mouth against hers.

He sipped. He nipped. He savored the shape of her mouth, the sweet taste of her. He felt Nikki's lips blossom under his probing. Heard her breathing grow raspy as he deepened the kiss with the intent to show her just exactly what he wanted to be doing with her at that moment.

"I told you this isn't a good idea," Nikki moaned as Scott nibbled on her lower lip.

"Sure it is." His voice was muffled as he pressed the tip of his tongue against her throat, where her pulse pounded in reaction. "You wear the sexiest perfume. That's what I remember the most from that first day. Other than noticing your legs." He moved his good arm upward, inching under her vest until he encountered bare skin. "You feel so good to me, Nikki."

She dipped her chin, pressing her forehead against his chest. "Please, Scott, don't do this to me. There's too much going on right now for either of us to even think of this."

Scott knew she wouldn't have displayed her vulnerability if she wasn't serious.

"When are you going to admit there's something brewing between us?"

She pulled back. "In this kind of work, emotions can get a person killed. And that means I could be killed just as easily as you. That means we both need to stay cool, calm and relaxed through this."

The idea of her being harmed hurt even more than his burns. He didn't like the conclusion he reached, but knew he had no choice.

"Then we'll put it on hold until the situation is settled."

Nikki wasn't pleased, either, because she didn't want to consider her growing attraction to Scott. But she already knew he was stubborn enough not to give in any more.

"I'll be right outside."

"You know, that old saying is right," Scott said to her back.

She looked over her shoulder. "What old saying?"

"'You can run but you can't hide.' I'll back off, but only a little. I don't want you to forget about me."

"I don't think there's any chance of that happening," she muttered.

Chapter 10

The house was four stories tall, ivy covered, with an old-world elegance that was as intimidating as hell. Luckily, Nikki didn't intimidate easily. Scott sat in the passenger seat just looking impatient.

Her four-wheel-drive vehicle, in need of a wash, looked out of place as she slowed to a stop in front of the dwelling. She turned to her passenger.

"If you don't behave, we'll drive right out of here."

"She's *my* daughter," Scott said grimly.

"And she's their granddaughter," she said gently. "Don't you think you have enough enemies after your sorry hide without adding them to the list?"

Scott didn't answer. He settled for a glare as he fumbled with the seat belt, until Nikki brushed his hands away and unsnapped it.

"I can tell this is going to be a real fun reunion," she murmured, climbing out of the truck.

She smiled brightly at the officious-looking butler who peered at her over the top of his spectacles as if she was something the cat had dragged in, if a cat would even be allowed to step onto the elegant Aubusson carpet.

"Mr. and Mrs. Winthrop are in the library," he informed them as he led the way down the elegant hallway. "I hope you are feeling better, Dr. Carter."

"Getting there." His face hadn't lost its grim expression. He leaned over and whispered in Nikki's ear, "Why hasn't he mentioned Heather?"

She gave a shrug. "Maybe she's chained in the basement," she whispered back, then smiled at the butler, who peered suspiciously at her. "I don't think he likes me."

"Don't worry, He doesn't like anybody."

The library was filled with books Nikki assumed to be first editions. There were several easy chairs and a couch near French doors that opened out onto a rose garden.

Randolph Winthrop stood by the windows. He was dressed in a dark, three-piece suit as if he was on his way to his office. Lucille Winthrop, elegant as only a former debutante could be, in a tailored, mauve silk dress, sat on the love seat.

"Scott." Her lips, colored a muted rose, barely moved in a smile. She lifted her head, silently inviting his kiss on her cheek. Her gaze cooled when she saw Nikki behind him and cooled even more when she noticed Nikki's bright pink cotton pants and pink-and-aqua-striped polo shirt. She turned back to her son-in-law. "You look very well. Please, sit down."

He had barely brushed her cheek with his lips. "Thank you."

"Scott." Randolph stepped forward and started to offer his hand. When he saw Scott's bandages, he quickly retracted. "Are you sure the hospital shouldn't have kept you another few days?"

"Other than my hands, I'm fine. Where's Heather?" He ignored Nikki's jab in the small of his back as he took the chair across from the love seat. He didn't care if he sounded belligerent. Randolph Winthrop tended to bring that out in him.

"She's visiting the new French ambassador's grand-daughter, who's staying for a few weeks," Lucille explained. "They've invited her for dinner."

Scott's expression darkened. "Did you even tell her I was coming over to pick her up right after I got out of the hospital?"

"This invitation was an honor for her," Lucille explained smoothly. "She'll associate with some very influential people who could do her some good as she grows older."

"Oh, right, just what she needs," Scott muttered.

"We also thought it would be better if we spoke to you first about something else," Lucille went on. She offered a chilly smile to Nikki. "Would either of you care for some coffee, or lemonade, since it's such a warm day?"

"All I want is my daughter."

"I'll be honest with you, Scott. We don't believe your home is safe for Heather right now," Randolph said. "Can you really ensure her protection? What if she had opened that box instead of you?" He held up his hand. "Not that I would wish that type of pain on you."

"Heather knows she isn't to open any mail or packages without having them checked out first," Nikki inserted. "Dr. Carter's opening that box was a mistake he won't repeat. As for Heather's safety, she has also been schooled in basic defense tactics, and I am certain that if anyone tried to grab her, she would be able to handle herself."

Lucille made a moue of distaste. "She told me about her classes. You've taught her to poke people in various parts of their body, and some elderly Oriental is helping you. Why, where you go isn't even in a safe part of town. After what happened before, I can't understand why you were even allowed in the house."

Scott forced himself not to show his temper. "Since Nikki was highly recommended by Mr. Larsen from the security agency and she had nothing to do with what happened to Renee, I saw no reason why she couldn't come in."

Nikki was doing a little forcing herself, to not show surprise at Scott's statement.

"If it hadn't been for her, there wouldn't have been those horrible, unwarranted accusations made about Renee and she would be alive today," Randolph said, glaring at Nikki.

"Mr. Winthrop, if you felt they were unwarranted, why didn't you fight harder back then to prove them wrong?" Nikki asked.

His face turned so red Nikki wondered if he was going to explode in front of her. "What are you trying to say, young woman?"

"Just that your daughter was arrested for treason and thrown into a federal jail. Yet every time the press tried to contact you, you had no comment to make other than that you knew your daughter was innocent," Nikki replied. "You didn't hire your own investigators or talk to an attorney. Why not?"

Scott turned to Nikki, astonishment written on his face. Then he turned to the older couple for their answer.

"Our attorney's recommendation was that it would be best we stay out of the entanglement," Randolph said stiffly.

"If you loved your daughter as much as you claimed, why would you listen to him?"

The couple didn't react to Nikki's bald question. Nor did they answer it. Lucille turned to Scott.

"Scott, we still feel Heather should stay with us until this unfortunate episode has ended."

Nikki saw the light of battle in Scott's eyes and feared what would happen next. "What about a compromise?" she offered, determined not to let them ignore her again.

Randolph looked down his nose at her. "Such as?"

"Why don't we consider letting Heather visit her grandparents for a few days while her father is home recuperating from his accident?"

Scott exploded instantly. "No way!"

Nikki held up her hand for silence. She turned to Scott. "Right now, you can do very little with your hands because they're still so sensitive. Once Heather sees your burns, she's going to be scared to death to even touch you. They'll look much better in a few days, when she comes home." She looked at Renee's parents. "Don't you agree that would work?" She didn't think anyone would argue with her compromise. And if they dared do so, she wouldn't hold herself responsible for the consequences.

Scott looked warily at his in-laws.

"I guess that would be acceptable," Randolph said uncertainly.

"Heather is enjoying herself with us," Lucille pointed out, as if in self-defense.

Scott looked at Nikki and realized what was going on. She didn't want Renee's parents as his enemies and had found a way to defuse their cold anger.

"All right." He knew he wouldn't have any other choice but to agree.

They lingered a few moments more to settle on a day and time to pick Heather up, then left. Nikki could swear the older couple looked relieved when she and Scott regretfully declined to stay for dinner.

"Well, I'd place that last half hour right next to a trip to the dentist." Nikki started up the truck engine and left it idling for a moment.

"About as close as you can get to it." He grinned. "Since we don't have the kid, how about we have dinner at a restaurant? We can go for something she wouldn't appreciate the way we would."

"Which means anything that isn't a hamburger or spaghetti. I vote for seafood." She put the truck in gear. "And I know just the place in Georgetown, if you can wait that long."

He settled back in the seat. "I can wait."

The restaurant Nikki chose had the homey atmosphere of a neighborhood tavern. The fragrant aroma of cooking permeated throughout the large dining area, where after a short wait they were seated in a booth.

"This is nice." Scott looked around. "I've never been here before."

"I once took a couple classes over at the university, so I learned about all the eating places in the area."

Scott opened the menu and perused the offerings. "What do you recommend?"

"Everything. I usually choose the beer-batter shrimp, though."

"How about some wine?"

Nikki shook her head. "I like to keep my wits about me. I'll stick to ice tea."

Scott cast a few covert glances around the restaurant. "Are you saying we're not even safe here?"

"Just call me paranoid." She looked up at the waiter, who appeared by their table, and flashed a smile at him. The man straightened under her attention and asked if they cared for a drink before dinner.

They both ordered ice tea and told him they would wait to order their meal.

"Are you sure you're not too tired for this?" Nikki asked, noticing the shadows under Scott's eyes.

"Are you kidding? I've had almost complete bed rest for the past few days, with room service, although the cuisine was nothing to write home about." He rolled his eyes. "You can only have so much Jell-O before you're convinced you'll turn into some red, disgusting blob." He smiled at Nikki's chuckle. "Hey, you should do that more often."

She was still smiling. "Do what?"

"Laugh. Giggle. Whatever you want to call it." He leaned across the table. "You seem more like a woman instead of a bodyguard." He whispered the last word.

Nikki leaned forward until their noses almost touched. "How do you know there aren't other bodyguards in this place?"

He shook his head. "No way. There couldn't be."

Nikki turned and scanned the restaurant again. Out of habit, she had given it a once-over when they'd entered, but she wanted one more look. Her lips tilted at the corners as she turned back to Scott.

"Are you sure?"

Scott glanced around as if he was interested in the many plaques adorning the walls and not the diners. It was a few minutes before he shook his head. "You're kidding."

"I'd say there were at least three in here, if not more."

He was amazed by her answer. "How can you tell?"

"It's a look they have. They're constantly glancing around, watching the door when anyone comes in, and they sit facing the entrance." She kept her voice low. "Also, their delightfully bland jackets are generally a bit more tailored than usual. To accommodate their sidearms," she added.

Scott turned a little green. "If this is what you've been doing for the past five years, I feel sorry for you. No one should have to live that kind of life."

"Some choose it."

"I can see your choosing to remain in the background."

"I told you I was only doing this as a favor for Harvey. I am definitely having the beer-batter shrimp."

Scott realized her abrupt change of subject was due to the waiter returning.

"I'm going for the scampi," he said, after taking another quick look at the menu.

When they'd chosen dressings for their salads, the waiter again left them alone.

Nikki stared into her ice tea glass as if the amber contents held all her answers. "For the past four years I have been teaching step aerobics and women's self-defense classes at a fitness center in Baton Rouge," she said quietly. "The year before that, I put so many miles on my car, traveling from one end of the country to the other and back again, that the dealer was amazed it was still in one piece when I wanted to trade it in."

"Why so much traveling?" he asked.

She shrugged. "I had trouble settling in one place. Maybe because I'd grown up going from one place to another. Maybe because I was trying to escape memories." She gave him a hard look. "And don't bother asking about what I mean about that, because I won't tell you."

Scott sat quietly for a moment, mulling over her words. "Why did you go into a line of work so completely different from your training?"

"Because it *was* different. I didn't have to carry a gun. I didn't have to take on a new identity or worry about tackling drug smugglers or murderers. I didn't have to wear a uniform and I didn't have to pray I wouldn't screw up my next assignment, which would reflect more on the admiral than on me. No pressure."

"So why did you come back?"

"Guilt." She looked up at the ceiling. "You know, this really isn't a great subject for dinner conversation. Why don't we switch to something more exciting?"

"Such as? We can't discuss your work. We can't discuss my work. What does that leave? I know—what plays or musicals we've seen," he suggested. "Heather has turned out to be a fan of the theater, and we try to take in a couple productions every few months. How about you?"

"I'm lucky if I see a movie before it comes out on video," she admitted. "I've worked a lot of nights and weekends."

Scott didn't like what he was hearing. "What about a social life? You had to have had one."

"Did I?" She shook her head. "I was having enough trouble adjusting to civilian life. Oh, I had dates, but the overzealous ones didn't like going out with a woman who could snap their bones without breaking into a sweat."

He had to grin at that. "Did you snap any?"

"No, but I almost ruined one man's perfect smile because he thought dinner and dancing meant thanking him in bed."

"I'll make a note of that." Scott leaned back as the waiter set their salads in front of them. He picked up his fork.

"What else did you do down there? Other than Cajun dancing."

Nikki smiled at the memory of their dance on the back lawn. "I learned how to be a girl," she said softly. "You see, the admiral didn't know how to raise a girl, so he didn't bother trying. It was easier to raise me the same as my brothers. I wasn't supposed to cry any time I broke a bone, and dolls were for sissies. I mainly wore jeans and wore a dress only for special occasions. He didn't feel we required a housekeeper, so it was our job to keep the house clean. We all had our own chores and heaven help us if we didn't have them done. If nothing else, my brothers learned what a vacuum cleaner was and how to wash windows." Shadows darkened her eyes to a deep gold. She reached for the pepper and sprinkled some on her salad. "Back then, we thought we were slaves, but I guess it had its uses. We all grew up very adaptable and able to take care of ourselves. My brothers are better cooks than I am. Although, unlike Matt, I never blew up an oven. I stick to easy foods that didn't require fancy cooking."

Scott burst out laughing. "He blew up an oven?"

Nikki nodded. "He had a science experiment that needed to be heated. At the same time, he had baseball practice. He figured if he put it in the oven on low heat, it would be okay. Instead, the experiment blew up, leaving gobs of the grossest-looking slime all over the interior. The oven couldn't be cleaned out and had to be replaced. Matt had to work at a fast-food restaurant to pay for it."

"Now, my parents would have insisted he figure out where the experiment went wrong," Scott said. "When I went through my chemistry phase, I was more interested in cooking up the most disgusting and smelly concoctions guaranteed to make a person sick. My mother liked the idea of seeing her son accept the Nobel Prize for chemistry, but was glad when her kitchen was returned to cooking family meals instead."

"What got you interested in computers?"

"Stepping into a computer lab and switching on a system for the first time. I took a programming class and realized I'd found my niche."

"And why did you start the designing?" Nikki took another bite, frowned and added more pepper to her salad.

Scott closed his eyes and thought for a moment. "I honestly don't know. Five years ago, I designed something for the navy that was a success. Because of that, I tried again. This time hasn't been as lucky for me. To be honest, I don't think my heart is in it."

"Because of what's been going on?"

"No, I just realize I'd rather work with something more life-affirming." He frowned as he watched her add more pepper to her salad. "You already put pepper on that."

"I know." She sprinkled a bit more on a lettuce leaf. "I happen to like a lot of pepper. I think it has to do with all the spicy food I've been eating the last few years."

"If you put pepper on your shrimp, I'm out of here."

Nikki smirked. "You're out of luck, because I have the keys."

Scott found his hands stiff and a bit uncooperative as he ate his dinner, but he refused any assistance from Nikki.

"The doctor said not to baby them too much. I need to keep them flexible," he told her.

"Keep them flexible, yes, but don't suffer for it." She winced in sympathy as she watched his awkward movements. "I'll put some of that ointment on them for you when we get back to the house."

"Good," he murmured, aware the ointment also had a painkilling property.

Their drive back to the house was made in comfortable silence punctuated by soft music from the radio.

"And here I thought golden oldies were all rock and roll," Scott commented.

"Not all of them." Nikki's gaze kept returning to the rearview mirror.

"What's wrong?"

She wasn't surprised he noticed her distracted air. "Just making sure no one is following us."

"Think someone would?"

"There's a truck back there that likes to stay in the same lane we do and changes lanes when we do. Too bad I couldn't get a bazooka attached to the truck."

"A bazooka?" he repeated.

She nodded. "When I bought this four-wheel-drive, I asked the salesman why I couldn't have a flame thrower or bazooka as an accessory. He thought I was joking. I tell you, if I had one, no one would bother me on the road."

Scott shook his head. He almost wished he had had a few drinks during dinner. He was sure the conversation would have made more sense. "Lady, you are sick."

"No, just an aggressive driver. Okay, he pulled off. If no one else shows interest, we should be all right."

When Nikki later passed the car holding one of Harvey's operatives, she flashed her lights twice and drove on. When she rolled down the driveway, she was relieved to see the lights burning in several rooms, courtesy of a central timer. She activated the garage-door opener and waited for the door to roll up.

Scott hopped out of the truck once it stopped in the garage. "I'll let you shut off the alarm, since it would probably go off by the time I could punch in the code."

"Good idea." She headed for the keypad and punched in the number, waiting for the red light to turn green before they crossed the yard. A motion-detector light over the back door flashed on as they walked across the grass. At the door, Nikki flipped up a hidden panel and punched in another code, waiting for the click to indicate the door was unlocked.

"Would you like some decaf or something else to drink?" She walked into the kitchen and switched on a light over the sink.

"No, actually, the day is catching up with me. I think I'll go to bed and let the TV put me to sleep."

"All right." Nikki pulled a bottle of lime seltzer out of the refrigerator and unscrewed the top. After filling a glass with ice and the bubbly water, she carried it into her bedroom and set it on the table by the bed, then changed into a pair of cotton pajamas. Suddenly she noticed her purse on the bed. And remembered she still had Scott's medication.

She quickly crossed to his room, knocked on his door and called out, "Scott, I have your medication and ointment. Remember, you need to put it on?" She waited a moment but could hear only the muted hum of the television set. "Scott?" She opened the door and peered inside. For a moment, she wondered if he was more tired than he'd let on and had passed out. She stepped inside and noticed the covers on the bed pulled back and a sitcom on television. "Scott?"

Nikki almost jumped when the bathroom door opened and Scott walked out. "What's wrong?" he asked, grasping her shoulders.

She tried to look at anything but his bare chest and the towel hitched around his hips. "I had your antibiotics and ointment in my purse," she murmured.

He stepped back. "My ointment. You don't mind putting it on?"

"I already said I would." She waited to see what he would do next. She didn't expect he would climb into bed, but he did. "Would you like to get your pajamas on first? This is a bit greasy."

Scott's face broke out in a broad grin. "And here I figured an observant person like you would notice there were never any pajamas in the laundry."

"Oh." She coughed to cover the squeak that erupted from her throat, then forced herself to walk over to the bed and sit on the edge.

"This might help." Scott opened the bedside-table drawer and drew out a handkerchief, placing it on the quilt.

"Yes, thank you." Nikki opened the tube and squeezed a bit of the contents onto the back of Scott's hand. Trying to be as gentle as possible, she used her fingertips to smooth the salve across the angry red skin, which felt a little scaly to the touch as the injured layer was sloughed off. All too soon both Scott's hands were covered with the emollient, but she didn't stop carefully drawing invisible circles on the second one.

"Nikki."

His low voice commanded her to look at him. She slowly raised her head.

"Don't go back to your room."

Nikki had known the moment would come. Logic told her that it would be a mistake. That she shouldn't become emotionally involved with him because letting down her guard could get one or both of them killed.

Her senses told her something else entirely the moment his mouth touched hers in the gentlest of kisses.

"Look at it this way." A wry smile curved his lips, but the heated expression in his sapphire eyes was a great deal more elemental. "I'm kind of powerless in here. Maybe you should stay for further protection."

She didn't have to stop to think.

"Yes," she whispered.

Chapter 11

Scott kept his hands lightly resting against her sides as he leaned forward and kissed her once more. This time, the pressure deepened; there was no longer a light and teasing touch. This time, he wanted his kisses to tempt her with the promise of more.

Nikki leaned into his embrace as he lay back against the pillows.

"Now, this is the way to cap off an evening," he murmured, trailing a row of nibbling kisses along her jawline, stopping at the corner of her lips. "Much better than having that night nurse come tuck me in for the night."

"She didn't seem all that bad." Nikki gently raked her nails through the slightly damp, dark hair on his chest, fascinated with the way the crisp hairs curled around her fingers. "She was very efficient."

"Efficiency is overrated," he whispered, turning his attention to her ear.

Nikki shivered as his tongue dampened a patch of skin along the shell-like exterior and he then exhaled a puff of warm air, cooling the moistened area.

Scott slid over toward the middle of the bed, silently inviting Nikki to swing her legs up and stretch them alongside his, with only the quilt and her pajamas between them.

The bedside lamp sent an intimate golden glow over them as they did nothing more than stare at each other for a long, silent moment.

"Scott?" She spoke in a low voice, unwilling to break the spell weaving a hot, silken web around them.

"Yes." He also spoke quietly.

"Would you rather I took off my gun myself or would you rather do it?"

For a moment, Scott wasn't sure if she was serious or not. Until he noticed the twinkle in her eyes. A slow grin stretched across his face.

"If I decided to be the one to take it off, would I have to search you to find it?"

"Yes."

"Would it be easy to find?"

She used her fingertip to trace the slight arch of his eyebrow. She ran her nail along his jaw as she dipped her head to murmur in his ear and tickle it with the tip of her tongue. "Not exactly. You see, I have a permit to carry a concealed weapon."

Scott suddenly turned and picked up the handkerchief, quickly wiping the rest of the ointment off his hands.

"You need that on to help your burns heal!" she protested.

"Sweetheart, now that I have you in my bed, I don't intend to have you slip out of my grasp because of some damn ointment," he told her, throwing the handkerchief to one side and turning back to her. When one hand slid up under her pajama top, his palm held only a slight slick residue that transferred itself to her skin.

Nikki moaned deep in her throat when he cupped her breast, shaping the plump mound with his palm and teasing her nipple with his thumb while his other hand efficiently unfastened the buttons. He parted the fabric and rested his gaze on her bared chest. He lightly fingered the pale tan lines along her shoulders. He smiled as he noted the dark pink color shading her cheeks. Obviously, Nikki wasn't used to being so blatantly admired. He vowed he was going to show her just how unique she was.

"Beautiful, like rare roses," he murmured as he leaned forward to taste her. "Hmm, no gun hidden there. I guess I'll have to keep looking."

Nikki felt hot and cold at the same time as Scott's mouth fastened on her nipple, drawing it deep into his mouth. Needing to keep herself grounded, she dug her fingers into his shoulders. But even that didn't help as she felt the electricity race through her veins, from the tip of her nipple to deep within, where her body began to ache for more of him.

She shifted her legs, urgently pushing away the quilt so she could lay over him. His knee rubbed gently against her aching center, creating a friction that sent waves of heat throughout her body.

He slipped his hands inside her pajama bottoms, ruffling the golden-brown curls and finding her hot and slick against his fingers.

"No weapon hidden here, either," he said thickly, stroking her with his fingers.

"I guess I already took it off and left it in my room," she said breathlessly, unable to stop her hips from moving against him as his fingers danced along her sensitive core.

"Darlin', you're decidedly overdressed for the occasion. I suggest we take care of that right now." Desire thickened his drawl as he reached down and pushed her pajama bottoms down over her hips and legs. They and her pajama top landed on the floor in record time.

With nothing between them, nothing more to hide behind, they were now free to explore each other with sensual abandon. Scott discovered a tiny mole behind Nikki's left knee and branded it with his lips. He found the scar along her side where she had been knifed and soothed it with his touch.

Nikki traced Scott's appendectomy scar with her tongue, delighting in his body shivering under her hands and mouth.

"Do you think we're going to be able to take this slow and easy?" she murmured, curling her tongue around a copper nipple that beaded at her attention. She inhaled the clean smell of lime on his skin from the soap he'd used during his shower, which now mixed with his own musky scent, heated by his arousal.

Scott muttered what could have been a curse or a prayer as he reached for her with hands that trembled with need.

"Right now, I'd like nothing more than for us to take this slow and easy, since we have all night without any interruptions. I want to take the time to map every inch of your body with my mouth," he said in a ragged voice. "I want to make outrageous suggestions in hopes of making you blush again." He smiled when she did just that. "At the same time I want to bury myself so deep in your body it will feel as if we're one. And I have an idea once I'm there I won't want to leave."

Nikki placed her palms along either side of his face. Her fingertips encountered the lingering dampness in his hair and felt the slight sandpapery texture of his cheeks.

"Tonight is all ours. Tonight we will create memories to hold us through whatever might happen in the days to come," she said softly, rubbing her lips against his, once, twice. Her eyes glowed a deep golden color, the sparkles of green and bronze shining iridescent in the lamplight.

His lips tipped upward. "Hey, there's no reason to make it sound as if one of us is going off to war, sweetheart. As far as I know, neither of us is shipping out in the morning. So don't worry about trying to seduce me into bed. You've already got me here. And I don't intend leaving anytime soon."

"And—that's—where—I—intend—to—keep—you," she said, punctuating each word with a kiss planted everywhere but his mouth. Each time, her lips lingered a bit longer, her tongue tasting the salt of his skin. When her mouth finally reached his, they both felt ready to explode with need.

This time, Scott took the initiative, thrusting his tongue into her mouth, sinking deep into the warm moisture of her mouth in the same way he wanted to sink into her body.

She tasted like hot nights covered with red silk. When their mouths parted, she whispered words just as dark and arousing. And when her hand circled and caressed his erection, he nearly shot out of his skin. He gritted his teeth against the pleasure-pain as she stroked him in a slow, even motion.

"Do you like that?" she asked in a breathy tone, drawing her teeth across his lower lip.

"More than you know."

Her fingers tightened against him. "Oh, I think I have a good idea."

Her body heat released her perfume. The vanilla and cinnamon, coupled with her own personal scent, brought forth an erotic fragrance in Scott's nostrils, arousing him even more, if that were possible. He placed his palm against her abdomen, feeling the muscles tense under his touch. He slid his hand down further, dipping into her center, feeling her slick moisture. He breathed in sharply as she contracted the deep inner muscles against his invading fingers. He felt her body jump and heard her soft moan when he stroked the tiny nubbin.

"Nikki, I'm already so hard I'm surprised it hasn't broken off," he said hoarsely. "Teasing wouldn't be a good idea right now."

Her eyes glowed like a cat's and her body moved against his with the same feline grace. "Who's teasing?"

Scott wasn't about to waste any time. He pulled open the nightstand drawer and fumbled inside for a moment until he drew out a foil packet. Nikki plucked it out of his hand and, with careful deliberation guaranteed to drive him insane, rolled it down his aroused length.

Muttering again, Scott grasped Nikki's waist and moved her under him.

"There won't be any 'slow and easy' now," he said between gritted teeth, looking down at her.

She reached between them and touched him. "I didn't think there would be."

After one sure thrust, Scott felt as if he had come home. Nikki's body was a tight silken sheath that welcomed him, and her muscles contracted to hold him securely. He had to clench his teeth as he withdrew because she felt so good he didn't want to leave. He felt her long legs wrap themselves around his hips as she tipped herself up to him for a deeper penetration.

With each thrust, Scott felt the emotional connection with Nikki grow stronger. The sensation of their souls merging at the same time as their bodies did intensified with each stroke. He looked down at her face, stunned by the beauty he saw there. Her cheeks were flushed a bright color, her lips parted and moist, but it was her eyes that ensnared him. What she had trouble saying he sensed could be read in her eyes. He could feel the tension within mounting and wondered how much more she could take. But he wanted even more from her. And he knew how to get it.

"Go ahead, honey, come apart for me," he muttered against her lips as he reached down between them to touch her core again. He'd barely brushed against her when Nikki shattered in his arms. His thrusts increased, deepened, as she arched up to meet him. Bare seconds later, he felt the explosion from within and he joined her in a shattering of bright lights.

Time seemed to stand still for Nikki. She could feel the dampness of Scott's skin as he reluctantly parted from her and left her for a moment. She lay against the rumpled sheets, positive she'd never be able to move again. And so satisfied she was surprised she wasn't purring.

When he returned, he brought a damp washcloth, which he gently stroked across her body. She started when the damp cloth passed over her still-sensitive nipples.

"I'd say that was one for the record books," Scott said lazily, stretching out beside her and pulling her back into his arms.

"You seem pretty sure of yourself." She curved her body around his, content to rest her cheek against his chest. She teasingly ran her fingers over the line of hair arrowing down to his waist.

He chuckled, gathering up her errant hand and kissing each fingertip. "Honey, as much as I'd love to, I think right about now I don't have the energy for more than talk."

Nikki retrieved her hand and slid it across his chest, resting her open palm against his shoulder. His skin was warm and damp to the touch.

"That's more energy than I have," she murmured around a jaw-cracking yawn. She could feel the events of the past few days catching up with her; her body relaxed until it felt boneless.

Scott brushed a stray lock of hair away from her forehead. "Go to sleep, Nikki. We can talk in the morning."

She chuckled softly. "You've been doing too much lately. You need the rest as much as I do." She smiled as he kissed her forehead and closed his eyes.

Two things happened in rapid succession that jerked the lovers awake. The alarm went off first, with the sound of breaking glass following in close succession.

"The perimeter alarms! Someone's on the property!" Nikki leapt out of bed and pulled on her pajamas. She was buttoning the top as she raced out of the room.

"Nikki, wait!" Scott had to stop long enough to find a pair of jeans. He moved into the hallway, hopping on one leg, pulling denim up the other as he smelled a noxious odor and heard Nikki's graphic curses.

"Oh my God," he breathed, stopping at the door to her room. He grimaced at the sight before him.

Nikki's bedroom window was broken and smoke filled the room, a nauseating odor was creeping out into the hallway.

"Talk about a top-of-the-line stink bomb." Scott coughed. When Nikki came out, he gently shoved her to one side and reached over to close the door.

"Don't touch the doorknob!" she warned, grabbing hold of his arm. "We might get lucky and find fingerprints." She used the hem of her pajama top to grasp the side of the door and swing it closed.

He looked at her, incredulous at what she was implying. "You think whoever did this would have tried to go through the house?" He started coughing again as the smoke crept under the closed door. "We've got to get out of here." He grasped her hand and pulled her back to his bedroom. He headed for the phone and picked up the receiver, then cursed as he realized there was no dial tone.

"The alarm company automatically cuts off the phone line, and they will contact the authorities," Nikki reminded him, cupping her hands around her mouth as she coughed. "Which means Harvey's people will be alerted."

Scott looked at her clothing, smudged by the smoke, and took in the less-than-attractive odor coming from her. He hated to think he smelled like that, too.

"Do you think anyone is going to wonder why you weren't in your bed when this happened?"

The grim expression on her face unsettled him and had him wondering if she wished she hadn't made love with him.

"No one will know. By the time you got in there, I'd already messed up my bed, and I was in the room long enough for the smell to permeate my clothing, although I don't think it took all that long, considering how strong it was. Right now, the last thing we need is any speculation about us. And no, I don't regret what we did," she said quickly, anticipating his next question. Her faint smile erased the lines of tension from her face. "I only wish we didn't have other things to worry about. I'd say we were just given a hell of a warning." She grimaced as she heard the strident wail of sirens in the distance. "I'll go out and meet them." She looked over her shoulder. "Before you see anyone, I suggest you zip and snap first."

Scott dropped onto the bed. He ran his fingers through his hair and exhaled a deep, pent-up breath.

"Makes you wonder if someone's trying to tell us something," he muttered, getting up with a weary sigh and going in search of a T-shirt as he zipped and snapped as suggested. When he walked down the hallway, he found he had to hold his breath as the smell coming from Nikki's room grew even stronger. By the time he reached the front of the house, the living room was filled with agents.

Scott stood back and admired the way Nikki handled the men with professional ease, even as she stood there in pajamas. He wondered if anyone noticed the whisker burns on her throat, or her swollen lips. Being trained agents, they should. For their sake, he hoped no one would comment. He had no doubt she would go after their heads if they did.

He smiled as he watched more than one agent give her a wide berth after getting a whiff of her clothing. The viscous smoke and nauseating odor from the bomb clung to her pajamas and wouldn't allow anyone to be in her vicinity without feeling sick from the fumes.

"How long do you think it was from when you heard the perimeter alarms go off to when your bedroom was bombed?" one man asked her.

She didn't have to think about it. "Mere seconds. Whoever did this didn't waste any time. They probably figured they would run in, do the job and get the hell out."

Another agent finished talking into his cellular phone and disconnected his call. "Harvey's on his way."

Nikki was not pleased with that piece of news and took her irritation out on the man. "I told you he didn't need to be bothered."

"Hey, if we didn't call him, he'd have our heads the minute he heard about this," the agent informed her. He looked over at Scott. "Dr. Carter, are you all right?"

"Just fine," he assured him. "After all, it wasn't my room that got bombarded with a state-of-the-art stink bomb. Whoever cooked it up was an artist," he added, admiration coloring his voice. "I am very impressed."

"Considering everything else, why would they bother with something so juvenile?" another agent asked with a snicker.

Nikki walked over to him until he got a good whiff of her clothing. "Have you ever smelled a skunk that's just been run over, Farley?" she asked.

The man turned a little green and shook his head.

"Well, this should give you a pretty good idea what it smells like," she said pleasantly. "It's not very nice, is it?" The man shook his head again, now looking even greener. "Remember it," she advised.

"Where is your daughter, Dr. Carter?" one of the men asked. "Is she all right?"

"She's staying with her grandparents for a few days. It was decided she would be better off there after I was discharged from the hospital today... or should I say yesterday. After this, I'm very glad she's not here. She doesn't need any more traumas."

"We'll check the room for prints, but I doubt we'll find any," the first man said. "And we'll check outside, too."

Nikki nodded. "I have an idea this was more a hit-and-run incident. A scare tactic."

"Did it work?"

"All it did was tick me off," she said flatly. "Right now, all my clothing smells as if a hundred skunks had been let loose in my closet. I'll probably never get the smell out of them."

"Don't worry, my dear, we'll replace your wardrobe," Harvey said as he walked in.

Nikki hid her smile. Even in the middle of the night, the man looked as if he'd just come from his office. There was nothing rumpled about him.

"You won't hear me turn the offer down."

Harvey looked at Scott. "Are you all right?"

"Other than wishing the fumigators hadn't done such a good job, I'm fine. And very grateful that my daughter is with her grandparents tonight."

With narrowed eyes, Harvey looked from Scott to Nikki. He kept his gaze on Nikki the longest. She returned his look with a bland smile.

"Next time, I'd prefer a more-conventional wake-up call."

Harvey walked over to her. A slight wrinkle of his nose was the only sign that he noticed the odor. "What else is going on here?" he asked in a low voice.

"Until our uninvited visitor, I was having a decent night's sleep," Nikki lied without a qualm. Not by a blink of an eye did she give any hint she wasn't telling the entire truth. "What I want to know is, why is this escalating?"

Harvey took her arm and led her aside. Out of the corner of her eye, Nikki noticed Scott watching them curiously.

"One of our people picked up something from one of his contacts earlier today," he said quietly. "There's still that faction out there that wants Scott's weapon. They're antsy because he hasn't finished it and they feel if they can obtain his notes, they can go ahead and finish it themselves. There's even word they'd prefer to have him out of the way permanently."

Nikki kept her face carefully blank. Not by a flicker could she betray her dismay. "Are you saying what I think you are?"

"Mr. Larsen!" One of the lab personnel came down the hallway carrying a plastic bag. "This was obviously thrown in with the bomb."

Harvey took the bag from him, looking through the clear plastic at the note inside. "The witch got off lucky this time, Carter," he read out loud.

"How poetic," Nikki murmured, taking the bag from the older man.

"This is all insane," Scott muttered. "If they were so desperate, why didn't they try to break into my lab?"

"They probably know they'd be locked out of your computer and wouldn't have the time to look for what they needed," Harvey replied. "We'll have a cleaning crew in here first thing in the morning and have the window replaced. As for you—" he turned back to Nikki "—buy what clothing you need to replace what you lost and send me the bills."

"Don't worry," she assured him. "I'll be more than happy to send you the bills. And believe me, my taste isn't cheap."

He smiled and nodded. "I'll want a full report first thing in the morning," he told his agents.

Nikki went into the kitchen and brewed coffee. She had an idea it would be badly needed. After informing everyone it was there for the taking, she retreated to the hallway outside her bedroom, watching the crew sift through the debris.

"I'd say you won't be finishing the night in here, Ms. Price," one of the men said.

"I can sleep in Dr. Carter's daughter's room," she replied. "There's still a bit of an odor in there, since it's so close to this room, but nothing like in here."

The woman photographing the room stopped and shook her head. "If I were you, I'd think about sleeping in the good doctor's room," she quipped before completing her duties. "Although I don't think I'd get all that much sleep!"

By the time the lab personnel left a few hours later, having collected every piece of evidence they could find, and the window was boarded up, Nikki felt ready to drop. With a sigh of relief, she watched the van's taillights disappear down the driveway. She knew one of the agents would be standing guard at the end of the road.

Scott walked up behind her and curved his arms around her chest. She raised one hand and rested it against his wrist.

"Sweetheart, let's not invite the neighbors the next time we have a party. They always leave such a mess," he said.

Nikki laughed unwillingly. "Does that mean I can blame you for this, since I didn't invite them?"

He reared back and looked at her with mock amazement. "*Me?* I didn't invite them. I thought you did!"

She shook her head.

Scott shrugged. "Nothing like party crashers to ruin an evening." He turned her around. "Come to think of it, I shouldn't be calling you sweetheart, because there's nothing sweet about you. How about a shower?"

She closed her eyes and smiled. "That sounds heavenly."

"Better yet," he whispered in her ear as he steered her down the hallway to his bedroom, "how about a shower for two?"

"Two as in you and me?"

"Exactly." Taking her hand, he led her into the bathroom.

He reached into the shower and turned on the water. Once he decided the temperature was comfortable, he turned back to Nikki. She had already shed her pajamas and dropped them into the wastebasket with distaste.

"And now to get you all fresh and clean again." Scott shed his jeans and T-shirt and stepped into the shower, pulling Nikki after him. "No offense, but right now I don't think I'd want you in my bed."

She laughed as the water hit her fully in the face. Scott turned her around so the spray would hit the back of her head, then picked up the soap and began lathering it between his palms. After setting the bar back in the soap dish, he ran his hands over her shoulders and down her arms. It wasn't long before the strong odor was replaced by the tart aroma of lime. His hands slowed as they trailed across her breasts.

Nikki closed her eyes as warm pleasure took over her senses. Her weariness was soon replaced with arousal and she felt her nipples tighten under his light touch. The rose-colored tips poked through the white foam as he drew circles around each breast. His fingers slowed with each circular motion until they reached her aching nipples.

"Feel good?" he murmured, ducking his head to nibble her earlobe.

Unable to speak, she settled for a slight nod of the head.

His palms flattened against her nipples, rubbing gently.

"Better?"

Again she could only nod.

"While you're very tempting there, I should remember I promised to get you all squeaky clean."

Nikki almost moaned in sorrow when his hands, still slightly rough from his wounds, left her breasts. She opened her eyes and watched him lather his palms again. This time, he ran them across her belly and lower, to gently scrub the golden-brown curls at the apex of her thighs.

"I guess I should make sure you're clean everywhere." His voice grew huskier as he inserted a finger inside her, then two.

Nikki couldn't stop moving her hips against him in blatant invitation for more. The more he stroked her, the tighter the tension in her body grew until she felt as if she was a rubber band stretched to its limit.

"No, I have to remember my job," he said.

She bit her lip to keep from screaming in frustration when his hands left her.

This time, he poured out a dollop of his herbal-scented shampoo and rubbed his palms together before combing his shampoo-coated fingers through her hair.

Nikki had never thought having her hair shampooed could be a sensual experience until now. Scott's fingers lightly kneaded her scalp as he gently scrubbed her hair clean. She closed her eyes and tipped her head forward while he massaged the sensitive skin along her nape. She could swear she felt his touch clear down to her toes.

He quietly instructed her to close her eyes as he tipped her head back to rinse the soap from her hair. He ran his fingers through it, making sure each strand was thoroughly rinsed. The procedure was repeated with a rich conditioner gently rubbed into her scalp.

By now, Nikki's body was one raw, sensual nerve. She wondered if Scott would resist if she jumped on him here and now. She slowly lifted her head and stared at him. She didn't have to speak. Her emotions, for once, were openly displayed in her gaze.

"Well." Scott coughed to clear his throat. "I guess you're clean enough."

She smiled as she turned to pick up the bar of soap and rubbed it briskly between her palms until she worked up a thick lather.

"Maybe I am, Doctor, but now I think it's your turn for a good scrubbing."

Nikki worked at a leisurely rate as she began soaping Scott's neck, tracing his collarbone with her fingertips. From there she covered the broad expanse of his chest, paying special attention to his nipples. When she reached his flat belly, his breathing grew ragged.

And when her hands cradled his erection, it didn't matter that there wasn't any soap on them. They were still slick and caressing as she slowly stroked his steely length.

"Nikki." His voice was rough in her ears and he thrust his hips forward as she caressed him with fingers filled with magic.

"Oh, no, it's my turn," she whispered, a secret smile curving her lips. "You've had your fantasy. Now I'm having mine."

Except Scott was past allowing her to have her way with him. A dark haze floated before his eyes and he knew he had to be inside her within seconds if he didn't want to lose his mind.

A gasp escaped her lips when he abruptly spun her around so he could step into the spray. The moment he was rinsed off, he propelled her out of the shower. He whipped two towels off the rack, wrapping one around her and the other around his hips.

"Wait a minute. Scott, I'm not even dry!" she protested as he none too gently pushed her into the bedroom. "We'll get the sheets all wet."

"It's a warm night," he said roughly, steering her toward the bed. "They'll dry. Besides, think of the number of accidents that occur in the bathroom, particularly the shower. I don't intend to be one of those statistics."

It was only because Scott didn't want their lovemaking to be on the carpet, either, that they even made it to the bed. The moment Nikki bounced onto the sheets, Scott followed her down taking only seconds to protect her before he thrust into her with one long, deep stroke. She cried out in pleasure as his movements grew fast and urgent, until they both shattered at the same time. Nikki's impassioned cries blended with his moaning her name, and that was when both knew their lives had taken another turn. They both refused to acknowledge the cold darkness that threatened the warm light brightening their lives just now.

Chapter 12

Nikki woke up as abruptly as she'd fallen into an exhausted sleep after she and Scott had made love that second time. She lay in his arms, relishing the closeness, the security he offered even as he slept. Curious to see what would happen, she tried to edge away from him. She was allowed to move only a scant inch before he mumbled in his sleep and tightened his embrace. Smiling, she contented herself with lying there for another moment before she carefully extricated herself from his arms and crept out of bed.

It wasn't until then that Nikki remembered she didn't have any clothing. She took a quick look in Scott's closet and chose one of his shirts, pulling it on and buttoning it up. She ran her fingers through her hair to smooth out the worst of the tangles and sneaked a smidgen of Scott's toothpaste.

She moved swiftly past her bedroom, eyeing the closed door, and headed for the kitchen. After tuning the radio to a station specializing in sixties rock and roll, she rummaged through the refrigerator for ingredients to make French toast. Pretty soon she was singing along with the radio as she fried bacon in the electric frying pan and dipped bread in a bowl of egg batter flavored with vanilla and cinnamon.

She knew the moment she wasn't alone in the room, but didn't turn around, since she knew who the intruder was. She merely smiled and leaned back when a pair of arms snaked around her chest and a damp face nuzzled her throat.

"Can I tell you a secret?" Scott murmured in her ear as he turned her around for a soul-stealing kiss.

"What?" she asked as soon as she regained her breath.

He kept her in his embrace as he leaned his upper body back, playfully bumping his lower body against hers. The rough denim fabric of his jeans was pleasantly abrasive against her bare legs.

"As much as I hate to tell you this, you can't carry a tune worth a damn."

She surprised him by not taking offense. "I know."

"Then why do you crucify a great song?"

She bumped her pelvis against his. "Because I woke up in a good mood and the song fit the occasion. That's why."

He held up his hands. "Good reason. Say, isn't it time to put more ointment on my burns?"

She shot him a wry look. "Very cute, Carter. This is how it all started last night. How about some breakfast instead?"

He arched an inquiring eyebrow. "Before or after?"

She planted her palms against his chest and pushed him back a few steps.

"Breakfast now. I'm starved. For food, you sex maniac," she enunciated as he playfully leered at her. "And if you're smart, you better stoke up. I'd hate for you to get tired too quickly."

He uttered a low growl. "I wouldn't worry about that, if I were you." When she pointed toward the cabinet, he decided to let her have her way—for now. He grabbed plates, silverware, mugs and glasses, then poured juice into the glasses and coffee into the mugs.

"What happens today?"

"A crew will be over in about an hour to clean everything up," she replied, forking French toast and crisp bacon onto the plates he handed her. She pulled a glass pitcher of maple syrup out of the microwave and carried it to the table. "By this afternoon, you won't even know a stink bomb had gone off in that room."

Scott pushed his food around on his plate. "You sound as if you're familiar with the procedure."

"Not personally, but I know that Harvey's men are excellent at making sure nothing looks out of place." She drizzled syrup in a corner of her plate and dipped her French toast in the golden-brown puddle.

He shook his head in amazement. "This is like something out of a B movie," he muttered.

"Not entirely. In a B movie we would have had a dead body in the room to worry about along with everything else. And one of us would have been accused of the murder."

Scott grimaced at the idea. "No thanks."

"I agree, bloodstains are very difficult to get out of carpeting," she said, dipping another bit of toast into the syrup.

Scott was hungry, for food and for Nikki. Watching her eat was another sensual experience for him. She was a woman who enjoyed herself. He had seen and felt that last night. Today she attacked her meal with gusto. He wondered what other surprises were in store for him where she was concerned.

Sensing his gaze on her, Nikki looked up. "What? Isn't your food all right?"

"It's just fine. Very good. I was just wondering how you got to be so beautiful." He wanted to grin when her cheeks turned a deep pink and she fumbled for her coffee mug. The ever-efficient Nikki Price, who didn't turn a hair when her bedroom was bombed, blushed when paid a compliment.

"I am not beautiful," she muttered into her coffee.

He shook his head. "Nikki, you need to take a good look in the mirror. You're one gorgeous lady."

"You forget something. I spent my formative years playing football and baseball and climbing trees and having no idea what lipstick was. That meant I didn't need to look in the mirror very often." She forked up a piece of toast, dipped it in syrup and held it before his lips. She smiled as he opened his mouth and bit down.

"What's your secret to sexy French toast?" he whispered after he finished chewing.

She pursed her lips in a sensual pout. "Vanilla powder and cinnamon."

He returned the gesture by stabbing a piece of toast with his fork and holding it out to her. "Next time, let's try the vanilla powder and cinnamon on each other."

Nikki was rapidly warming to the game. "The syrup might work even better."

"Hmm." All of a sudden his eyes darkened and started to glaze over.

"Scott? Scott?" She sharpened her voice. When she received no response, she snapped her fingers in front of his face. "Scott Reynolds Carter!"

"Maybe that will do it," he muttered, setting his fork down. "Yeah, it just might."

Nikki was starting to worry. "Scott?"

Without a word, he rose from the table and almost ran for the door leading to his laboratory.

Nikki sat back in her chair, stunned by the abrupt change in him.

"All you had to do was say so if you didn't like the French toast," she called after him with a gurgle of laughter. She didn't expect an answer and didn't get one.

Nikki finished her solitary breakfast and did the dishes in record time. She had put the last plate away in the cabinet when a knock sounded at the door.

"At least they won't find us rolling around on the kitchen table," she murmured, heading for the front of the house.

Lost in his work, Scott barely heard a few faint thumps and bumps overhead as he sat hunched over his computer. His fingers raced over the keys, his gaze fixed on the monitor as he watched numbers change and formulas recalibrate before his eyes.

"This could do it," he muttered. "It has to be the reason." He punched the Save key and brought up the directory. He frowned as he realized something appeared to be missing. He scrolled downward but still couldn't find what he was looking for. "Dammit, where is that file?"

When the elusive file refused to appear, Scott gave up and keyed in his modem so he could dial in to the institute's computer, where he knew it would be stored in his private files.

The moment the high-pitched tone echoed over the computer's speakers and the letters appeared on the screen asking for his password, he typed out his personal code. And swore profusely when the screen went blank seconds later.

"It can't be a power surge doing this. Not with all the protection we have against them." He repeated the sequence and received the same results; except this time, the words *Unauthorized Password* flashed across the screen. "What the hell is going on?"

Scott didn't waste any time in snatching up his cordless phone and punching in a phone number held in his computerlike memory.

"Dr. Westin."

He didn't bother to identify himself. He had an idea David Westin could easily figure out who his caller was.

"Do you want to tell me why I can't get into the institute's mainframe?"

"Carter, how are you feeling?" Much to Scott's anger, the man acted as if he had spoken to him only the day before. "I didn't realize the hospital had released you yet."

"I was discharged yesterday," he snapped. "I just want to know why I'm locked out of the computer."

"It was a recommendation made purely for security reasons."

Scott silently damned the officious man's manner. "Whose recommendation?"

"It was the board's decision. Considering what has gone on, and your proposal to work from your home part-time, they feared the institute's computer could be compromised. Of course, there will be no problem in your accessing the mainframe when you are working here. But for the time being, you will be denied access from your home computer."

Scott silently counted to ten in Latin, then in French. When his temper didn't dissipate, he counted again.

"Dr. Carter?" Dr. Westin inquired. "Are you still there?"

He took a deep breath. As much as he wanted to lose his temper, he knew it wouldn't do any good with David Westin, who merely turned into an ornery mule any time anger was directed his way. He didn't want David as an enemy, but he didn't want him feeling as if he'd won this battle, either.

"I'm still here, David. And as long as I work from here, I'll expect to have no problem dialing in when necessary. I'm sure I'll have no trouble accessing the computer by the end of the day."

"The end of the day?" the administrator exclaimed. "This is the weekend, Carter. I can't authorize that without the board's approval, and you know it."

"David, since I've known you, you've done a lot of things without the board's approval. Telling the computer to allow me access is nothing more than a minor technicality. I'm sure there won't be any reason why I can't be in on Monday to run some tests I can't run here at home. I'll see you then." He didn't care if it sounded like a threat. In fact, given the mood he was in, it would have been very appropriate. He hit the disconnect button and lowered the antenna.

He had no idea how long he sat in his chair, staring at the blank computer screen while anger and frustration warred inside him. Along with something else that had been growing inside him for the past few months.

"Hey, Scott, how many weapons have you designed on computer?" he said out loud. "Oh, I don't know, four or five. Two of them were snapped right up. The others are still in the planning stage and coming along like mud." He linked his hands behind his head. "So, what are you going to do when they're finished? Design another weapon? Make up a video game? Wash cars for a living?"

His first indication that he wasn't alone was the whiff of vanilla and cinnamon coupled with something exotic. This time it wasn't associated with French toast. His second hint was a pair of arms stealing around his neck.

"Isn't there a saying about people who talk to themselves?" Warm breath tickled his ear as a tongue did something a lot more erotic.

He smiled, leaning back in the chair until his head hit a pillowy softness.

"That's only if they're answering themselves."

"You were answering yourself." Nikki began massaging the tight cords along the back of his neck. Her fingers dug into the taut muscles, kneading until they began to loosen. "Having trouble?"

"Nothing but. I've been locked out of the institute's mainframe."

She circled around until she stood by his side. "What?"

"You heard me. Westin locked me out." He muttered a pithy curse under his breath. He was glad to see she'd added a pair of his jeans to the shirt she had borrowed. At least he didn't have to worry about Harvey's crew getting a good look at her legs. He could still remember the feel of them wrapped around his hips. The memory alone was arousing.

"Can they do that?"

"He said the board gave him the authorization." He tipped his head back. "Everyone gone upstairs?"

She nodded. "There's a new window installed, the carpet has been cleaned and disinfected, the drapes and all the bedding replaced." She ticked each item off on her fingers. "I told them Harvey promised me his gold card, but they only laughed. It seems he told them I'd say that." She shook her head. "And here I thought I could go shopping."

Scott grasped Nikki by the waist and pulled her onto his lap. "I didn't think you were the shopping type."

"I didn't use to be." She looped her arms around his neck. "But down in Baton Rouge I made some friends who were shopping maniacs and they taught me everything they knew." She lowered her voice. "Do you know there are stores that sell nothing but very sexy lingerie?"

He swallowed. He didn't tell her Renee had spent hours in those shops and squandered a small fortune on pieces of lace and silk that hadn't held his attention during those last couple of years. But he found the thought of Nikki in something sheer and sexy a tantalizing idea.

"Yeah?"

She smiled a slow, sweet smile. "Yeah."

He brushed a stray lock of hair away from her face and tucked it behind her ear.

Nikki looked around the room, littered with computers, printers, scanners and varied computer parts. She knew Scott kept a small refrigerator down here so he wouldn't have to go upstairs to get something to drink. For a moment the thought that his work life was as sterile as her personal life crossed her mind.

"I want to ask you something and I want a serious answer," she said. "You led basically a sheltered life. No sports, no outside activities. Yet you turned out fairly normal. You're affectionate and outgoing. Everything a typical scientist isn't. How did it happen?"

Scott was surprised by her question. "How did it happen?"

She nodded.

His chest rose and fell as he took in a deep breath, trying to formulate his answer.

"My parents were overprotective because they felt they were raising a world-class scientist." He offered a deprecating grin. "But they were also very loving people. They believed hugs took away the hurts."

"The last time I was hugged I was eight years old. My mother had hugged me because I'd gotten all the words right on my spelling test," Nikki murmured. "Three days later she was gone."

He imagined he could feel the pain she was experiencing. "How did she die?"

"A blood vessel burst in her brain," she said softly. "One moment she was standing there telling us to set the table for dinner. Then she got this strange look on her face and next thing we knew she fainted. The doctor said she was dead before she hit the floor. We stayed with one of the other naval families until our father came back from his assignment." Bitterness coated her words. "He opted to forgo compassionate leave, considering his assignment, and arrived home four days after the funeral. That's when he told us we were his children and tears weren't allowed. Girls were no exception."

Scott could only do one thing—he wrapped his arms around her and held her in a tight embrace. He didn't use words, but allowed his body to speak for him as he buried his face in the bright cloud of her hair. For once she hadn't tied it up in a ponytail and he was grateful.

"Scott," she said in a small voice.

He wanted to tell her he wished he could absorb her pain. He wanted to give her all the laughter and joy she deserved.

"Uh-huh?"

"Have you ever thought of making love in this chair?"

He was positive an electric charge had stopped his heart.

"This chair?"

She nodded.

He coughed to clear his throat. She had managed to spring another surprise on him.

"The chair we're sitting in?"

"I'm not talking about that chair over there without the arms that's meant for people who have bad backs." Her words were muffled against his shirtfront.

Scott sensed that what she needed was comfort, but the images flying through his mind had nothing to do with comfort. As Nikki rotated her hips in his lap, he realized her thought processes were following the same path.

He planted a hand on either side of her head and brought her face up for a thoroughly deep, thoroughly satisfying kiss.

"I guess there's no harm in running an experiment to see if it will work."

Scott noticed that Nikki deliberately stayed out of the family room while he talked to Heather on the phone. He was frustrated that his daughter wasn't with him, but at the same time he was grateful she hadn't been there last night. Partly because of the bomb, and partly because he knew that if she had been, he and Nikki wouldn't have made love. He cradled the receiver between his shoulder and ear as he lightly rubbed his palms against the couch's nubby fabric. With his burns healing, he found that his skin itched constantly.

"Grandma is taking me with her to her garden club tomorrow after I get out of school," Heather announced. She lowered her voice. "It sounds real boring, but she said she wants to show me off."

Scott couldn't help smiling. "Just pretend you're interested, okay? For Grandma."

"I will. But if I start sneezing around all those flowers, I'm gonna ask to go home. Dad? When can I come home? I miss you a lot."

He swallowed against the emotion clogging his throat. "Soon," he said finally. "I just thought you might like to stay with them right now, and they're real happy to have you there."

"Yeah, but Grandma gets this funny look on her face when I practice my self-defense moves and yells. She says what I'm doing isn't ladylike, but I told her nobody's ever gonna get me as long as I remember what to do."

As he listened to her chatter, he asked himself if what he was doing was right. "I think she understands."

"Is Nikki there? Can I talk to her?"

"Just a second." He angled his head toward the kitchen, where he knew Nikki was popping corn. "Nik! That kid we used to have living here wants to talk to you! You know, that real little pain in the neck? That short person?"

"Dad!"

He muffled his laughter as his daughter's aggrieved protest reached his ears.

"Oh, you mean that kid who constantly demanded homemade muffins and never picked up her clothes?" Nikki's voice was equally loud as she walked into the room carrying a large bowl of popcorn. "Please don't tell me she's begging to come back. Just when we got rid of her!"

"I heard that! And I know you're just teasing me!" Heather's shout was perfectly audible as Nikki traded the bowl of popcorn for the receiver.

"I bet over there you pick up your clothes," Nikki said. She laughed at Heather's reply. She spoke to the girl for several more minutes before hanging up.

"She misses us."

Scott grinned. "Yeah. I wonder if that means she'll appreciate us more when she gets back."

She dropped onto the couch and stole a handful of popcorn. "Probably not." As they bantered back and forth, Nikki realized the scene was very domestic. Mom and Dad in front of the TV after talking to their daughter on the phone. And that comfortable feeling was the last thing she wanted, because she knew once the assignment was finished, they would be, too.

Scott picked up the remote control and turned the TV off. He stood, taking the popcorn bowl with him, then held out his hand.

"It's too pretty a night to sit in here. Let's go outside and indulge in a few romantic notions."

She allowed him to pull her to her feet. "I hope you realize you're destroying all my conceptions of a logical, cold-blooded scientist."

"Good." His smile remained fixed. "It took a pretty big upheaval in my life, but I decided you have only one chance to live your life and you may as well make the most of it."

Nikki took the bowl from him and kissed him from one corner of his mouth to the other, until he parted his lips for her questing tongue.

"Then, Dr. Carter, if you play your cards right, you just might get lucky out there."

The office was again left in shadows, thanks to a dimly lit lamp near the window. The occupant waited behind the highly polished desk for a visitor who opened the door without knocking.

"You're late."

"I wanted to make sure no one saw me come in here. Why aren't we discussing this on the phone as per usual?"

"Because tonight I wanted to see your face. Your little stunt last night went very well."

The visitor took a seat on the black leather couch set against a far wall. "I knew it would. Juvenile in a way, but it made its point. I'm sure Ms. Price wasn't too happy to come out smelling like a skunk that's been dead for a year. The odor from that kind of bomb also permeates any fabric in the room, so she's out a wardrobe, too. I wonder how many scrubbings it took to get the smell out of *her?*"

"I won't cry over it if she has raw skin. She's doing her job and we're doing ours."

"Why hasn't he finished that damn weapon yet?"

"I have no idea, but pressure is mounting for him to finish it soon. Right now, he's been slowed down by our surprise package, but that's all right. It's given us time to work on breaking into his files in the institute's mainframe. He's encrypted his files, but we're working on breaking the codes."

"If you felt the package made a point, why the bomb?"

"Because Nikki Price is known not to scare easily. Her bastard father raised her to fear nothing, and he hasn't been much help on this at all. I'm hoping the destruction this last surprise caused gave her something to think about."

"And if it didn't?"

"Then we'll just have to think of something else, won't we?"

Chapter 13

"Give me one good reason why I can't go with you," Scott argued.

"I can give you the best reason possible. You need to work. I'll call so someone can come over and stay in the house while I'm gone."

"I can work anytime, but you're not that lucky when it comes to buying your new wardrobe." Scott directed a lazy smile over her lean body. She was wearing another one of his shirts, this time a soft cotton teal polo shirt with the buttons undone. Luckily, she'd had a pair of jeans in the laundry, so she wasn't totally without her own clothing. "Although I have to say I like the way you wear my clothes, you would probably prefer something that fits a little better. If I go, you won't have to call in someone to baby-sit me while you're gone."

"Men don't like to shop."

Scott wondered if her father had instilled that belief in her.

"I admit it's not at the top of my list of most-fun activities, but the way things are going, maybe you're in need of a protector as much as I am."

Nikki looked up, snaring him with that deep honey-brown gaze of hers. "Does it bother you, having a woman guarding you?"

"No, and not because of the other, either." He obliquely referred to their lovemaking. "You've shown you know your job and that's what counts."

Nikki thought of the files she had read again and again, and wished something would spring out. Not for the first time she thought of asking Scott to read them. But how would he feel, reading the cold, clinical reports detailing Renee's death and autopsy?

"I'll be ready in an hour," she said finally. "Don't worry, it won't take me long. I don't intend to break Harvey's wallet."

Scott had seen the number of plastic bags carried out by Harvey's people. It had been recommended that they not be left in the trash because of the smell.

"If I were you, I would."

Within sixty minutes, Nikki and Scott were out of the house, heading for a nearby mall.

"No exclusive boutiques?" he teased.

She shook her head. "Not my style."

The moment they stepped into the two-story mall, Nikki learned that Scott viewed shopping as an experience to be savored. Instead of heading for the nearest department store, he suggested one of the boutiques.

"That would look great on you." He pointed to a dress in the window.

She shook her head as she studied the melon silk slip dress. "Not exactly the type of dress one would wear on duty."

His lips brushed her ear as he answered, "You have to go off-duty sometime. Besides, everyone would be so busy looking at you in that barely there dress that you could carry an Uzi and no one would notice. Come on, let's see what else they have. Maybe a little something with hidden pockets.''

In the end, Nikki let Scott have his way. The moment they walked into the elegant shop, she knew she wouldn't find anything in there, but she was amused by the saleswoman's response to Scott's lord-of-the-manor pretense.

"Darling, wouldn't this be perfect for the Worthington affair?" he asked, gesturing toward a black gown that Nikki knew had to be expensive just by its simplicity.

"It's lovely, but I'm certain Buffy will be wearing something similar and we just can't be seen wearing the same thing!" she replied in a haughty voice, going along with the game and enjoying herself in the process.

"Perhaps madam would care to look at something else? We have many lovely evening gowns," the saleswoman suggested, ignoring Nikki's casual wear. She had assisted enough customers to know that just because a person wore jeans that didn't sport a designer label didn't mean she didn't have money.

Nikki turned to Scott. "Why don't we shop for you first and then come back?"

She smiled at the clerk as she grabbed his hand and pulled him out of the store. "You really must behave."

"Or?"

She kept hold of his hand as she walked purposely toward one of the department stores. "Or I will have to hurt you."

"Hmm, kinky. I like the idea."

Scott sensed shopping with Nikki would be different than the few shopping trips he'd endured with Renee. And he was right. He had no time to lounge or grow bored as he watched Nikki shop. She scanned the racks, pulled off outfits and walked on to the next department, finding more. She paid for her purchases and looked around.

"You can stay here," she told him, loading his arms with bags. "I can see you from where I'll be."

"Nik, I'm not five years old. I won't talk to strangers and I won't let anyone offer me candy to lure me away," he grumbled. "Why do I have to stay here?"

She looked to her left before leaning over and whispering fiercely, "Because the last thing I need here is your assistance."

Scott watched her walk toward the lingerie department. "I'd be more than willing to help."

Nikki chose several nightgowns, uneasily aware that the ones she was selecting weren't the type she used to wear. Instead of cotton, they were silk and lace. The same with bras and underwear.

"I'm nuts," she muttered, picking up a soft peach silk-and-lace bra and matching bikini panties.

"Pick up that dark blue set, too." Warm breath tickled the back of her neck.

She shook her head. She wasn't going to tell him she had deliberately bypassed it because the deep color reminded her of Scott's eyes. That was a reminder she wouldn't need when this assignment was over.

"Hmm." He fingered the spaghetti straps of a skimpy chemise the same brilliant blue. "How about this?"

She didn't look at it. "I don't think so."

"I do." Scott carefully pulled it off the display hanger, checked the size and walked toward the sales desk.

Nikki practically raced to grab his arm. "What are you doing?"

"You won't buy it, so I will."

"No one buys my lingerie."

"Things change, Nikki." He disentangled himself from her grip and approached the desk while digging in his back pocket for his wallet.

Nikki could feel her face flaming as she returned to pick up the items she'd dropped when she'd run to catch up with Scott.

"Stubborn man," she muttered, pulling her composure together and dredging up a smile for the sales clerk who approached her.

Scott smiled at Nikki as he handed the clerk his credit card and later accepted his package.

"Shoes next?" he asked Nikki, who looked a little disgruntled.

She nodded. "And some makeup."

Nikki should have known that once Scott started butting in, he wouldn't stop. He picked up a tester bottle of the perfume Nikki wore and inhaled it, promptly informing her that it smelled much better on her skin. He immediately purchased dusting powder and body lotion.

To the delight of several sales clerks in cosmetics, he stuck to Nikki's side as she chose blusher, eye shadows, lipstick and mascara.

"You women go to a lot of trouble," he commented, running his finger across a demo eye shadow and inspecting the color on the pad of his finger.

"Surprising, isn't it, when most of you men aren't worth it," she quipped, picking up her bag and handing it to Scott with a smile.

He gasped and buckled his knees as if the weight was pulling him down.

"You should have gone to your lab. And I wish you hadn't bought that chemise," she muttered as they walked out of the store.

"Call it a reward for taking less than eight hours to pick out one outfit. You didn't even try anything on."

"I'm a pretty standard size," she replied.

Scott glanced at his watch. "How about lunch?"

"How about I drop you off at the institute? I thought you wanted to meet with Dr. Westin today."

Scott's expression darkened at the man's name. "Meet with him? I'd like to throttle him. I tried six times last night and couldn't get into the computer."

"Maybe he couldn't get the authorization to get you back in," she said placatingly.

He shook his head. "I don't think he had it to take me out in the first place. He just wanted to show me he could do it." He gestured. "Come on, let's get something to eat. And no more talk about Westin. I don't want him ruining my appetite." He took her arm and guided her inside the restaurant.

They were seated immediately. As Scott set the bags down by the table, Nikki glanced covertly around. The hairs on the nape of her neck had prickled uneasily and she hoped she could find the reason.

There were several couples dining at other tables. Two tables were filled with women and several others had either one or two men seated at them. Most of them appeared to be employees of the mall stores or area businessmen. No one seemed to have any interest in them, but Nikki didn't expect them to.

As much as she hated any reminder of her father, the thought that he had schooled her well in paranoia kicked in. Adam Price believed that if everything seemed too right, something had to be wrong.

"What's going on?" Scott had noticed her preoccupation.

"Nothing."

"The hell there isn't. You look like a bird dog on point. What did you see?"

Nikki was impressed. No one before had ever noticed when she kicked into her protective mode.

"What makes you think I saw something?"

He leaned across the table. "Hey, sweetheart, maybe no one else can spot this other side of you, but I can." Keeping his smile directed on her face, he shifted his eyes from side to side. "You'd think they'd come in wearing trench coats and snappy fedoras, wouldn't you? Shouldn't they talk out of the sides of their mouths or something?"

"They only do that in dark bars." She inspected the menu then looked up. "Could I make a suggestion?"

"Anytime."

"Don't keep anything new on the institute's computer. Back it up and keep the disk with you."

His expression altered as he absorbed her words. "Do you think Westin could be behind this?"

"Just because he checks out doesn't make him lily-white." She purposely kept her voice low. "After what's happened in the past week, I don't think you should trust anyone."

Scott waited while the waitress stopped by to ask if they cared for something to drink. "I think we can order now." He glanced at Nikki, who nodded.

After the woman left with their orders, Scott turned back to Nikki.

"I don't like living like this," he said quietly. "You're telling me I'm going to have to look over my shoulder and suspect everyone, including the people I deal with in my work."

"That's what happens," she said flatly. "I've dealt with seamen and officers who seemed like the kid next door. They looked as if the worst thing they'd ever done was steal an apple from a neighbor's tree. One attacked me with a knife. Another shot at me. That's an excellent reason not to trust people."

Nikki pretended to concentrate on her ice-tea glass, but out of the corner of her eye she watched a man leave one of the tables and head for the rear of the restaurant.

"Sorry to pop your paranoia bubble, but don't forget a customer can find public telephones and rest rooms back there."

She ignored Scott's sarcasm.

"Yes, they can."

Scott's stomach suddenly felt unsettled as the waitress set his lunch in front of him. He made a pretense of eating, but was now eager to leave.

"You're right, I should get to my lab," he murmured after settling the bill. When Nikki didn't reply, he looked up.

Scott couldn't understand why the compassion he saw shadowing her eyes angered him. Unless it was because he knew she realized how much he hated the world she had learned to accustom herself to.

"Just drop me off at the institute," he said crisply once he'd stowed the packages in the back of Nikki's truck. "My driver will take me home when I'm ready."

She merely nodded before walking around to the driver's door.

With a minimum of fuss, Nikki drove to the institute, ignoring Scott's orders not to bother coming in with him. She escorted him to his laboratory door and peeked inside.

Cully looked up from a tall stack of computer printouts. He grinned and called out to her. Kay's expression as she turned to Scott revealed that she wasn't as pleased to see her.

"I thought you had a driver bringing you in, to be on the safe side. What help would she be?"

If he noticed her tone was accusatory, he preferred to ignore it. "I offered to help Nikki run her errands, so she dropped me off here when she was finished," he replied, walking over to Cully and looking over his shoulder. "What did you find out?"

"The power pack isn't stable and the casing looks to be the same way," he replied. "I ran these figures ten times and they all say the same thing." He looked at his boss's hands, still a bright pink where the skin had peeled, and winced. "Ouch. Man, that must have hurt like a son of a gun."

"I've known better days," Scott said dryly, leaning over Cully and scanning the lines of a printout. "Where did you find the first problem?"

Kay turned to Nikki. "I'm not trying to be rude, Ms. Price, but this is a high-security area for a good reason. While it was all right for you to accompany Dr. Carter here, it wouldn't be right for you to remain and hear data without having the proper clearance."

Nikki itched to take the younger woman down a notch or two. "Kay," she began, deliberately using the graduate student's first name. "My father is Admiral Adam Price." She decided imparting this bit of information wouldn't hurt. "The same Admiral Price attached to the Pentagon. Honey, I was born with a top-secret clearance pinned to my diaper."

After dropping her verbal bombshell, she smiled at the two men and walked out.

Scott saw dark storm clouds gathering on Kay's face. *Big mistake, Nikki,* he thought to himself. *I'd say you've made an enemy.*

"Did Westin call and say anything about my being readmitted to the mainframe?" he asked, eager to break the frigid silence.

Cully shook his head. "Haven't heard a thing, but then, I only got in a couple hours ago. Kay got here first. Did you hear anything, Kay?"

She had already returned to her computer and was diligently typing in data. "Not a word."

Scott snatched up the phone and punched in David Westin's extension, only to be told by his secretary that he was in conference and had left orders not to be disturbed.

"Tell him I want to hear from him as soon as he comes in," Scott instructed. Frustrated, he slammed the phone down in its cradle. He turned to Cully. Thank God he had his work to help him deal with his frustration. "All right, let's look at what we've got."

Scott soon lost himself in the intricacies of a laser gun he had once foreseen as the weapon of the future, something that could be easily hand held and replace larger guns. Now all he saw was a dream spiraling downward.

"The prototype can be ready by the end of next week if they have the plans by first thing tomorrow," Kay announced.

Scott looked up. "What?"

She didn't seem to care that his quiet voice held a dangerous note. "We can have the prototype ready for testing in a week. We test it out and make everyone happy."

"Kay, you're not listening to me. And you're not listening to Cully. It's obviously not ready if it fails all the tests we've done on the computer."

Kay took a deep breath. "And I told you before—just because it fails on the computer doesn't mean it will fail in real life. And if there's a problem, let it come out so we can see what it is and fix it!"

If Scott's gaze could have been turned into a weapon, Kay wouldn't have been standing there.

"It needs to be ironed out now. That way I don't have to worry about anyone being injured the way an earlier test turned out. Also, let me remind you that this is *my* project, not yours."

Kay threw up her hands. "Why do I bother? You know, I don't need this garbage." She snatched up her backpack and stormed out of the laboratory.

"She's been doing a lot of that lately," Cully said. "You'd think it was her butt on the line instead of yours."

"Thanks a lot for your vote of confidence," Scott said wryly.

"Just telling it like I see it. Don't expect to hear from Old Man Westin anytime soon," he advised. "The man hates your guts."

"Yes, well, the feeling is mutual," Scott muttered.

Cully leaned back in the chair, lacing his fingers behind his head. Whistling a popular rock tune, he stared at the ceiling. Suddenly, he lunged forward, whooping with joy.

"We are really stupid!"

Scott wondered if Cully's many hours at the computer had finally fried his brain. "Speak for yourself."

Cully spun around in the chair so he was facing Scott.

"Virtual reality," he announced with the dramatic aplomb of a circus ringmaster. He waited, looking about as smug as the proverbial cat who ate the canary.

"Virtual—" Scott stopped. His eyes lit up. "Why not? It would work."

"We write the program and set it all up. That way we can see it in action—"

"Without having to worry about having a prototype built," Scott finished.

Cully nodded. His expression was expectant as he watched his boss pace back and forth. "Does this mean you like my idea?" he ventured.

Scott leaned over Cully. "You could get a raise out of this."

"To a whole nickel an hour?" he quipped.

Scott grinned. "Maybe even a dime." He twisted away, rifling through another stack of printouts. "Okay, let's get to work on that program."

"Kay's going to be really teed off that we left her out of this."

Scott dropped into his chair and turned to Cully. "She wasn't here when the idea came to you. Besides, she'll be in on the testing. That's all that matters to her."

"Hey, it just came to me. Honest." He held up the two-fingered Boy Scout salute.

A corner of Scott's mouth tipped upward. "You're using the wrong hand."

Cully quickly switched hands. "Look at it this way. If she stayed, she'd only sit around and complain that building a prototype was the only way to show those anal-retentive types we know what we're doing. You know it and I know it."

Scott booted up his computer. He'd turned it off with the vague idea of going home. But after Cully's suggestion, the last thing he thought of was leaving.

"Let's get to it then."

Nikki put her purchases away as soon as she arrived at the house. Her nose wrinkled at the faint astringent odor of fresh paint as she stepped inside the closet and pulled out hangers.

"There is no way I'm going to let my new clothes smell like paint," she murmured, placing the hangers on the door instead.

The bag holding Scott's purchase still lay conspicuously on the bed when she finished.

Nikki took out the manila folders holding the reports on Renee. She'd looked them over many times and still hadn't been able to find what she was searching for. She sighed heavily as she carried them into the family room. The odor coming from the paper was an unpleasant reminder of the night before.

"Nothing like spending the afternoon doing a little light reading," she said wryly, dropping the papers onto the carpet.

The hours passed with Nikki reading every word over several times and studying each photograph until she was positive she was going cross-eyed, and to no avail. When it grew too dark to read, she switched on a lamp, turned on the television for background noise and absently glanced at the clock.

"Obviously, our boy genius got a brainstorm," she murmured, dropping down onto the carpet. She flipped back to the first page of the files with the intention of starting all over again.

This time as she leafed through the papers she used a pen to highlight words and phrases that caught her eye.

By the time Scott arrived home, it was closer to dawn than dusk and he felt as if all his muscles had been twisted into pretzels.

He walked into the house, surprised to find the alarm off and a light still burning in the family room, with faint sounds coming from the television. He headed in that direction with the intention of telling Nikki she needn't have waited up for him.

A memory unwillingly popped into his brain. He had encountered a problem with a formula and had gotten so involved in unraveling the mystery, he had forgotten to call Renee and tell her he'd be late. By the time he got home, she had worked herself into a temper and accused him of everything from having an affair to living a secret life elsewhere. He winced as he remembered the accusations. And here he had done it again, gotten so involved in his work that Nikki must have wondered what happened to him.

"No wonder Renee hated me." He walked into the room and found Nikki curled up sound asleep on the carpet. She had obviously been awake enough at some point to pull a pillow off the couch and slip it under her head. For a moment he was tempted to pick her up and carry her to bed. But he suspected that if he tried, he might end up being thrown over a piece of furniture. He settled for turning off the TV.

Nikki immediately roused at the absence of sound. "Hmm, decided to come home, did you?"

Guilt automatically set in. "I'm sorry I didn't call."

She waved away his apology as she sat up. "It's not as if you'd run off to Paris for dinner. I didn't worry, since you had ample protection over there while you worked."

"I still should have called," he insisted.

She looked up with eyes still heavy from sleep. "Did you come up with a good idea?"

"Cully did."

"Then no apology is needed." She nodded in understanding. Her jaw opened in a wide yawn. She glanced at the wall clock hanging over the television set. "Considering the hour, you might as well have stayed there to begin the new day. Did the two of you get it all ironed out?"

"Yes, but I won't be going back there until this afternoon."

"Then that's all that counts." She rose to her feet and stretched her arms over her head. "Did you get anything to eat?"

"Cold cheeseburgers and cold coffee around midnight."
Nikki wrinkled her nose. "Sounds appetizing."

Scott's weariness disappeared as he looked at Nikki,
delightfully rumpled in red cotton shorts and a red-and-
white T-shirt that bared her midriff when she raised her arms
over her head. She had left her hair down and it hung
around her face in loose waves. Her lips looked slightly
pouty. She yawned again.

"You must be exhausted." Without even thinking about
it, she took his hand and guided him out of the room, tapping the light switch along the way.

"I was," he said, eyeing her bare legs with great interest.
He was amused to notice her toenails were painted red to
match her shorts.

By now Nikki had fully awakened. She was surprised by
the glow of desire in Scott's eyes.

"Do you realize it's been a good three days since we've
had a decent night's sleep?" she asked.

"Only three days, huh?" He backed her against the wall,
a hand planted against the smooth surface on each side of
her. "I guess we're both past due for some much-needed
rest."

"I guess we are." Her husky tones matched his. She
leaned against the wall, arching her upper body just enough
to get Scott's attention.

He fingered the slightly gaping neckline of her T-shirt.
Unable to resist, he took a quick peek inside. Her bra was a
soft cream confection covered with lace and dipping low
enough to reveal her slightly rounded breasts.

"Just how tired are you?" he asked.

She arched against him like a cat. "Unlike you, I had a
nice long nap."

He smiled at her matter-of-fact voice, which warred with
the dancing lights he could see reflected in her eyes from the
night-light burning in the hallway. "A nap sounds good, but
you know, working the way I have tends to get me wired.
Tense."

When Nikki reached out, she didn't finger the polo neckline of Scott's shirt but his belt buckle. She traced the simple brass device, then lowered her fingers to trace the zipper straining against his arousal.

"Yes, I can tell. You know, I've read that a lot of tension isn't good for a man. Perhaps a hot bath would help ease that . . . tightness you must feel."

He lowered his face until his mouth was a breath above hers. He wanted to know where this teasing side of hers came from. "I was hoping you could think of something hot."

Her smile was the kind that brought to mind silk sheets and wild sex even as her fingers found their way around the waistband of his jeans.

"I usually can come up with ways to relieve tension," she murmured breathlessly.

By now, Scott was past speech. His mouth covered Nikki's, causing sensations that shot all the way down to her toes. He parted her lips with his tongue, thrusting inside with the urgency his body demanded he repeat with another part of his body. He tore her T-shirt up and over her head and scrambled for the tiny fastening at the front of her bra. Her breasts swelled at the moist heat of his mouth suckling her, creating electric shocks throughout her body.

"I don't know about you," he said hoarsely, tearing his mouth away from hers, "but I'm too damn old to make love right here, although the way I feel right now . . ." he paused to take a deep shuddering breath ". . . anything is possible."

Nikki tore open his belt and unzipped his jeans. "Think back to young and horny days," she enunciated, reaching inside his jeans and encircling his hardness. Her eyes, blazing dark golden lights, snared him. "What do you say?"

He grasped her around her waist and lifted her onto him. Their mouths fused the same moment their bodies did.

Scott felt an exultation as Nikki accepted him as if she had accepted him for years. That was when he knew this woman meant far more to him than just a protector. And there was no way he was ever going to allow her to leave him.

Chapter 14

At first Scott wasn't sure what had awakened him. He
narrowed his eyes and looked around to see what could have
disturbed his sleep.

The faint light spilling through the narrow opening between the drawn drapes told him it was early morning, and
the warmth curled up next to him told him Nikki was still
asleep.

He lay there, content to have Nikki's head resting against
his shoulder. Except something kept nagging at his memory. Something disturbing. The longer he lay there, the more
nagging the thought became.

He closed his eyes and forced himself to relax in hopes the
thought would form in his mind. As it did, a chill stole over
his skin.

Neatly typed sheets with words highlighted in bright pink
and notes written in the margin flashed in his memory. And
photographs. Damning black-and-white photographs of
papers and a body lying in a jail cell, then the body draped
in what appeared to be a white sheet in clinical surround-

ings. Renee's body. Those papers were still lying on the family-room floor.

Scott held his breath as he carefully disengaged himself from Nikki. She mumbled and curled up in a tight ball. He couldn't help but smile at the faint frown furrowing her forehead when she reached out in her sleep, and couldn't find him.

He found the jeans he'd worn the night before lying on the floor next to Nikki's shorts. He pulled on his pants and zipped them up, but didn't bother to snap them before leaving the room.

Sensing he would need fortification to look over the papers, he detoured via the kitchen and brewed a pot of coffee first. Carrying a filled mug into the family room, he sat down and picked up the papers, pointedly ignoring the Top Secret stamped in red on each sheet.

The more Scott read, the sicker he became. He felt as if acid was dripping into his stomach as he read Nikki's reports about Dr. Carter's home life. About her finding his papers and a roll of microfilm among his wife's things and her recommendation that Mrs. Carter be taken in for questioning.

There were reports written by the agents who'd arrested Renee. Reports with Harvey's signature detailing Renee's interrogation. Neatly typed depositions made by Renee. And, lastly, reports graphically describing her death and the subsequent autopsy.

Bile rose in his throat as he studied the gruesome photographs of her body lying in the jail cell, then in the morgue.

Words spilled from his lips. Vile, hateful words against the system that had destroyed a woman in such a manner. He held the photos up, prepared to tear them into pieces so that no one could ever see them again.

"I should have known better than to leave them out."

He looked up, but he didn't see Nikki Price, his lover, standing in the doorway looking like an angel in one of his colored T-shirts, her hair tumbling down around her shoulders. As he stared at her, he didn't see the woman who had made such magic with him last night that he'd sworn he'd died and gone to heaven.

"This is so ridiculous it's sick." His throat hurt as he spoke. "Renee had her faults, but she didn't deserve any of this. It wasn't in her to do something like this."

"That's the conclusion I came to."

His beginning diatribe was halted by her calm words.

Nikki walked over to Scott and dropped to the floor, sitting cross-legged next to him. She didn't try touching him; it was as if she knew he would reject any physical overtures from her. She kept her expression free of emotion as she watched him.

"I have spent I don't know how many hours going over these reports, and there's something in them that just isn't right," she said. "Yesterday, I tried calling the medical examiner who performed the autopsy, but he's since retired and I can't get his new address. The current M.E. refuses to discuss the case because it's considered closed, and an M.E. I used to know is no longer in the area."

His mouth opened and closed as he tried to force his sluggish brain to form words he badly needed to say. "Why?"

"I don't know, Scott," she said honestly. "That's why I've looked over every word hundreds of times. The only questions raised in my mind are in the autopsy notes."

He flicked the appropriate stack of papers with his fingers. "I read them."

"Obviously, you're not used to reading such things. I'm not, either, which is why something kept eluding me until last night." She shuffled the papers until they covered the autopsy photographs. She saw no reason for Scott to have to look at them again. "The conclusion drawn was that she died of poison."

"I know," he answered dully, feeling the bitter pain rise up again.

"So if she was poisoned, where are the results of the toxicology reports?" she asked. "You can't say someone was poisoned unless you run a toxicology screen to determine what kind of poison was taken. There's no report here and no poison named. To me, that's sloppy work. And these people aren't known for sloppy findings. Especially if there's an important court case involved."

Scott thought of the findings he had read and what he had missed. "Do you think the report's disappearance was deliberate?"

"Could be."

"Harvey?"

She shook her head. "That's not his style. He'd rather have you read something and argue with him, so he can show you how he's right and you're wrong. Harvey loves nothing more than engaging in a verbal battle." She gathered the papers together and pushed them into their respective folders.

Scott thought for a moment. "Who else would have access to these papers?"

"More people than I'd like to think. If someone has a high enough security clearance or has the ability to break into computers and bypass the codes, he can gain access without a qualm."

Scott glanced at the folders in her hands and felt the sorrow rise up again. This time the boiling acid seemed to come from his eyes. He had no idea tears were rolling down his cheeks.

"I somehow felt her stealing the reports and killing herself was her way of getting back at me because she sensed I had stopped loving her," he said in a low voice that shook with emotion. "I hadn't told her yet, but I couldn't see our having a future together any longer. If I had told her, the divorce would probably have been dirty, but maybe with a clean break she would still be alive today."

Nikki moved closer now, putting her arms around him.

"No, Scott," her low voice urged him to listen to her, "don't give in to self-pity. Get angry. Get good and mad because someone made sure Renee died so the case would be closed."

"What are you saying?" he demanded.

"I have a hunch their case wasn't as airtight as they thought it would be. But if she died, supposedly by her own hand, it would automatically be assumed she was guilty and the case would be closed. Get mad, Scott, and make sure this person pays," she urged.

Scott wrapped his arms around her, taking solace in Nikki's warmth, the life flowing through her veins. His tears flowed down his cheeks and dropped onto her face. He thought of a woman who had died needlessly.

But if she hadn't died, if the hell hadn't started up again, he wouldn't have seen Nikki again. Wouldn't have found out he was falling.... The word refused to form in his mind. For the moment, it didn't seem right.

"What can I do?"

She didn't hesitate with her first request. "I'm going to find a medical examiner we can trust. Someone who can explain some of these terms to us. I want an explanation as to why a toxicology screen wasn't run. The more I've read, the more confused I've gotten."

He pulled away from her and stood up. He felt a thick fog surround his brain. "I've got to get out of here," he muttered, striding down the hall. Moments later, he returned, wearing a T-shirt tucked into his jeans and carrying a brown leather jacket.

Nikki jumped to her feet and followed him. "Where are you going?"

He didn't stop as he walked through the kitchen toward the back door. "Out."

"Out where?"

"Out where I don't have to see anyone or talk to anyone." He pulled open the back door and headed for the garage.

Nikki remained fast on his heels. She winced as the bottoms of her bare feet touched the rough surface of the driveway's asphalt.

"Scott, don't do this." She hissed a low curse when he wheeled his motorcycle out of the garage. She ran over and stood in front of him, as if by blocking him, she could keep him there. "You're not taking off on that. You can't go anywhere alone."

The ferocity in his expression would have frightened another woman. But Nikki wasn't just any woman. She stared back, not exhibiting one whit of fear.

"My life is in the toilet," he stated, spitting out each word. His face was contorted with pain. "My existence has been threatened, my daughter terrorized, my car bombed, my guest room ruined and I've been locked out of my work. I always felt that Renee didn't steal my notes and now you're looking at points that could prove it, evidence that says she was killed because her death would automatically make her look guilty. So for now, I intend to do something I have control over, and that means getting the hell out of here." He pulled his helmet onto his head.

"I want to go with you."

"Dammit, Nikki, can't you understand? I don't want you with me. I want to be alone." He angled the bike so he could roll it around her. Without looking at her, he climbed on, started it up and gunned the engine a moment before racing off.

"Damn." Nikki felt the frustration knot her insides as she stared at his retreating figure. She ran back into the house, her first thought being to call Harvey and arrange to have Scott picked up. She had just grabbed the receiver and started to tap out Harvey's number when she suddenly slammed the receiver back in the cradle.

She stood at the kitchen window, looking out at the garage and wondering if she could try to catch up with him. But he could be anywhere by now!

"If anything happens to him, Harvey will take a piece of my hide," she muttered, raking her fingers through her hair. "Right after I do the same thing to myself."

She poured herself a cup of coffee and stared at the phone, while her brain raced through problems real and imagined. When the worst occurred to her, she muttered a pithy curse. She stared at the cabinet that held bottles of whiskey and brandy. She seriously thought about adding a stiff shot to her coffee.

"Oh, Scott, I hope this escape of yours is worth it."

The longer Nikki thought about it, the more things suddenly started to fall into place. She ran back to the guest room, hunting for her private address book. From there, she headed for the family room, where she gathered up the file folders and ran back to the kitchen.

"Brad," she said the moment the phone on the other end of the line was picked up. "It's me. I need some help."

"Nik, you've been gone for five years, with not a word out of you during all that time, and you think with one phone call I'll help you?" her brother asked. "Get a life."

"I need you to help me prove that Renee Carter didn't kill herself. I think I can also show who was really behind it."

"That case is not only closed, it's out of my jurisdiction. Try some other sucker."

As always, she ignored his protests. "I want to talk to the medical examiner who autopsied her body. And I want to talk to an independent medical examiner to ask questions about the report that was filed. The diagnosis was poison, but there was no toxicology screen run."

"Why aren't you talking to Harvey about this? Isn't this his territory? He could get what you need in seconds."

"He wouldn't agree with what I'm doing. He's convinced he was right in the beginning. I want someone out of the loop. Someone who can give me an impartial opinion."

"Then what about Dad? He has a hell of a lot more contacts than I do," he suggested. "What makes you think I have the contacts you need?"

"I'm not asking the admiral, I'm asking you. Besides, you owe me."

"I owe you zip."

"Who took the blame for the broken living-room window?"

"That was more than twenty years ago!"

"Who took the blame and who vowed to help me?" she pressed.

Nikki listened to Brad's imaginative curses. "Right now, I'm not sure if I'm crazy or you are. You have a fax machine?"

"Dr. Carter does, in his office."

"Okay, fax the papers to me and I'll hand carry them over to a medical examiner who's trustworthy and see what he says. And I'll see if I can find out where the other one is." He gave her a fax number. "No one else will see them but me."

"You won't tell anyone you're doing this for me?" What she was really asking was that he not tell their father.

"Dammit, Nik, no, I won't tell anyone." He paused. "Look, don't run off again without a word to anyone, okay?"

"When I resigned from the navy I was also out of the family, remember?"

"Only because you made it that way. Just a second." She could hear faint sounds as he muffled the mouthpiece with his hand. "Look, I've got to go. Fax me the papers and I'll see what I can do."

She blinked rapidly as she felt tears burn her eyes. "Thanks."

"Yeah, well, now we're even."

Nikki sorted the papers and carried them down to Scott's laboratory. Finding the door locked delayed her only about four minutes as she easily picked it. The moment she faxed the paperwork to her brother she felt as if part of the load had been taken off her shoulders. She trusted Brad not to tell anyone what he was doing. But as she thought about it, she realized she hadn't asked him how he was going to make sure no one knew who the subject was. If Harvey found out, she knew he would be furious with her for bypassing him, for not trusting him. Except right now she wasn't sure who to trust.

Nikki sat in Scott's chair, imagining she could feel his warmth surrounding her. She tucked her legs up, wrapping her arms around them. She rested her chin on her knees, looking as forlorn as a grown woman could.

"I made the major mistake a bodyguard can't afford to make. I got emotionally involved. I put too much trust in him instead of relying only on myself."

Scott had no idea how long he rode the highways leading him away from the city. He didn't glance in his side-view mirror to see if he was being followed. In the mood he was in, he didn't care. All that mattered was the road unwinding ahead of him like a broad silvery-gray ribbon. He didn't want to think. He didn't want to feel.

After a while he coasted to the side of the road and rolled the bike into a rest stop, not halting until he reached the far end of the lot. He hoped anyone driving in would take the hint that he wanted to be left alone.

Scott sat at a far bench staring at the countryside, but he didn't see any of it. He rested his elbows on the wooden table in front of him and buried his face in his hands.

"Scott, do you honestly think I would do such a thing?" Renee had screamed at him the day the two agents showed up unexpectedly with an arrest warrant. "I may hate your work, but I have the sense not to break into your computer and steal files. I don't even know how to turn the thing on!"

All he'd done was stand there, stunned by the agents' accusations. Even then only certain words seemed to pierce his shock: *stolen files, sold them, secret bank account,* and the most damning of all, *treason.*

Renee had been handcuffed and hustled out of the house before Scott could come out of his stupor. By the time he'd returned to the present, Heather was in tears and he was trying to figure out what had just happened. He hadn't learned anything for two days, until Harvey came to see him and explained, in detail, what they had found and how the evidence pointed to Renee. By the time Scott was able to find an attorney willing to handle the case, Renee was dead. That was when he'd learned that Nikki was the main force behind the evidence gathering. Ultimately, he had blamed her for Renee's death.

"She's making up for what happened then," he said out loud, frowning as he racked his brain for every memory he could conjure up from that time. A knot tightened painfully in the pit of his stomach. "Why are you out here instead of back there helping her? She asked for your help and all you could do was run. Not a good move." He started to get up, determined to go back and face Nikki, when a faint noise from the bushes caught his attention. He froze, suddenly wondering if someone was back there with a gun. When the sound was repeated, he realized it was an animal whimpering.

"I must be nuts," he muttered, slowly making his way toward the noise. He parted the bushes, fully prepared to make a run for it, until he saw the black-and-tan form lift its head. "Oh damn. Hey, boy, it's okay," he crooned to the puppy as he slowly crouched down. "What's wrong, are you lost?"

The small dog shied away at first, wary of the human.

"What happened to you?" When it scrambled to one side, a badly chewed burlap bag was visible under its gangly body. Now Scott knew the puppy wasn't lost; it had been dumped at the side of the road. "Okay, let's see if we can get you to the animal shelter or something. I can't leave you here." He slowly reached for the puppy, and this time the young dog allowed him to pick it up.

The moment Scott picked up the puppy, he knew he wasn't going to go to the trouble of finding an animal shelter. Not when a pair of big brown eyes, shining with trust, looked up at him.

"Oh sh—" He exhaled a deep breath. "Congratulations, boy, you found a sucker. Heather's been wanting a dog, so it looks like you're it."

He unzipped his jacket and wrapped the edges around the dog as he walked back to his motorcycle. Once he climbed on, he zipped up the jacket as far as possible to keep the puppy secure.

"Do us both a favor, boy. If you've got to pee, let me know. Okay?" He received a wet kiss as his answer.

It wasn't until Scott started back for the house that he realized just how far he had traveled.

"Maybe having you with me will save my butt," he told the puppy, which snuggled inside his shirt and promptly went to sleep. "Nikki might not be inclined to shoot me once she gets a look at you."

By the time Scott drove up his driveway, the sun was down. He was cold from the wind on the road, sore and hungry. He looked around, surprised not to find scores of government cars parked around the house. Even the house wasn't blazing with lights; there was one burning in the kitchen and one in the family room.

He parked the motorcycle in the garage and carried the drowsy puppy to the lawn, waiting while the pup sniffed around and did his business.

"Good boy," he praised. "Come on. Let's face the music."

The puppy scrambled along beside him, uttering soft yips as he went.

Scott tested the back door and found it unlocked. He cocked his head, listening. The faint sound of the television was all he heard.

When he entered the family room, he found Nikki curled up on the couch. He knew she had to have heard him enter, so she must be purposely ignored him.

"Hi," he ventured.

She didn't turn around. "Have a nice ride?"

"Yeah."

Her voice was soft, empty of all expression. "Where did you go?"

"Maryland."

"Nice place to visit."

At that moment, the puppy made his way to the couch and propped his front paws on the cushion. Nikki looked down.

"Well, who are you?" she asked the dog, who promptly yipped. She looked over her shoulder. "You went to Maryland for a puppy?"

"Actually, he found me." Scott hoped it was safe to venture forward. "Someone dumped him near a rest stop. I couldn't leave him there."

Nikki laughed when the puppy pushed himself up onto the couch and crawled into her lap, covering her face with slobbering kisses.

"Scott, this isn't a puppy. This is a small horse." She giggled when the puppy tried to climb up her chest. "He's got German-shepherd markings, but it's obvious he isn't a purebred, which might be why he was dumped." She grabbed hold of him and held him up for a good look. "The other half might be collie or retriever. It's hard to say just now, although it's obvious he's a large breed. Look at those paws. He's going to be huge when he grows into them."

"He was dumped because his mother was a little too popular one night?" Scott was disgusted at the idea.

Nikki shrugged. "Maybe it was prom night," she quipped. She rubbed her face against the puppy's fur. "Are you hungry, little guy?"

"We're both starved."

Nikki set the puppy on the floor and stood up. "The puppy I'll feed. *You* are on your own."

Scott followed her into the kitchen. "I didn't get a chance to stop to eat."

Nikki took some cooked chicken out of the refrigerator and tore it into bite-size pieces. She set the plate on the floor and filled a bowl with water. The puppy immediately had his nose in the plate, eating hungrily.

It wasn't until Nikki turned her attention to Scott that he saw the lines of strain around her eyes and mouth.

"I had no idea where you were for all these hours," she said softly.

Scott winced. He would have preferred her yelling at him than that dangerously soft tone. "I had to get away."

She leaned against the counter, her arms crossed in front of her chest. Her body language told him she wasn't willing to listen to anything he had to say.

"By all rights, I should have called Harvey. He would have had you picked up."

"And brought back like a wandering five-year-old."

"You can't just go out without protection like that. That is why I'm here." She took a deep breath. "I had no idea if you were lying by the road bleeding to death. Or if someone had followed you from here and decided to kidnap you because they were dissatisfied with the delay in your work."

Scott felt as if his feet had been glued to the floor. He stared at Nikki, seeing the shine in her eyes that had nothing to do with the lighting. What he saw were unshed tears, tears she was using all her self-control not to shed.

"Oh, Nikki." He stepped forward with the intention of taking her in his arms.

"Don't touch me, you bastard!" She punched him in the stomach. Hard. "I am so angry at you I could shoot you myself!"

The puppy looked up, then returned to his meal.

Air whooshed out of Scott's lungs as the burning pain radiated upward.

"Damn, that hurts," he wheezed.

"You're lucky I didn't hit you any harder!" she cried.

"You could have hit me harder?" He lightly ran his hands over his abdomen, positive he'd find something broken.

"I was worried sick about you!" she railed. "I thought you were dead! I *wish* you were dead!"

He smiled, surprised at this new side to her personality. "No, you don't." This time he was a little more cautious when he took her in his arms. "I'm sorry," he murmured in her ear. "But I had to get out and think things through."

She sniffed, still unsure if she wanted to accept his apology.

"Besides, how can you be angry when I brought you home a present?"

"That puppy is not a present."

"Sure he is." He nuzzled her throat, inhaling the exotic fragrance that was all hers. "I knew he needed a mom and I immediately thought of you."

"Somehow that isn't reassuring." Her arms crept around his waist. "Most men bring home flowers or candy."

Scott's heart quickened at her choice of words. If she thought of this as home, he was one step closer to proving to her she belonged here full-time. And not as a bodyguard. "I wanted to be original."

"That you are." Her soft sigh shuddered through her body as she lifted her face. "Just how hungry are you?" Her words were muffled as she ran her hands up under his T-shirt, pulling it up and over his head. It barely settled on the floor when her teasing fingers snaked their way into the waistband of his jeans.

He sucked in a deep breath as she cradled his hardness.

"Depends on what you're offering."

Nikki unbuckled his belt and unsnapped and unzipped his jeans. "You put me through hell all day today. You really should be punished."

His own hands burrowed under her shirt. He was pleased to discover she wasn't wearing a bra and that her nipples immediately hardened at his touch.

"This kind of punishment I'm more than willing to endure," he said hoarsely, starting to push her shorts down her hips.

"Wait." She covered his hands with hers. "Not in front of the puppy."

He stepped back and took several deep breaths to slow his racing pulse.

"He'll be fine on his own." He grasped her wrist and started to playfully drag her out of the kitchen.

"He's a puppy!" she protested, laughing and digging in her heels.

"No problem. Come on, Nikki, we're losing the moment." Muttering something about "stubborn women," he took matters into his own hands by picking her up and throwing her over his shoulder in a fireman's carry.

"Scott!"

"Be quiet and let me act like a caveman." He playfully hit her on the butt. "I've never done this before and I want to make sure I get it right."

The moment they reached the bedroom, Scott leaned over to rip the covers off the bed before dropping her unceremoniously in the middle.

"Scott." Nikki held him back as he dropped down beside her and started to reach for her. "We can't solve all our problems with sex."

He kissed her in such a deep, probing way that she thought for sure her soul had merged with his.

"We don't have sex," he corrected. "We make love. And this isn't about solving problems, but making a vow to each other." His expression changed from teasing to serious. "I love you, Nikki. It took a lot of miles and freezing my butt off, but now I know how I feel and I don't intend to let you get away."

Her breath caught at his declaration. "Are you sure?" she whispered.

He wanted to grin at her stunned expression. If anyone needed to know how much she was loved, it was this woman. That was something he intended to make sure she knew every day of their lives together. But he'd save that part of his intentions until another time. He figured one shock a day was enough.

"As sure as I can be." He took her in his arms again. "I love having a woman who can throw me, shoot me and probably inflict all sorts of torture."

Nikki pulled him toward her. "Right now I'm not entirely sure if I dare say the same thing to you, because of what's going on. But when it's over..."

He stopped her with a breath-stealing kiss. "When it's over, I'll make sure you say anything you want. Until then, this is my show."

When Scott entered her, Nikki sensed the difference. She felt his love enveloping her and wanted nothing more than to wrap it around both of them and stay in that safety zone until their lives could be normal.

Scott roused when he felt Nikki leave the bed. He vaguely heard her leave the room and later speak to the puppy in a low voice; then he heard the sound of the laundry-room door closing.

"Don't leave me again," he mumbled when her warm, naked body cuddled up against him.

"I wanted to check on our new arrival." She traced his ear with her lips, biting gently on the lobe.

"He's probably fine."

"Oh, yes, he's peachy keen. So far he's piddled on the kitchen floor, chewed your T-shirt and mauled one of the family-room pillows." Laughter rang in her voice.

Scott rolled over, taking her with him. "I'm glad to hear he's found a way to occupy himself."

Chapter 15

"**W**hat makes you think you can get away with this?"

The moment Scott heard David Westin's furious voice, he knew the man had heard of Cully's and his endeavors.

"Hello, David, yes, I'm doing very well. Thank you for asking." He doodled on the pad of paper near his elbow.

"I don't know what has happened to you over the past few years." The administrator sounded as if his temper was hanging by a mere thread. "You are definitely not the same man we asked to join us here. At that time you were serious about your work, dedicated to finishing your research. Now you're flippant, you defy authority and, from what I understand, you aren't even close to finishing your project."

Now it was Scott holding on to his temper. *Kay.* The name ran through his brain and he vowed the young woman was going to receive the lecture of her life. He'd already warned her about not talking to David. Obviously, she didn't understand the ramifications of what she had done. By the time he finished with her, she would understand her error. In spades.

"What makes you think you can justify the expense of testing your weapon using this virtual-reality method, which is nothing more than a child's video game?" David demanded. "What do you expect to accomplish?"

Scott silently counted to ten. If there was one thing he hated, it was explaining himself. Especially to a pompous jerk like Westin.

"It's the best way to find the bugs in the weapon."

"I thought building a prototype and testing it would show you the same thing and would be considerably more viable."

Scott automatically replaced the word *viable* with *cheaper*. He was familiar with David's feelings on spending money. He continued doodling as he argued, "In virtual reality we can put the weapon through more extensive tests."

Scott suddenly cocked his head to one side. Nikki had just walked into his laboratory; he could tell by the sexy fragrance of her perfume. He looked over his shoulder and watched her approach, the puppy on her heels. They hadn't been able to come up with a suitable name for the rambunctious canine, who already behaved as if the entire house was his playground and Nikki and Scott available playmates. In less than twenty-four hours, he had chewed a pair of Scott's running shoes, two of his T-shirts and one of Nikki's sandals. He'd even gotten into Heather's room and chewed on a few of her stuffed animals. Nikki had made a quick visit to a pet store and picked up food and every kind of puppy toy available to keep him out of trouble. She had also made an appointment with a veterinarian. While there, she'd learned the puppy was in excellent health; he'd whimpered only a little when given his shots and had piddled on the doctor's shoes.

Dr. Westin? she mouthed the words.

Scott grimaced and nodded. "David, read my lips," he went on. "This is a better way to test it. I was given carte blanche for this project and it will be done my way," he informed the man.

"This is not the way, Carter, and you will find that out."

"All I've learned so far is that you haven't reauthorized my entry into the mainframe," he reminded him. "I suggest you get on it."

Westin's reply was to slam down the phone.

"A bit gruesome, but an excellent depiction of the man," Nikki commented, looking over Scott's shoulder. Her fingers dug into his tense muscles, rubbing the stiffness out of them.

Scott looked down at the pad and laughed. He'd drawn an amazingly accurate picture of David Westin with a hangman's noose around his neck. The eyes bugged out and the mouth hung slack.

"It needs a little more defining." He redrew a few lines until the picture looked like something out of a horror movie. "Better."

"What's this about virtual reality?"

He twisted his neck from side to side as he felt the tension leave his body, thanks to her talented fingers.

"Cully came up with the idea of testing the weapon by using a virtual-reality program."

"Can that be done?"

"It requires some work on our side, but, yes, it can work. We intend to make it work." He spun his chair around and dragged her between his spread knees. He ran his hands along her bare legs. "You know, it's almost like the real thing. Some say even better. In years to come it will replace video games."

Nikki rolled her eyes. "When are you going to the institute?"

He glanced at his watch. "In an hour. I called Cully and Kay and warned them to be prepared for another long day."

She nodded. "You might want to take your new son with you. Especially since he seems loath to let you go."

Scott looked down and found the puppy happily sprawled on the floor with his pant leg in his mouth. The dog's tail thumped on the floor as he blissfully chewed on the fabric.

Scott grimaced and tried to disengage his pants from the puppy, who thought it was a game and responded by growling and pulling on them harder. Scott muttered an earthy curse.

"No, he already did that in the family room." Nikki crossed her arms in front of her chest. "I'm not here to housebreak a dog, Dr. Carter. I am here to make sure no one maims your body. Although, after the morning I've had, I'm very tempted to do a little damage."

"That bad?"

She looked down at the puppy, then back up at Scott. "Take him with you." She turned on her heel and walked out, closing the door after her so the dog was left behind.

Scott reached down and scratched him behind the ears. "Well, boy, I hope there's room in that doghouse for both of us."

Nikki reached the kitchen just in time to hear the phone ringing. She skirted a chewed rawhide toy and grabbed the cordless receiver, pulling up the antenna.

"Carter residence."

"It's me," Brad said. "Remember where I took you for your birthday and promptly lost you?"

She stilled. "Yes."

"Meet me there at two." He hung up.

Nikki carefully replaced the phone in its cradle. The prickles of sensation along the back of her neck told her she was going to be given some interesting information.

"What?" It was Scott's voice.

She spun around. "Nothing."

His response was decidedly profane. "What?" he repeated, more forcefully this time. "It's about me, isn't it?"

"It's about Renee's death. I asked one of my brothers to do a little checking for me. He has sources I don't," she replied. "He obviously didn't want to tell me over the phone, which worries me that he suspects the phone might be bugged. I'm meeting him this afternoon."

"I'm coming with you."

"No. You have to go to the institute, remember?"

Scott's head snapped up. "Yes. Dammit, Nikki, there isn't any way I can work while something like this is going on. I need to know!"

When she spoke, her voice seemed to have come from a deep freeze. "You're probably going to hear things you won't like."

"What's so new about that? So far I haven't heard all that much I do like. This time I promise not to run," he said quietly.

She slowly nodded. "All right, but Junior will have to stay in the garage while we're gone. And you will have to do whatever I say, with no questions asked."

"I have so far, haven't I?"

"Not exactly, but I'll take that as a yes."

Scott saw the strong family resemblance the moment he met Brad Price in the mall at the Smithsonian. Tall, with hair a few shades darker than Nikki's sun-lightened locks and trimmed short, he was an intimidating sight in his summer uniform.

"Damn, Nik, you got even uglier over the years." Brad flashed a crooked smile at his sister. "There's no way I want to admit I'm related to you."

She grinned back. "Jealous?"

He stared at her sage green-and-cream-checked cotton walking shorts and matching vest. He shook his head. "This is a new look for you."

"No, I'm just more used to it than you are." Nikki stepped forward and hugged him.

Brad was surprised by her sign of affection, then angry as he noticed her companion. "Dammit, did you have to bring him?" he demanded.

"Yes, he needs to know, Brad. Even more than I do."

He glanced around. "Let's walk."

With Scott on one side of the officer and Nikki on the other, they strolled across the grassy area in front of the row of world-famous museums.

"You can forget about the retired medical examiner. He died of a heart attack two years ago," Brad began.

"Damn!" She grimaced. "I'd hoped we could learn something from him."

"We can't from him, but his assistant is still alive and is now working in Delaware."

She shook her head, trying to assimilate his words. "Delaware? Why there?"

"He's the big cheese over there, that's why." Brad lowered his voice. "I phoned him at home last night. He was not pleased to hear why I called."

She felt that tingling along the nape of her neck. Something was about to happen. "What did he say?"

"That they were told to consider the case strictly hush-hush. It went under wraps supposedly because of her husband's government contacts."

"Meaning?"

"Meaning that was why no toxicological screen was run."

"Then how could they conclude she died of poisoning?"

"The symptoms given by the guards indicated atropine poisoning."

Scott winced as he heard the pronouncement. "Damn, why?" he muttered.

Nikki's mind worked overtime. "Are you saying she wasn't found dead? That she was alive and they let her suffer?"

"The way this guy understood it, the guards claimed they thought she was faking it to get some attention. She had already complained about her cell and the food, so they were told to ignore anything else she might try. Supposedly she complained about intense thirst and then had trouble talking as she went on about her eyes not focusing properly." He paused. "She was left alone after they told her to quit faking and settle down. I asked this guy about symptoms for atropine poisoning. It causes mania, psychotic behavior, convulsions, coma—just to name a few. In the end, her circulatory and respiratory systems collapsed. She was probably given a superlarge dose, because it happened quickly.

"During the exterior examination of her body, the pathologist found shedding of skin along her face, neck and upper body. That's a well-known symptom of atropine poisoning. They have no idea how it was administered, since there wasn't a hypodermic found near the body and they didn't bother to look for puncture marks."

Nikki swallowed the bile rising up her throat. She took a quick glance at Scott and felt his pain radiating outward. His face was paper white with shock.

"She didn't deserve to die that way," she whispered, feeling a painful pressure in her chest. "No one would. Did he say anything else?"

"I was lucky to get that much out of him. He told me not to call him again or he would have to take appropriate measures," Brad said wryly.

Nikki had to smile at his disgruntled tone. She knew her brother wouldn't have taken that well.

"Thank you."

"Hey, there's more."

She stilled. "What?"

"I didn't like what he told me, so I did some checking up on him. The guy didn't have the credentials for his cushy job and there were others vying for it who did. Since he got it, he had to have had connections. So I did some more snooping, and what I found out made me glad I'd covered my tracks as I went along." He glanced at Scott. "This had to have been an inside job."

"You're saying someone we're trusting now is behind all this?" Scott asked.

Brad nodded.

Scott licked his lips. "Could—" he cleared his throat in hopes of getting rid of the obstruction in it "—could she have been killed because she had an idea who was behind the theft?''

"I wouldn't be surprised. She might have tried to bargain with the person. She could have threatened to expose him if he didn't make sure she was released," Brad replied. "Except it backfired on her."

Scott shook his head. "Renee had guts. If she could have found an easy way out of there, she would have taken it. And I can't say I would have blamed her."

"Even if it cost her her life?" Brad asked bluntly.

"You idiot! You couldn't have put it another way?" Nikki punched him in the arm. She sensed the pain Scott was feeling and hated his hearing everything so bluntly.

Brad glared at his sister. "For once, think with that mind you're supposed to have," he ordered. "None of this could have happened unless there was someone on the inside who knew everything that was going on. I'd bet my career that the same person involved back then is involved now. The bomb that destroyed your car. The package delivered to your house with that caustic powder. The stink bomb through Nikki's bedroom window. It's probably all from the same person."

"If Brad is betting his career, he's one-hundred-percent sure he's right," Nikki muttered, glancing around vaguely. Were they being watched? She felt as if they were, but lately, she wondered if her fear for Scott was making her go overboard. "Do you feel anything?" she asked her brother.

He remained still for a moment. "Nothing. You know, paranoia only works for spooks."

Nikki made a face at being compared to a CIA agent.

Scott, feeling the tension, couldn't help but look around. "Dammit, I hate this," he said between clenched teeth.

Brad turned and pushed his face into Scott's. "Listen to me, *Doctor,* you were the one who chose to design a weapon a lot of people don't want to see manufactured—people with the money to ensure you don't finish it. People who will do *anything* to stop you."

Scott refused to back down. He looked into eyes the same rich honey-brown shade as Nikki's. And with the same anger darkening the orbs.

"You do your job, Commander. I'll do mine."

"If my sister breaks even a nail because of you, I will make what's happening to you now look like a picnic," he whispered fiercely.

"Surprising you should think of her welfare now instead of five years ago when she was really hurting," Scott whispered back, with the same ferocity in his voice.

The animosity between the two men escalated with each second as they waged a visual battle. For a moment it looked as if they would come to blows.

Nikki stood back, impressed with Scott's ability to hold his own. She remembered her many battles over the years with her older brother. The few she had won had been hard fought and she usually carried bruises and scratches afterward.

"Gentlemen—and I use the word loosely—we are in a public place, where fisticuffs would only draw attention to us. And that's the last thing we want, isn't it?" she murmured, moving in close to Scott's side. She smiled when Brad's gaze cut from him to her, silently gauging what was going on. "Just remember, big brother, I'm employed to protect the good doctor here, not you. Besides, I don't think the Pentagon would appreciate your being involved in a public brawl that I would have to break up." She offered him a smile that would have perfectly suited a shark. "I'd hate to break a few bones in the process."

"I don't need a woman to fight my battles for me," Scott muttered.

At the same time Brad barked, "Don't act so tough with me, little sister."

Nikki reached over and wrapped her fingers around Brad's arm, pressing down on a nerve. She smiled when he flinched.

"That's what happens when you settle for a desk job," she said pleasantly. "Now, I thank you very much for the information, but please don't get too involved. And make sure the admiral doesn't find out."

He shook his head. "He has connections I couldn't dream of having. Dad can help you where I can't."

"No thanks. As it was he stormed into Scott's house acting like an outraged father. As far as I'm concerned he gave up his parental rights years ago." She glanced around. "Do you have anything else to tell us?"

Brad stared at her incredulously. "I break a lot of personal codes to get you this information, then you tell me to back off, inflicting a little pain in the process, and now you have the gall to ask if I have anything more?"

She flashed her shark's smile again. "Do you?"

He shook his head in disgust. He turned to Scott. "All I have is a hunch here, but my hunches are usually pretty accurate. I think you'll find the culprit close to home."

"And you accuse your sister of paranoia."

"No, I just prefer to be careful." Brad looked around. "And you better do the same." He started to walk away, then turned. "If you don't want to rejoin to the navy, there are plenty of other positions you could look into that could use your qualifications, Nik. No one can say you weren't well trained."

"I'll think about it." For a moment, something—regret?—flashed across her face. "Don't let all those staid types drag you down."

He smiled. "I'll try not to."

Nikki watched her brother cross the mall, his back ramrod stiff in his khaki uniform.

"I was considered inferior because I was a girl," she said softly. "So I fought harder than anyone to show them I was as good as they were. But it took my graduation from the Naval Academy and later assignment with Naval Intelligence to prove it. I discovered just how stubborn I was when I realized that the only person I needed to prove myself to was me. That's when I knew it was time to get out and do something for myself."

She took Scott's arm and smiled brightly up at him. "Come on, I intend to drop you off so you can play with that specialized video game you spent all night working on." She started walking so swiftly he had no choice but to go along. "And while you're doing that, I'm going to do a little snooping."

Tension wrapped coils around his stomach. "Are you talking about doing something dangerous?"

"Only if I'm caught."

Scott noticed the lights dancing in her eyes, the excitement lighting up her smile. He feared she was discovering the life she was perfect for. And when the time came, she would walk away from him without looking back. He had to find a way to make sure that didn't happen.

"One more thing," she went on. "Do you know how to shoot?"

"I know enough to point."

Nikki shook her head. "I'll find you a good gun and show you what to do."

"I have a gun," he admitted. "I bought one when this all started." He lowered his voice. "It's not registered."

"I know. I found it when I searched your house the first day I was there. I was just waiting for you to tell me." Nikki looked around. "Now, it's a matter of showing you how to use it properly. I'll talk to Harvey about getting it registered."

He shouldn't have been surprised to learn she had searched his room. He should have been angry that she had invaded his privacy, but somehow he wasn't.

"Is there anything about me that's not a surprise to you?"

Nikki leaned over and whispered something in his ear. Scott's eyes widened with shock as he listened to her. She smiled back when he stared at her.

"You asked."

He suddenly discovered the day had heated up a good twenty degrees.

Chapter 16

"Considering the amount of security at the institute, how do you intend to snoop?" Scott asked once they were settled in Nikki's truck.

"That will depend on how much of a crash course in computers you can give me and if I can break into Westin's computer." She eased out of the parking space and soon entered the heavy flow of traffic. "Also, I need to know whose offices are on what floor."

"We all have our offices on the same floor. How much do you know about computers?"

"I can turn one on. I understand how to use a mouse with Windows and I know how to read a menu." She ticked the items off on her fingers. "Pull up files, print files and download to a disk."

Scott groaned. "There is no such thing as a crash course. I can do the snooping a hell of a lot faster myself than I could teach you. You forget, I was a hacker way back when. There isn't a system I can't break into."

Nikki thought about it. "Can you do it from the house?"

"No problem."

"What if you're still locked out?"

"That's been taken care of."

"All right, then I'll check out a few other things while we're there."

Scott's stomach knotted up again. "Who do you suspect over there?"

"Everyone."

After that pronouncement, he chose not to say anything more during the drive to the facility.

Nikki flashed her brightest smile at the security guard as the man nodded at Scott and waved them through.

"Who's in actual charge here?" she asked, nosing the truck into the space reserved for Scott.

"Westin. Most of us are too busy to bother with placating the investors or fooling around with the paperwork. He has an office staff that handles it all, and we voted him in."

"He didn't offer to take the position?" Nikki dug into the glove compartment, slipping a small packet into her skort pocket before she climbed out of the truck, activated the alarm on it and followed Scott toward the entrance of the sprawling, five-story brick building.

He shook his head. "No, he was in the midst of working out a mathematical formula for NASA."

"What was it for?"

"I never asked. He stays out of my computers, I stay out of his way. Hi, George," he said, greeting the guard at the door. "Ms. Price will be accompanying me down to the dungeon. Can you issue her a pass?"

The man in a security-guard uniform grimaced. "Dr. Westin said no one goes down there without his authorization." He lowered his voice. "You know what a stickler he is for the rules. I have to follow his orders."

"Then please call him and explain the situation."

The older man looked apologetic as he keyed into the computer that Scott was now present in the building. "He's not in today, Dr. Carter. Something about a family emergency."

"Then don't worry, George, because I'll take full responsibility for Ms. Price's presence," Scott insisted, leaning over the counter and picking up a laminated guest badge that sported a bright orange circle in one corner. He handed it to Nikki, who clipped it to her vest pocket. "I'll make sure he knows I overrode your objections." He gestured for Nikki to sign the register, then led her toward one of the rear elevators. "George, do you want to hit the release button? Thanks." He waited until the doors slid open, then guided Nikki inside.

"The dungeon?" She noticed the elevator started to descend, although Scott didn't push any buttons.

"It's more or less a top-secret lab facility," he explained. "And it's already set up for virtual reality. Someone used it a year ago for a space program. You do know what virtual reality is, don't you?"

"I saw it used in a movie. Does that count?" Nikki watched several buttons flash before the elevator coasted to a stop.

"Close enough."

"Does the institute handle a lot of top-secret projects?" she asked, just as the door slid open, revealing a dimly lit tunnel.

"It handles its share."

"Why didn't they insist on having a metal detector installed at the entrance?" She followed him down the tunnel.

"Since we're more-or-less known for our peacekeeping projects, not many people would think to wear a gun in here, except for security." Her silence alerted him. He whipped around. "You mean you're..." He shook his head in disbelief as he gazed at her. "Where?"

She held her arms out from her sides. "Care to frisk me and find out?"

"Hold that thought for later when I can do that frisking at my leisure. I'd hate to think I could miss a hiding place." He walked on, battling frustration and anger. He thought of the days when his life had been calm and serene. Thanks to an unknown faction and Nikki's return to his life, those days were long gone.

"There's a stairway nearby, too, isn't there?" she asked, ignoring Scott's muttering that he had a good idea of what she was planning to do and he didn't want to think she was crazy enough to do it.

"The stairs are used for emergency purposes," he replied.

"Where are they located?" Nikki asked, waiting as Scott punched in a code on a keypad set in the wall by a metal door. A buzzer sounded, the red light on the keypad turned green and the door silently swung inward with a whoosh of air.

Scott jerked his thumb over his shoulder as he walked in. "They're down that hallway. You walk until it forks, then you go to the left." He frowned at her. "What are you planning?"

"It's better you don't know," she whispered. "Oh, look, my favorite person."

"What is *she* doing here?" Kay demanded. She stood near Cully.

"I've been invited to observe a virtual-reality experiment," Nikki replied, perching herself on a nearby stool. She wondered if Scott's assistant would appreciate hearing her comments on her straight denim skirt, which barely covered the essentials, and a lacy knit, sleeveless top that faithfully outlined her feminine curves. "How did you get so lucky to be included? I thought you disagreed with Dr. Carter and with Mr. O'Brien's idea."

"Naturally I'd be here. I've worked with Scott on this project ever since he joined the institute," Kay retorted. "Besides, they need one sane person here."

"If you two don't mind? And Kay, I don't want to have to remind you again who's in charge here." Scott walked between them. He turned to Cully. "How does it look?"

The younger man made a circle with his thumb and forefinger. He picked up a helmetlike object fitted with wires trailing into a computer and held it out.

"I think it's only fair that you do the honors."

Scott accepted the helmet and turned to Nikki. "It's as if there's a mental screen fitted into the helmet, so I'll see everything I'm doing." He picked up a pair of odd-looking gloves that were also fitted with wires. "With these, I control firing of the weapon."

Nikki gazed curiously at the strange devices he held. "What will you be firing at?"

"I designed some space-age creatures and tough-looking mercenaries for Scott to battle to make it more realistic," Cully explained.

"The test won't show a thing," Kay scoffed.

Nikki turned to the younger woman, deliberately keeping her gaze innocent. "As I asked before, if you feel it's a waste of time, why are you here?" She heard Cully's muffled snort of laughter.

Kay's lips thinned. "*I* have a right to be here. You don't." She turned to Scott. "Shall we see if this works?"

Scott paused in fitting the helmet on his head. "Kay, if you have such negative feelings about this test, you don't have to stay."

She looked stricken by his comment. "It's not that," she protested, quickly backpedaling to regain lost ground. "I just don't want anyone to think you're wrong in what you're doing."

Nikki waited until Scott had slipped on the gloves and helmet with Kay's help before she spoke up. "You know, maybe I shouldn't be here for this. Is it all right if I wait upstairs in your office?"

Scott shot her a searching look. She smiled back, looking as innocent as vanilla pudding.

"I'll take you up there."

"What about the test?" Kay argued.

"It can wait a few minutes, Kay," he told her, placing the helmet and gloves on the table. "Nikki may be wearing a high-security visitor's pass, but she doesn't know where my private office is and I don't think it would be right for her to just wander around."

"Go on," Cully advised, studying his computer monitor. "I can do a little fine-tuning while you're gone."

"I'll be back in five minutes or so." He took Nikki's arm and walked out with her. "Any reason for that?" he said under his breath.

"No one will think anything about my being upstairs," she murmured. Instead of heading for the elevators, she turned toward the door marked Stairs. "I'd rather go this way."

"There are security cameras on the floor we'll be heading for," he told her.

"All right."

She trod lightly up the metal stairs, since she knew her footsteps would echo in the cavernous stairway. When they reached the fourth floor, she pulled on the door, breathing a curse when it refused to open.

"They didn't use to lock these doors," Scott said.

"Not to worry." Nikki pulled the small packet she'd taken from the truck out of her skort pocket. Muttering how out of practice she was, she finally picked the lock and pushed the door open.

"Didn't I read somewhere it's illegal to have those?" Scott heaved a sigh as he followed her

"It's illegal to own an unregistered gun, but I notice that didn't stop you from getting one." She scanned the discreet nameplates alongside the doors. "Who's Dr. Frazier?"

"Botanist."

She read another. "Dr. Reese?"

"Astrophysics."

"Where's Dr. Westin's office?" She looked around.

"Down the hall and to the right."

Nikki headed in that direction with Scott behind her. She started to turn the corner when the sound of a familiar voice stopped her cold.

"You are digging yourself in so deep you'll never be able to pull yourself out of this mess."

Nikki inched toward the end of the wall so she could glance around the corner just in time to watch her father walk out of David Westin's office.

"You do things your way. I'll do them mine," the administrator replied coldly.

The admiral muttered something under his breath that Nikki couldn't catch. She was so stunned to see him there, she barely felt the comforting warmth of Scott's arm wrapped around her waist.

"This is a very delicate matter, Westin. Don't screw up, or you'll find yourself in more trouble than you can imagine." Adam Price's threat was explicit. "You better start working with us or be prepared for the worst."

"As long as the money is there, you have nothing to worry about."

"I hope not." Adam's cold voice chilled even Nikki. He turned on his heel and headed for the elevators.

David waited until the admiral had reached them. "Don't forget to get off on the second floor and take the rear exit when you leave," he called after him. "Remember, I'm not here today."

Adam's gaze was frosty as he stared at the man. "I hope you're as careful with everything else." He stepped into the elevator as soon as the doors slid open.

Nikki inched her way back down the hallway until they reached Scott's office. Scott quickly keyed in his code to unlock the door, dragging her inside with little ceremony.

"Sit down," he commanded, pushing her onto a chair and forcing her head between her knees.

"You idiot! I'm not going to faint!" She batted at his hands, but he refused to release her.

"You looked like you were. You're as white as a sheet."

She took several deep breaths to clear her head. "If you found out your father might be a..." She couldn't finish the statement.

"Traitor." He said it for her.

She shook her head. "No, there's something very wrong there. He's so red, white and blue he could qualify as a flag."

Scott walked over to the small refrigerator in a corner of the office and pulled out a bottle of cold water. He filled a glass and handed it to her. "Then what do you think we just heard out there?"

"I don't know." She sounded miserable.

"Are you going to ask him?"

"And have him give me a song and dance that it's none of my business? That I left the navy and therefore have no reason to question him? No, thank you." She sipped the water, grateful to have something to dampen her parched throat. "No, he'll tell me I'm a fool for even daring to question his integrity. And he'll be right." Her hands trembled as she set the glass on the desk. She stood up. "I need to get into Westin's office and see if I can find anything from his files."

"Lock picks won't work on these doors. They're all controlled by an electronic code we've each chosen," Scott pointed out, glancing at his watch. "None of us know the others'."

"Are there any files listing anyone's codes?" she asked.

"In the computer."

She nodded. "You go on back downstairs. I'll see what I can do from here." She looked at his computer.

Scott reached over and turned it on. He tapped out several keys. "That should keep you busy for a while. Come down when you're ready."

Nikki didn't look at the computer monitor until Scott had left the office, closing his door behind him. When she did, she realized she was looking at icons detailing a variety of computer games.

"If he can do it, I can do it," she muttered, using the mouse to ask for additional files. She clicked and waited.

Nothing happened.

"All right." She typed in *H-E-L-P* and tapped the Enter key. Again nothing—until the screen suddenly exploded in a rainbow of colors, then turned blank except for words neatly printed across it: *The only games you'll play with my computer are the ones I say you can.*

She thought about throwing the mouse across the room. "And he called *me* paranoid."

Scott faced a rugged man holding a weapon three times the size of his. The animated creature didn't waste any time in shooting at him. Scott ducked and lifted his hand and pressed the firing button. A stream of light flashed from the weapon and eliminated his enemy.

"Got him!" he said with satisfaction.

"Hey, we're only beginning," he could hear Cully saying. "Be on the lookout for anything."

Scott suddenly seemed to turn around and face a creature he was convinced was a product of a horrible nightmare. This battle lasted longer and the creature evaded his shots. Eventually, he was dispatched.

Scott had no idea how much time had elapsed when he felt his hand turning very warm. He looked down and realized the warmth was coming from his weapon.

"What the hell?" The words barely left his mouth before the weapon burned his hand. Yelling in pain he was positive he felt, he jumped back, just as a fiery explosion engulfed him.

"Scott, what happened?" Kay ripped the helmet off his head as he struggled to pull off the gloves. "Are you all right?"

He shook his head. "I knew there were problems." He took several deep breaths. "The housing can't contain the power the way it should. The gun exploded in my hand."

"Wow," Cully breathed. "You figured there was something wrong with the case and you were right. What are we going to use to hold the power?"

Scott shrugged. "I don't know. We need to research it more."

"Building a prototype would have shown us the same thing without the extra expense," Kay pointed out.

Scott looked over her shoulder toward Nikki, who had returned to the room and now sat on the stool she had perched on when they'd first arrived.

"I'm sorry," she said simply.

"Better we find out this way than endangering lives." He turned to Cully. "Why don't we wait until tomorrow to check this out further? Our usual time."

"I'll be here."

"Why not get into it right now while it's all fresh?" Kay suggested. "I'll even drive you home, so your housekeeper won't have to wait around. I'm sure she must be bored with all this technical talk."

"You forget that Dr. Carter has been through some rough times lately," Nikki replied with a bland smile. "He needs his rest." She hopped off the stool.

"Thanks a lot for making me feel a hundred years old," he muttered as they entered the elevator.

"Whatever works," she said airily.

"So what did you come up with?"

She rested her forefinger against her lips. "Who knows where the ears are and who's listening," she whispered. "Wait until we're out of here."

As they walked through the lobby, Scott handed Nikki's visitor's badge to the guard and showed her where to sign out.

"By the way, Pete, did Dr. Westin come in today?" he asked casually.

"No, sir, he had a family emergency and said he wouldn't be in," he replied, keying the information into the computer that Dr. Carter was no longer in the building.

Scott nodded. "Have a good evening."

"Family emergency," Nikki mused as they walked to her truck. She deactivated the alarm, which automatically unlocked the doors. "If security has a computer to show who's in the building and who isn't, how can he get in and out without anyone knowing it?"

Scott didn't like the thoughts creeping through his mind. "It means he either has a hell of a lot more computer knowledge than any of us thought he did, or he has help."

"We need to break into the computer, Scott, and see what he has." She gunned the engine and roared out of the parking lot. "And we need to do it tonight."

Scott closed his eyes. Hacking had been a hobby for him years ago, and the old adrenaline started pumping through his body. Still, he remembered all the laws he'd broken back then and how lucky he'd been not to have gotten caught.

"Do you realize what you're asking?"

"You told me you can do it. You were the hacker of all hackers. And there's a plus. You know this computer."

"Yes, but I prefer doing it when I'm feeling a little more alert," he protested.

She was unconcerned. "I'll make lots of coffee."

True to her word, Nikki set a pot of coffee brewing before she took the puppy outside. When the coffee was ready, she carried it down to Scott, who sat at his computer, his fingers flying over the keyboard.

"Where did this come from?" he muttered, scowling at the rows of numbers and letters scrolling across the monitor. "I'm blocked here. I'll have to go back and try another way."

Nikki looked over his shoulder as she set a mug of coffee by his elbow. "How do you do this?"

"They put in security codes to block outsiders," he explained, his gaze focused on the screen. He frowned and fumbled for a pair of glasses. Slipping them on, he returned to the screen. "I have to bypass the codes and traps until I can get in. *Yes!*" He pumped his arms up and down over his head. "I'm in."

Nikki looked at the clock. It had taken Scott two hours to break into the computer without leaving a trail back to him.

"Already?"

"I am good."

"Yes, you are, my love." She kissed his cheek.

Scott continued typing, pulling up menu after menu until he found the one he wanted.

"I can't believe this. Most of those idiots use their birthdays for their security codes," he muttered, still typing. "Westin and I are the only ones who don't." He started tapping the Print Screen button.

Nikki watched information roll across the screen, but found it meaningless.

"I'm in Westin's files," Scott said eventually.

Tired from watching the screen, Nikki had curled up in one of the other chairs, with the puppy valiantly trying to crawl into her lap. By now she was half-asleep and the dog was nestled against her. She straightened at his announcement.

"What's there?" She put the dog down on the floor and walked over to him, looping her arms around his neck and looking over his shoulder.

He didn't answer as he continued scanning various files and printing them out. He looked up with an expression that told Nikki to prepare for the worst.

"More than either one of us figured on," he said slowly.

Chapter 17

Nikki walked over to the printer and picked up the pages already run off. "What are these?"

"Mathematical formulas." Scott kept his attention on the screen as he quickly downloaded what files he could. "Uh-oh."

She looked up. "What?"

"Traps. No problem." He started chuckling.

"What's so funny about traps?"

"Whoever wrote this program didn't know I bypassed traps like this years ago." He suddenly muttered a curse. "Backup traps. This guy is good. I'm going to have to be quick or they'll find out I was in here."

"You can't let them know you were."

He didn't turn from his work. "I don't intend to."

Nikki went back to her reading.

"These are more than mathematical formulas," she said, quickly turning pages. "They're some kind of code."

Scott held up his hand for silence. He continued typing for another ten minutes before disconnecting the modem and switching off the system. He turned his chair around.

"What makes you think it's code?"

"Using mathematics for codes isn't anything new. It's been done for years," she explained, handing him several sheets of paper. "If you look at these series of numbers, you'll see an order to them. The trouble is, I have no idea how to interpret them."

Scott left his desk and rummaged through a file cabinet. "I may have a program that can do it. During my hacker days, I used to design programs to break codes." He pulled out a computer disk. "This one might work."

Nikki pushed her chair forward and sat by Scott's side as he patiently worked through each file.

"You are a wonder," she murmured, amazed at what she was watching.

"I try."

By the time Scott had broken the codes, Nikki had brewed another pot of coffee, and both of them sported headaches from lack of sleep and all the caffeine they had drunk.

"I can't read anymore," she moaned, rubbing her eyes. "How can you?"

"Sweetheart, I used to sit at my computer for days without thinking about sleep," he told her. "Why don't you go on upstairs to bed? I'll be up soon to shower and get back to the institute. Will you call and make sure my driver picks me up?"

Nikki dragged herself up the stairs. "Sleep sounds great." She yawned.

After making the call, she headed for her bedroom. Exhaustion had finally overridden the caffeine and she dropped into bed with her clothes on.

She barely roused when a warm body curved around her.

"You're in the wrong bed, Price," a male voice murmured in her ear as strong arms wrapped around her body.

"We both need our sleep," she mumbled, smiling as the warmth of his body surrounded her.

"And we'll get it."

Nikki slept, not waking until the alarm went off. She watched Scott climb out of bed and head into the hall. She lay under the covers, listening to the homey sounds of the shower running and drawers opening and closing. Much later, he stopped in the doorway.

"I'll read over the papers and see what I can learn," she told him. "I should call Harvey and tell him about the admiral and Westin and what you've found."

"Remember what your brother said. Don't trust anyone."

"I refuse to believe Harvey could be in on this. He's even more Mom-and-apple-pie than the admiral," she argued. Then she held up her hands in surrender. "All right, I'll wait until I see what we have. Deal?"

"Deal. You know, you're a very tempting sight right now." He ran his finger down her cheek.

"I think you should stay home," Nikki said suddenly, experiencing that inexplicable feeling that she knew not to ignore.

"I have to. I made a decision last night." He looked away. "I'm scrapping the project."

She sat up. "What?"

He nodded. His expression was resigned.

Nikki's heart went out to him. She knew this was not a decision he had made lightly. "Can you get away with that?"

"I had a clause put in my contract that gave me the right to cancel the project if I felt it wasn't working. And it isn't."

"It just might be nerves because of everything that's happened. Once this is all settled, it could all fall into place for you."

Scott shook his head. "I realized I don't want to design something that will destroy when I could design something that could benefit. The weapon is too unstable in the only housing available at this time for that kind of power. I think it might take years of research before the right case could be manufactured."

"They'll want all your notes."

"I'll hit a few keys and they'll all be gone. No one will be able to retrieve them. I'll make sure of that."

"People have tried to kill you for that research," she said. "Harvey has been waiting for that weapon to be completed."

"Then someone else can try. I'll use the escape clause in my contract and look around for something more fulfilling." He cupped her face in his hands. "And then we're going to have a long talk. About us."

She suddenly felt very frightened. "Scott—"

He stopped her words with a deep kiss. "Later." He kissed her again and left.

"Scott!" Nikki called after him, but her only answer was the sound of the front door closing.

The puppy's whimpering caught her attention and she hustled him outside. While he was out, she took a quick shower and dressed in fresh clothing. Then she went downstairs and gathered up the papers Scott had printed out only hours before.

As she read, things started making sense.

"Not now!" she muttered when the doorbell intruded on her studies. She jumped to her feet and went upstairs.

The moment she opened the door, she wished she hadn't.

"What the hell do you think you're doing?" Adam Price swept into the house, right past her. His face appeared carved from stone as he glared at her.

"I've been doing the job Harvey hired me for."

"You were caught breaking into the institute's computer last night," he snapped.

"I have better things to do than break into a computer." She wasn't really lying, since Scott was the one who had broken into it.

Her father stepped closer to her as an intimidation tactic. But it didn't work with Nikki.

"You know very well what I'm talking about." His voice was dangerously soft. "The good doctor has returned to his old ways. He was a hacker a lot of computer-security personnel remember only too well."

She didn't bat an eyelash, while inside she was screaming at him. She saw her father as a lot of things, but a traitor wasn't one of them. What was going on?

"No, I don't know what you're talking about."

The man took a deep breath. "You met with Brad yesterday outside the Smithsonian. He told you things he had no right to."

"Amazing. You have spying down to such a fine art, you even use it on your own son," she answered mockingly. "I guess he didn't realize he shouldn't be seen with me."

His jaw muscles flexed with barely repressed anger. "Harvey put you in this job because all you'd have to do would be baby-sit the man. Instead, you taught his daughter self-defense, didn't properly intercept a mail bomb, were an alleged victim of a stink bomb and played spy in the process. I told him you'd screw up and I was right."

Nikki put herself on instant alert. "Harvey's in on this, too?" She could feel her temper quickly reaching the danger level.

"He does what he's told." Adam looked around. "Where's the information you stole from the computer?"

"Tell me what I supposedly stole and I'll tell you if I did."

He looked as if he could cheerfully murder her. "You just can't do anything right, can you? Think about it. Westin was behind Carter's wife's murder. He had the connections to smuggle the drug used to kill her into the jail and he had the medical examiner under his thumb. He's more than a mathematician, he's an expert in gathering information and collects cash from various countries looking to expand their knowledge. He's in the perfect position to do just that. And for now, he wants Carter's notes on the weapon he's developing because he has a client willing to pay big money. He also has many others on his payroll willing to help him get it."

"Tell me something I haven't already figured out. Where are you in this?"

"He thinks I'm on his payroll, while I'm gathering my own evidence that will put him away for life."

"That's what you say. Why were you at the institute yesterday?"

He appeared surprised. "You saw me?"

"You and Westin, who supposedly wasn't in due to a family emergency," she replied. "Anyone who overheard you would think the worst."

"I don't explain to anyone."

"I know that and you know that, but let's pretend you do." Nikki stared daggers at him. "Scott is going to the institute this morning to scrap the project and destroy all his notes."

"What?"

She smiled, not used to seeing her father look stunned.

"He ran a virtual-reality test on the weapon yesterday and it exploded. He doesn't have the heart to design new weapons any longer. He has an escape clause that will give him the out he needs and he's taking it," she told him.

"And one of his assistants is on Westin's payroll," the admiral countered. "I wouldn't be surprised if they make sure Carter doesn't get out of the building."

Nikki froze. No wonder she'd felt so unsettled this morning. "And I have an idea who it is." She ran from the room.

In no time, she had changed her clothes and snatched up her gun. When she returned to the entryway, she found her father struggling with the puppy, who was cheerfully chewing on his pant leg, oblivious to the fury on his face.

"Can't you do something with him?" he demanded, vainly trying to shake him off.

"Be grateful dogs like you," Nikki muttered, dragging the puppy through the house and into the laundry room, where his water dish and food bowl were kept. She was heading out the kitchen door when Adam approached her.

"I'm going with you."

"I was the one hired to protect Scott."

Adam studied her set expression. "You've fallen in love with him." Disgust colored his voice as he mentioned an emotion he had erased from his nature years ago.

"Yes, I guess I have." She dropped a second cartridge clip in a pocket and made sure her gun was nestled snugly against the small of her back. "Hard to believe, isn't it? The Prices aren't exactly marriage material, but maybe I can break the curse. Because if he asks, I'm saying yes."

"You won't last."

She pulled open the door and stopped in the doorway. "Oh, yes, I will. Just to prove to you how wrong you are. Hit the latch on your way out." She ran to the garage and was gone in seconds.

As Nikki drove to the institute, she ran over various scenarios in her mind. What would she find when she got there? And could she expect her father to send backup?

"I'm sorry, miss, but I can't let you in," the security guard at the gate told her.

"I work for Dr. Carter. It's an emergency," she argued, not caring how much she had to lie as long as she got in. "His daughter was badly hurt and I need to pick him up to take him to the hospital."

The man hesitated. "Dr. Westin said no visitors today. Something big is happening with one of the projects."

"This is very important." She put on her best pleading expression. "Please, he needs to know about her."

"All right, but I'll need to call ahead."

"Let me talk to Dr. Westin when I get in there," Nikki suggested. "I'll make sure he understands this isn't your fault."

He looked relieved. "Okay." He activated the electronic gate.

Nikki barely waited for it to swing open before driving through. She kept one eye on the rearview mirror, comforted by the fact that the guard didn't pick up the phone to call the building.

"Let's find that rear door," she murmured, bypassing the visitors' lot and driving around the side to the employees' parking lot. She was surprised to see it almost empty and wondered what story had been given out to keep most of the staff home today.

Nikki eased into an empty space and crept out of her truck.

She encountered her first obstacle the moment she found a hidden side door with a security keypad by it.

"Birthdays," she murmured, tapping in a series of numbers she remembered. She smiled when the door clicked open.

Nikki slipped inside and found herself at the end of a hallway. She searched her memory for the stairway and found it with a minimum of error. She trod lightly so her footsteps on the metal wouldn't be heard.

She had nothing to go on but her senses. She kept her respiration shallow, her mind wide open as she tried to tune in to Scott any way she could.

His office, she told herself. *He'd go to Westin's office to tell him. Westin wouldn't dare try anything there, would he?* The moment she asked herself the question, she knew the answer. The man would do anything to achieve what he wanted.

When she reached the appropriate floor, she used her lock picks again and eased her way into the hallway. Feeling the prickles of unease intensify, she pulled her gun out of the small holster against her back and kept the barrel pointing upward, her fingers wrapped around the stock in a two-handed grip as she crept down the hallway.

"It doesn't have to be this way, Scott." Westin's voice was clear, coming from the direction of his office.

"The minute I cracked your files I knew it would be. You're already out of luck, David. I erased the files before I came in here to tell you."

"They can be retrieved, and I know just the right person to do it. Am I correct?"

Nikki held her breath as she inched her way along the wall. With the office door open, she could see Scott facing Westin, who held a revolver in one hand. The shadow of another person was highlighted on the wall.

"I'll get them," the other person promised. "I made copies and kept them under another name in a file only I can access. They're not up to date, but that's no problem."

Shock billowed through Nikki's body. Realizing she needed to pull herself together or lose her edge and perhaps endanger Scott, she quickly stiffened her resolve.

"Scott, it would be easier if you just gave me your files. I know you didn't have the time to erase them. There's a lot of money involved in this," David insisted. "Enough for all of us. More than you'd ever receive here. If you dispensed with your holier-than-thou principles, you'd see that."

"Money isn't the issue." Scott appeared reflective. "Tell me something, David. How did you arrange Renee's death?"

Nikki peeked around the door for a better look. She was impressed with Scott's calm exterior.

"You were needed and we decided she was the key. You were so angry at the world, you wanted to get away and we gave you that chance." David presented his story as if discussing a book he'd read the night before. "But we still had to keep an eye on you. Especially when things weren't going the way we wanted them to. You should have finished this project months ago. Actually, we planned our little acts of terrorism, if you will, in hopes you'd finish."

"No matter what decision I make, you'll kill me and you'll be caught. That's the way it works."

"You don't read a lot of mysteries, do you, Doctor? There are drugs out there that simulate heart attacks, and even an autopsy can't detect them," the third speaker volunteered.

That was when Nikki decided to make her move.

"And sometimes the cavalry shows up in time," she announced, stepping into the office. She swung her gun between David and his partner. "Drop your gun, Dr. Westin. I have had this horrible case of PMS lately and I just know that shooting you would be better than chocolate in cheering me up." Her voice hardened. "Drop it now!"

David smirked. "You're not that fast. If you shoot me, I shoot him."

"Yes, but if I shoot you in the gut he'll have a chance to duck, because you'll be in so much pain you'll probably miss him altogether." She barely glanced toward the person watching her warily. "You're the surprise in all this. I didn't expect to find you here."

Cully shrugged. "Going for a doctorate requires money and I was promised plenty of it. And no problems with my dissertation. All I had to do was keep tabs on Scott's research until it was ready to go. Since I always seemed to be on his side, no one suspected me."

"Until you left a few clues in the computer," Scott said quietly. "Once I saw your trail, I knew it was you."

"Surprise, Cully. You'll have plenty of years to obtain that degree," she said pleasantly. "Now, stand up very slowly and move toward Dr. Westin, who will now drop his gun and kick it toward me." She gestured again with her weapon. "Believe me, I've had a hell of a day. Don't tick me off."

David's beaten expression told her he knew he'd lost. Once the gun was pushed aside, Scott quickly picked it up and moved backward toward Nikki.

"I thought it was Kay," she told him.

"I did, too," he admitted. "It seems she's only hoping to be the first woman to head this institute. Her ambition turned out to be not as dangerous as Cully's and David's."

Westin's face darkened with fury. "You won't get away with this."

"That's what you think." Another voice chimed in.

Adam Price and several other men stepped into the office.

"What kept you?" Nikki asked.

"I wanted to make sure you wouldn't shoot me by mistake." Her father gestured for the two men to be taken into custody. "Dr. Carter, if you will come with me." He grasped Scott's arm and ushered him out of the office.

"Wait a minute!" Nikki started to follow them, but was stopped by one of the agents. She looked up. "Let me by."

He shook his head.

Nikki had the man on the floor in seconds, but she was still too late.

The elevator doors had shut and Scott was gone.

"Where is he, Harvey?" Nikki leaned over the man's desk.

"Dr. Carter and his daughter are in protective custody," he explained for what was probably the hundredth time.

Nikki hadn't wasted any time after Scott had been taken away by the admiral. She'd driven home at the speed of light, but found only the puppy, whimpering in the laundry room.

When she called the Winthrops, she'd learned that Scott had been by to pick up Heather, but the older couple hadn't been told anything, either.

For the past week, Nikki had alternated between storming Harvey's office and her father's. She hadn't learned anything from either of them. In fact, her father had even had security escort her off the premises with the threat that she'd be arrested if she showed up again. Harvey hadn't gone that far yet, but she could tell he was close to losing his temper.

"Nikki, considering everything, we had no choice but to put the two of them in protective custody," he explained wearily. "In fact, they will be entering the Witness Protection Program. There are now too many people who want him dead."

"He destroyed the files! Even Cully's hidden ones."

"Exactly. And the ones who wanted the weapon are furious with him for doing so." It was a no-win situation when so many had an interest in the weapon.

Nikki backed away at the pity in his eyes. "I need to see him, Harvey."

"Nikki, he's going to begin a new life," he said gently. "One you have no part of."

She stood still, unable to hide the hurt in her eyes. "Why not?"

"Because of the way you grew up. You need the constant excitement and danger. You feed on it. Come work for me," he urged. "You'll forget all about him."

Nikki swallowed the lump in her throat. "No." Her hands moved restlessly, as if she wasn't sure what to do with them. "No."

She left the office before she could disgrace herself by bursting into tears.

Nikki had moved out of Scott's house when she'd realized he wasn't coming back, and she had taken the puppy with her. Thanks to Brad, she had found a garden apartment where a dog was allowed. For now, she concentrated on discovering Scott's location.

"He's gone, Nik," Brad had told her when she'd begged him for the information. "You know very well why secrecy is involved. It's time to get on with your life. Come on, admit it, you wouldn't have been happy as some little hausfrau anyway."

She sniffed back the tears that had been threatening to spill since she'd realized Scott was gone.

"That's what you think," she murmured before hanging up. She turned to the puppy, which she had named Rusty. "All right, boy, what do we do? Go to work for ole Harvey? Go back to Baton Rouge and the fitness center? Or turn ourselves into such a pain in the butt that they'll want to get rid of us, too?"

Rusty barked.

She smiled. "I knew you'd see it my way."

Epilogue

"Are we always going to live here?" Erin Wright, aka Heather Carter, asked her father.

"That's right, kiddo." Gary Wright, aka Scott Carter, replied.

"But what about Nikki?"

"I explained to you why we had to take new names and move away." He faced their dinner with the same disinterest he'd felt toward food for the past three months, ever since Adam Price had roughly hustled him out of David Westin's office and out of the building. The admiral had explained that Scott had no choice but to enter the Witness Protection Program and that Nikki was now working for Harvey and was already involved in a new assignment. Scott hadn't even been given the chance to ask her if that was what she wanted.

As he looked around the house provided for them, he realized it was exactly what Nikki had described what seemed like a lifetime ago. A house that could be made into a home in a neighborhood where everyone knew everyone. There were Sunday barbecues, and he even mowed the lawn on weekends. The wives all stopped by to welcome him and offer hints as to where to shop for what and who to avoid. A few even hinted that they had eligible friends. But the last thing he wanted right now was to meet a woman. Not when one already had his heart.

He was teaching computer science at the small college and Heather was beginning horseback-riding lessons. The government had taken two years off his age and arranged a whole new life for him and his daughter in this small, midwestern town. Both sets of parents were upset with the situation, but he knew cutting all ties was his only choice and Heather understood.

Surprisingly, he didn't miss the big-city excitement and realized they had actually done him a favor. He was beginning to understand why Nikki had craved this sort of life while she was growing up. He only wished he could give it to her. While Heather missed Nikki's companionship, he missed her warmth in his bed and just missed her, period.

He heard the faint sound of the doorbell and his cleaning lady's announcement that she'd answer it.

"Mr. Wright?" Velma, who came in to clean twice a week, walked into the kitchen where they were just finishing lunch.

It still took him a moment to realize that was his name. He looked up with a smile.

"Yes, Velma?"

"There's somebody out front who says she has your dog." She looked skeptical. "I told her you don't own a dog, but she insisted I come in and tell you."

He was afraid to hope. "I'll, uh, talk to her." He slowly stood up.

Heather perked up. "A dog?"

"It could be a mistake," he murmured.

She started to bolt out of her chair, but he held her back. "Let me go first."

He walked to the front door and peered through the screen, which was still closed.

She was dressed in her usual bright colors, displaying a pair of tanned legs he well remembered. One hand held a leash belonging to an animal the size of a small horse. She stood with her back to him, surveying the neighborhood. A corner of his mouth tilted up.

She had been right. He'd swear the dog had already doubled in size. He hit the screen door with the flat of his hand, pushing it open as he stepped outside. Nikki turned at the noise.

"You said you have my dog?" He spoke casually, standing on the top step.

She held up a leash. "Rusty needs a home."

"Rusty?"

"I couldn't let him go without a name any longer. I was afraid he'd start answering to anything I said." Her voice wobbled.

He refused to hope. "Why are you getting rid of the dog? Do you have plans on going where he wouldn't be welcome?"

She shook her head. "Actually, we're sort of a package deal. Where he goes...I go." Her gaze was hungry as she watched him. "I like your house."

He now dared to hope. "It's got everything. Picket fence, nice neighborhood, a park two blocks over. Big backyard for the monster there. What do you think?"

Nikki blinked rapidly. "It sounds great," she whispered.

Scott opened his arms. She didn't waste any time flying into them. "My God, I've missed you so much." His words were muffled against her throat. "Your father said you went to work for Harvey."

Her reply about her father was decidedly unprintable. "Actually, I proved to be such a pain in the butt he and Harvey decided in the end it was better to get rid of me." She covered his face with kisses. "So you have to marry me. If you don't, Harvey will come after you with a shotgun.

Our lives won't be perfect right away. We'll have to go back for the trial. I'm pretty sure that Westin and Cully will be in prison for a long time.''

"I can't believe you're here, but now that you are, I'm not letting you go for anything." He cupped her face with his hands and covered her mouth with his. Their kiss deepened as they fought to assuage a long hunger.

"Wow, a dog! Nikki!" A smaller pair of arms encircled them both. "We've missed you!"

"Do me a favor, kid, and take the dog out back," Scott said huskily, pulling back and staring into Nikki's eyes.

"Is Nikki staying?"

"Yes," they said in unison.

"My name's Erin now," the girl whispered before running off with the dog following after her.

"How do we explain you?" He was so afraid he'd wake up and discover she was nothing more than a dream.

"Don't worry, *Gary,* I'll fill you in on my little history," Nikki murmured. "It seems we had a lover's spat before you moved here, but I finally saw the error of my ways. I admit, your new name will take some getting used to, but I've always been very adaptable."

He had to grin. He decided he was wide awake—she was here, and she was going to marry him. Now he saw his life as perfect.

"Can you adjust to nosy neighbors in a small town where everyone knows everyone else's business?"

She cocked her head to one side. Her eyes twinkled as she threw her arms around his neck.

"Just call me Mrs. Gary Wright."

*   *   *   *   *

COMING NEXT MONTH

#643 ANOTHER MAN'S WIFE—Dallas Schulze
Heartbreakers/A Family Circle
Gage Walker knew the value of friendship—enough to have taken responsibility for his best buddy's widow and young son. But his sense of duty had *never* included marriage—or fatherhood. Then he learned that Kelsey had a baby on the way—*his!*

#644 IAIN ROSS'S WOMAN—Emilie Richards
The Men of Midnight
Iain Ross had no idea that the woman he'd saved from drowning was the embodiment of his own destruction. Feisty Billie Harper seemed harmless—and charming—enough, but an age-old curse had rendered her his sworn enemy. But Iain was powerless to resist her—and their destiny....

#645 THE WEDDING VENTURE—Nikki Benjamin
Laura Burke would never give up her son. Timmy was hers, and no mob kingpin would take him away—even if he was the child's grandfather. Desperate, she turned to Devlin Gray, a man shrouded in mystery. Then she learned that Devlin's idea of protection involved trading danger for wedding vows.

#646 THE ONLY WAY OUT—Susan Mallery
Andie Cochran was on the run, struggling to bring herself and her young son to safety. Yet Jeff Markum was the only man she could trust—and the one man who had every reason to hate her.

#647 NOT WITHOUT RISK—Suzanne Brockmann
Emily Marshall had never dreamed of seeing police detective Jim Keegan ever again. He'd dumped her years earlier without warning—or explanation—and now he was masquerading as her "brother" to catch a drug smuggler. But the feelings that stirred between them were anything but familial.

#648 FOR MERCY'S SAKE—Nancy Gideon
Sheriff Spencer Halloway knew a person in hiding when he saw one, and Mercy Pomeroy was one woman who didn't want to be found. He couldn't figure out what a classy lady and her cute daughter could possibly fear, but he would move the heavens to find out....

ANNOUNCING THE

FLYAWAY VACATION SWEEPSTAKES!

This month's destination:

Beautiful SAN FRANCISCO!

This month, as a special surprise, we're offering an exciting FREE VACATION!

Think how much fun it would be to visit San Francisco "on us"! You could ride cable cars, visit Chinatown, see the Golden Gate Bridge and dine in some of the finest restaurants in America!

The facing page contains two Entry Coupons (as does every book you received this shipment). Complete and return *all* the entry coupons; **the more times you enter, the better your chances of winning!**

Then keep your fingers crossed, because you'll find out by June 15, 1995 if you're the winner! If you are, here's what you'll get:

- Round-trip airfare for two to beautiful San Francisco!
- 4 days/3 nights at a first-class hotel!
- $500.00 pocket money for meals and sightseeing!

Remember: The more times you enter, the better your chances of winning!*

*NO PURCHASE OR OBLIGATION TO CONTINUE BEING A SUBSCRIBER NECESSARY TO ENTER. SEE REVERSE SIDE OR ANY ENTRY COUPON FOR ALTERNATIVE MEANS OF ENTRY.

VSF KAL

FLYAWAY VACATION
SWEEPSTAKES

OFFICIAL ENTRY COUPON

This entry must be received by: MAY 30, 1995
This month's winner will be notified by: JUNE 15, 1995
Trip must be taken between: JULY 30, 1995-JULY 30, 1996

YES, I want to win the San Francisco vacation for two. I understand the prize includes round-trip airfare, first-class hotel and $500.00 spending money. Please let me know if I'm the winner!

Name_____

Address _____ Apt. _____

City   State/Prov.   Zip/Postal Code

Account #_____

Return entry with invoice in reply envelope.

© 1995 HARLEQUIN ENTERPRISES LTD.   CSF KAL

OFFICIAL RULES

FLYAWAY VACATION SWEEPSTAKES 3449

NO PURCHASE OR OBLIGATION NECESSARY

Three Harlequin Reader Service 1995 shipments will contain respectively, coupons for entry into three different prize drawings, one for a trip for two to San Francisco, another for a trip for two to Las Vegas and the third for a trip for two to Orlando, Florida. To enter any drawing using an Entry Coupon, simply complete and mail according to directions.

There is no obligation to continue using the Reader Service to enter and be eligible for any prize drawing. You may also enter any drawing by hand printing the words "Flyaway Vacation," your name and address on a 3"x5" card and the destination of the prize you wish that entry to be considered for (i.e., San Francisco trip, Las Vegas trip or Orlando trip). Send your 3"x5" entries via first-class mail (limit: one entry per envelope) to: Flyaway Vacation Sweepstakes 3449, c/o Prize Destination you wish that entry to be considered for, P.O. Box 1315, Buffalo, NY 14269-1315, USA or P.O. Box 610, Fort Erie, Ontario L2A 5X3, Canada.

To be eligible for the San Francisco trip, entries must be received by 5/30/95; for the Las Vegas trip, 7/30/95; and for the Orlando trip, 9/30/95.

Winners will be determined in random drawings conducted under the supervision of D.L. Blair, Inc., an independent judging organization whose decisions are final, from among all eligible entries received for that drawing. San Francisco trip prize includes round-trip airfare for two, 4-day/3-night weekend accommodations at a first-class hotel, and $500 in cash (trip must be taken between 7/30/95—7/30/96, approximate prize value—$3,500); Las Vegas trip includes round-trip airfare for two, 4-day/3-night weekend accommodations at a first-class hotel, and $500 in cash (trip must be taken between 9/30/95—9/30/96, approximate prize value—$3,500); Orlando trip includes round-trip airfare for two, 4-day/3-night weekend accommodations at a first-class hotel, and $500 in cash (trip must be taken between 11/30/95—11/30/96, approximate prize value—$3,500). All travelers must sign and return a Release of Liability prior to travel. Hotel accommodations and flights are subject to accommodation and schedule availability. Sweepstakes open to residents of the U.S. (except Puerto Rico) and Canada, 18 years of age or older. Employees and immediate family members of Harlequin Enterprises, Ltd., D.L. Blair, Inc., their affiliates, subsidiaries and all other agencies, entities and persons connected with the use, marketing or conduct of this sweepstakes are not eligible. Odds of winning a prize are dependent upon the number of eligible entries received for that drawing. Prize drawing and winner notification for each drawing will occur no later than 15 days after deadline for entry eligibility for that drawing. Limit: one prize to an individual, family or organization. All applicable laws and regulations apply. Sweepstakes offer void wherever prohibited by law. Any litigation within the province of Quebec respecting the conduct and awarding of the prizes in this sweepstakes must be submitted to the Regies des loteries et Courses du Quebec. In order to win a prize, residents of Canada will be required to correctly answer a time-limited arithmetical skill-testing question. Value of prizes are in U.S. currency.

Winners will be obligated to sign and return an Affidavit of Eligibility within 30 days of notification. In the event of noncompliance within this time period, prize may not be awarded. If any prize or prize notification is returned as undeliverable, that prize will not be awarded. By acceptance of a prize, winner consents to use of his/her name, photograph or other likeness for purposes of advertising, trade and promotion on behalf of Harlequin Enterprises, Ltd., without further compensation, unless prohibited by law.

For the names of prizewinners (available after 12/31/95), send a self-addressed, stamped envelope to: Flyaway Vacation Sweepstakes 3449 Winners, P.O. Box 4200, Blair, NE 68009.

RVC KAL